D0688613

BOOK TWO

QUARANTINE

the SAINTS

LEX THOMAS

QUARANTINE

the SAINTS

BOOK TWO

EGMONT
USA
NEW YORK

Powell's
08/2013
18.

EGMONT

We bring stories to life

First published by Egmont USA, 2013
443 Park Avenue South, Suite 806
New York, NY 10016

Copyright © Lex Thomas, 2013
All rights reserved

1 3 5 7 9 8 6 4 2

www.egmontusa.com
www.lex-thomas.com

Library of Congress Cataloging-in-Publication Data
Thomas, Lex.
The Saints / Lex Thomas.
pages cm — (Quarantine ; book 2)
Summary: The world inside an infected Colorado high school quarantined
by the government takes a startling turn for the worse when a new gang enters
the school and starts gaining power.
ISBN 978-1-60684-336-9 (hardcover) — ISBN 978-1-60684-337-6 (ebook)
[1. Survival—Fiction. 2. Gangs—Fiction. 3. Interpersonal relations—Fiction. 4. Virus
diseases—Fiction. 5. High schools—Fiction. 6. Schools—Fiction. 7. Science fiction.]
I. Title.
PZ7.T366998Sai 2013
[Fic]—dc23
2013008605

Printed in the United States of America

All rights reserved. No part of this publication may be reproduced, stored
in a retrieval system, or transmitted, in any form or by any means, electronic,
mechanical, photocopying, or otherwise, without the prior permission of the
publisher and copyright owner.

To our family and friends. For still hanging out with us after
we dropped off the face of the Earth.

BOOK TWO

QUARANTINE

theSAINTS

THE OUTSIDE. IT WAS A PLACE WHERE THINGS
were alive, where forests grew, where your friends weren't
trying to kill you, and the air didn't taste like dust. The door
to the outside was now open.

Hissing torches filled the dark hallway with red. Will held
Lucy's hand. They ran like mad down the hall, trailing the
rest of the Loners. They'd gone back to get their gang when
those gun-toting kids from the outside had opened the
doors. Will watched the Loners ahead of him dash around
the corner and pour into the front foyer. He heard happy
screams.

Will and Lucy burst into the foyer. Bright light streamed
in from the mysterious white room beyond the steel graduation doors. The rest of the Loners were already crowded at
the doorway, fighting each other to get through first. Half
of them were in tears. Sunburned kids from the outside

stood at the edges of the foyer, leaning on their rifles and waving the Loners forward.

Will and Lucy charged toward the light. Will wanted inside that room so badly, but the rest of the Loners were ahead of him. He and Lucy pushed against the backs of the Loner mob. The approaching thunder of running feet filled the halls behind him. The other gangs were coming. All of them.

"Faster!" Will shouted at the Loners in front of him, who were still passing through the graduation doors ahead.

Shrieks of joy echoed through the foyer as kids from every gang flooded into the foyer from hallways, and came charging down the central staircase. Clamoring students slammed into the backs of Will and Lucy, pushing them through the graduation doors and knocking them to the floor of the blinding white room beyond. If they hadn't scurried to the side right away, they would have been trampled.

The white room. It was uncharted territory. The only McKinley kids that had ever made it this far were graduates. Will squinted, trying to make his eyes adjust to the brilliant light that overexposed the room. This area must have been on its own generator. He realized that the entire, wide ceiling was one large panel of light, except in the center, where there was a giant mechanical contraption. It had eight metal arms that each held a hose with a spray nozzle at its end. The device's arms were drawn in on itself, like a dead spider. The floor and walls were all white ceramic tile except for an eight-by-eight-foot metal door to Will's left and an observation window by the ceiling.

Lucy's hands grasped Will's arm and lifted him off the floor. "Come on," she said. "Hurry."

Will and Lucy flowed with the crowd toward a door at the other end of the room. They fell in beside Belinda and Leonard, but the crowd around them had mostly become a patchwork of different-colored heads. They left the white room behind and entered a long corridor. They teetered at top speed, and clung to each other for balance. On either side of them, down the length of the hall, were holding cells, each with a thick, clear, plastic door. Hanging ceiling lamps revealed that each cell contained a cot, a sink, a toilet, and a desk bolted to the wall. Stacks of magazines lay on the floor of some cells, a deck of cards was scattered in another, and in the last cell, Will noticed that the walls were graffitied with permanent marker doodles. One was a happy-face sun looking over a graveyard.

The crowd bottlenecked again at the next doorway. People behind Will and Lucy started pushing harder, screaming to move faster. They squeezed into the next room. The doors in and out were airtight. Metal closets lined the walls. The little room was packed beyond capacity. A bunch of Skaters behind Will and Lucy pressed against the crowd with solid, continuous force. Will felt merged with the bodies around him, like meat through a sausage grinder. Finally, they were spit out through the second door. They stumbled into a wide room with a hall to the left and to the right. Outsiders blocked those passages and waved everyone forward.

This new room was lined with desks that must have once held computers and machinery, but now only tangles of wire remained. Desk chairs were strewn over the room. An American flag on a pole was tipping into a dead, potted palm. The place had been abandoned in a hurry.

"Oh my god," Lucy muttered, squeezing tight on Will's arm.

Will had already seen it. In the center of the wide far wall, beyond the writhing, multiheaded silhouette of the dashing crowd, sunlight streamed in from open double doors. He almost cried.

The crowd surged. Loners ahead were making it outside, into the sunlight. Kids from other gangs too. Will saw the outside in glimpses. Snowcaps on the distant hills. Clumps of luscious green grass sprouting up across the front lawn. Swaying trees. A pigeon flying in a quartz-colored sky.

"Yes, yes, yes," Lucy said on repeat, as they raced toward the doors.

One outsider stood at the exit, holding one of the doors open, as kids wrestled their way past him, fighting each other to get out first. The kid was tall, he had long white hair, and one of his eyes was so bloodshot that the white of his eye was a deep red.

"Keep going, keep going!" the red-eyed boy said to Will as he reached the doors.

Lucy tugged Will back. He looked back at her in a panic. What was she doing? They were only a few feet from freedom. Her face was taut with terror. Will heard the blast of a car horn.

"Bus!" Lucy said.

Will turned to see kids in front of him dive out the doors. A blazing yellow school bus was barreling toward Will, seconds from smashing into the building. The outsider kid hadn't seen it yet; he was still shouting at the crowd inside.

Will shoved Lucy to the side, away from the doors. He grabbed the outsider kid, and yanked him out of the way.

Will and the outsider hit the floor just as the bus plunged through the entrance. The impact jolted the entire wide room with a clap of metal against concrete. Chunks of ceiling dropped, nearly crushing them. Dust clouded the room. All the lights in the facility flickered and died.

For a moment everything was still and silent.

Will breathed in dry air. He was alive. The outsider pushed himself up and held his head, dazed. Coughs mingled with the creak of metal and the tick of a hot engine. People slowly began to rise around the room. The entire structure had collapsed around the crushed face of the bus, covering the doors and windshield with gigantic slabs of concrete. All that could be seen was the bus's front grille and bumper; not a speck of the outdoors was visible anymore. One unbroken headlight cut through the thick dust, and stared deep into the new darkness.

"No," Will heard himself say.

He was staring over at Lucy. She was unconscious. He scurried to her and took her head in his hands. He brushed her soft tangle of white hair away from her face. He touched her pale cheek; it was cool.

"Lucy. Wake up," Will said. All he wanted was for her big, beautiful eyes to open, some sign of life, but her body remained limp. He could feel his voice getting weaker with emotion. "Please," he said.

Still nothing.

All around, kids struggled to their feet. They pulled at the rubble, but the heaviest slabs stayed put, locked in place around the bus. There was no budging any of it.

The wailing began. Kids cried, and held each other. They beat at the bus with their fists. Dust still swirled in the headlight's path.

Will held Lucy's head gently in his hands.

"You can't leave me," he said. "You can't. Please, Lucy."

Lucy coughed. Her eyes fluttered open. She looked up at him, confused.

"Did we . . . ," she rasped. "Are we getting out?"

Will couldn't bear to look her in the eye.

"No."

2

THIS ISN'T REAL, LUCY THOUGHT.

"Are you okay?" Will said to her.

She was still on the floor. She stared at the mangled grille of the bus. It was one with the building now. Kids had given up trying to move the stubborn, concrete slabs that covered its front.

"I'm—" Lucy said.

She didn't know what to say. To say something would be to acknowledge that this was actually happening, that she'd seen nearly her entire gang escape McKinley before she could, and that the only way out of the school had been destroyed.

Everybody else was furious. McKinley kids had the outsiders backed up against the bus. They were screaming at them, asking desperate questions, with so many shouting at once that all Lucy could hear was one long, unintelligible blast of anger and confusion. The outsiders looked frightened. They had their rifles and pistols drawn and pointed at the McKinley kids.

The boy with the red eye stepped out in front of the other outsiders.

"Everyone, shut up!" the red-eyed boy said.

His voice carried, and the screaming subsided.

"We aren't the bad guys," the red-eyed boy said to the crowd. "We didn't drive this fuckin' bus in here."

Will squeezed Lucy's hand. She hadn't realized he was holding it, but of course he was. In the last two weeks, as the food had run out, as they began to starve, as death became a certainty for them, Will had always been there, holding her hand.

"Can you walk?" Will asked Lucy. He was looking at the outsiders, like he didn't want to miss a word of what they had to say. Lucy didn't either. She nodded.

Will helped her up, and they shuffled over to the teeming crowd around the outsiders. The room was hot with their breath. Anguished faces and torches extended back through the room, and down the hall beyond.

"Who are you?" a Varsity yelled.

"My name's Gates," the red-eyed boy said. "Look, just calm down. We're infected just like you. And we were trying to get you out of here."

"Bullshit!" a Freak shouted.

Gates's red eye flared. "It's not bullshit! You think we want to be trapped in this place?"

"Who was in that bus?" a Geek yelled.

"How the hell should I know?"

"Gates?" a Freak girl next to Lucy said in a trembling voice. Gates calmed at the sight of her worried face. She held a torch, and firelight licked the thin lines of scar tissue that stood out in sharp relief all down her forearm.

"Yeah?" he said to her.

"What's out there?" she said.

The crowd went quiet. It was what they'd all wanted to know for the last year and a half.

"Well . . . what exactly do you know?" Gates said.

"The military told us that the virus was spreading, and they were working on fixing it and we haven't heard anything since," Belinda said from the back of the room.

He blinked his way through what Belinda had just said, his red eye blinking much more than the other.

"Shit, I don't know where to start," Gates said. "Uh . . ."

The room waited patiently for any information he could give them. Gates seemed surprised by just how captivated they all were. A minute ago, they were a vicious, barking mob.

"Let's see," Gates went on. "The infection hit us about three weeks after you. Most of us went to St. Patrick's Academy down in Denton."

"The private school?" Will said.

"Yeah," Gates said, brightening a bit when he saw that it was Will asking. "We'd heard there was a quarantined school in Pale Ridge and all these people had died, but Denton is fifty miles south of here, and the news said we had nothing to worry about." His eyes unfocused as he got lost in the memory. "The day it hit us, it was school spirit day. All our parents were there. We were all out on the lacrosse field. One second it was fine, the next, parents were vomiting blood all around me. My mom—"

Gates cleared his throat and stopped talking. He looked out at the crowd of McKinley kids again.

"I'm sure this stuff is nothing new to you. Must have been the same here," he said. "But when the soldiers came for us, they didn't try to quarantine us, or capture us. They started shooting. Two hundred and thirty-two of us eventually made it out of there alive. We hid anywhere we could, and we stayed on the move. They were evacuating the whole state, and they were having a hard time. People driving over each other's lawns, and cars crashing into each other and shit. It was nuts. The virus was spreading so fast. The more kids caught it, the more adults died. Parents with teenagers were trying to get their kids out of the state before they caught the virus. It got real messy. Any soldier that saw a teenager with a bald head, they'd kill you. And it wasn't just the soldiers either. Everybody had guns. Fuckin' grandmas were shooting at us."

Lucy could hear the crowd get sick. Her stomach sank too. She thought of her own family trying to leave Colorado, scared they were going to die. Somewhere along the way she'd convinced herself not to think about whether her parents had died. She thought most kids in here had done the same. Now, those feelings took hold of her again.

"We ate what we could steal or what we could hunt," Gates continued. "We hid wherever we could. In the mountains, in the sewers. Empty barns. But we were never safe. They murdered so many of us. Some were lucky enough to phase out. There's only forty-two of our original group now."

"Are our families out there?" a sunken-chested Nerd boy said.

Gates looked at him, perplexed. "Were you listening?"

The Nerd boy continued to stare at Gates, like he hadn't answered him yet.

"No, they're not," Gates said.

The Nerd turned and walked back into the crowd.

Gates took a deep breath. "Since the evacuation, the only adults around have been military search squads. I take that back . . . there are a few nut-jobs out there that refused to move out, and every once in a while you'll get some angry bastards who come back to Colorado, wanting to kill any infected they can. That's probably who was driving this bus. But mostly, it's been soldiers and infected."

"They didn't let you turn yourself in?" Lucy said.

A flicker of a snarl upset Gates's somber face.

"No, they did," he said. "They drove these giant armored trucks around. They'd blast the same announcement over and over, that we wouldn't be harmed if we came forward and got into the back of the truck. They said they had a facility for the infected where they would be taking us, and we'd be safe there. A lot of other kids did turn themselves over."

Emotion choked Gates to a stop again. One of the outsiders, a girl with short white hair, walked to Gates and gave his shoulder a reassuring squeeze. He cleared his throat and dug his knuckle into his red eye, then started up again.

"But it was all bullshit," Gates said, and shook his head. "You can be sure they drove those kids straight to a gas chamber."

This boy is a liar, Lucy thought. He was playing with their heads with all this talk of murderous adults on the outside. He had to be a liar. *Please let him be a liar.*

"And then, you'll love this . . . that offer to turn ourselves in had an expiration date. They let us know that if we didn't turn ourselves over by their deadline, our refusal to come forward would be viewed as a hostile action. That's what they called it. Like we were the bad guys. They said that we would be considered 'deadly threats with intent to do harm.' Basically, turn yourself in or we're going to come kill you. And that's the way it's been since then; we run, they hunt us. Well, it was until about a month ago."

"What happened a month ago?" Lucy said, annoyed that this guy was pausing dramatically. He had the room riveted, and he knew it.

"The military picked up and left. Just like that. We'd been

hiding in the woods over by Tilsing Hills, and we stayed there for a week 'cause it seemed like it had to be a trick. But another week passed, and they still didn't come back. Eventually, we went ahead and walked into town. That first day we took whatever we wanted from the stores and houses we could break into. There were other kids like us, crawling out of their hiding places and passing through. We traded information, stuff we knew about where we'd been. Somebody said they heard McKinley was still locked up and you weren't being fed anymore. We figured somebody better let you out."

He smiled.

"You guys are kinda celebrities to the kids out there. You're the first ones. There wasn't an infected out there who didn't wish they could trade places with a McKinley kid. No one shoots at you in here. For whatever reason, you all got to stay safe in your high school, they even fed you."

Lucy found herself cussing uncontrollably, but she wasn't alone. The whole hallway was pissed.

"You got no idea what it's been like in here," a voice said, louder than the rest. Lucy knew it immediately. Violent pushed through the crowd with a slight limp. She didn't seem to care that the outsiders were tightening up on their guns. She stopped just ahead of the rest of the McKinley kids, and stood there fuming, with a sharp cafeteria knife in her hand. She looked so strong, like none of this had frightened her in the least. Violent could handle anything.

"Hold on. Hold on," Gates said, putting his hands up. "I'm not saying you had it easy—"

The crowd shouted over him. It didn't matter what he said; he'd crushed their dreams of what the outside could be, and now they were once again locked inside a place where there was no hope. They continued to shout questions and insults at the outsiders for nearly fifteen minutes, and they would've kept going all day if news hadn't come filtering through the crowd that something crazy was happening in the quad.

3

THE GRAY CANOPY THAT USUALLY HUNG

over the quad was now stretching toward the sky. It was as if God was outside the school, holding a giant vacuum cleaner to the middle of it. The canopy's center rose up into the air like a circus tent, and the gray material pulled taut, still clinging to the four walls of the quad. Will heard the heavy grinding of a distant motor. He saw the canopy start to pop away from the wall in different spots all around the quad's edge. With each pop came a puff of concrete dust, and the canopy would pull bits of wall away with it.

Nearly everyone in the school was there, staring up at the rising ceiling and freaking out. Belinda was to Will's left, Lucy to his right. A small group of Loners crowded in close around them.

The distant motor lurched. The canopy had reached the

limit of its elasticity. With a tremendous rip, the canopy tore away from the school entirely.

The quad was flooded with sunlight. Will had to shield his eyes at first. When he took his hand away, he saw a brilliant orange crane arm cutting diagonally across the blue sky. The heavy gray material of the canopy hung from the crane's cable like a wet towel.

Everyone gasped at the sight of the sky. Will's spirits soared into the boundless space above his head. Fresh air engulfed him. He took a deep breath in, and it made the air he'd been breathing for the last year and a half seem like car exhaust. He was practically outside. Kids were hugging each other around him. He saw Lucy smile. The crane turned slowly, and swung the giant canopy away from them.

Will scanned the bright, overexposed quad. Edges were sharper. Corners of the quad that once were lost in shadow were now found, and in the new light, they lost some of their menace. It went the same with people's faces. The dim, gray light that had shined through the old canopy used to paint deep shadows under their eyebrows, obscuring their eyes, turning their brows into cliffs and their eyes into chasms. In the clarity of full daylight, their eyes looked like normal teenage eyeballs.

He saw that there were tangled bushels of razor wire along the top edge of each of the quad's four walls. There were two people on the roof, standing behind the hip-high razor wire hedges. A man and a woman, in motorcycle helmets, both wearing scuba tanks on their backs. Air hoses curled over their shoulders and tucked up into their helmets. The man's helmet was black, the woman's lilac. He wore a canvas jacket and trousers. She wore a beige, zip-up hoodie and unfashionable jeans. There was a guitar amp, half covered in stickers, by the man's feet.

The man bent over and plugged a black microphone cord into the amp. It let out a harsh squelch of feedback. Will saw that the other end of the long cord was attached to his helmet.

"We represent a network of concerned parents," the man said in a muffled but strongly amplified voice.

The quad went silent.

"I'll get right to the point." The man continued, "We didn't plan on driving a bus into your school, but we had to do something. I know this may not be what you want to hear, but we have decided that we can take better care of you in here. We won't be letting you out."

"What the fuck?" Will said. The crowd's roar around him drowned him out. It was so malicious, so full of hatred, that it frightened Will.

Lucy was red in the face beside him. "You can't do this!" she screamed.

"Listen to me!" the man shouted. "The military wants you dead."

That got the crowd's attention.

"In fact, they think you're dead right now. I know because I knew the man put in charge of running McKinley for the military. I hounded him for months with requests to open up lines of communication with you. It never worked. But a month ago, he contacted me and told me that they were pulling out of McKinley and ceasing the delivery of food. He and all his men had to report to the front lines to aid in the effort to quarantine every uninfected teen in the country. See, they've given up on containing the virus. They're locking up all the healthy teens now, so that the virus can't spread. And they've passed a new law that makes it legal to kill an infected teen in self-defense, or if they come within twenty-five feet of you. I read that only one way. The government wants to kill the infected off. You all included. The last thing the man told me before he hung up was that he'd been given the order to kill all the students in McKinley before he withdrew."

Gasps rippled through the crowd.

"Thank God he couldn't go through with it," the man went on. "At least somebody in that operation had a conscience. He lied to his superiors and told them he'd filled the school with poison gas. And then he told me that McKinley was my responsibility now."

"Let us out!" an outsider screamed.

"We're only doing what is best for you," the man in the motorcycle helmet said. "In here, we can keep you safe. People are moving back to Pale Ridge. The government announced that they have done all they can to clean the virus out of Colorado, and the risk of running into an infected is nearly the same as anywhere else. If we let you out, we couldn't stop someone from killing you. Those kids who got out earlier, off hiding wherever they're hiding now, they'll have no one to protect them when the time comes. But we can keep you safe in here. We can defend this place. We're not going to leave. I need you to understand that. We won't leave you. No matter what."

"Whose parents are you?" a Geek girl called out.

The man paused before answering.

"We've talked to former graduates. We know what things are like in here, and we've decided that we can't tell you. We don't want our children to be targeted."

Kids began calling out their parents' names, and saying, *Mom? Dad?*

The woman in the lilac helmet elbowed the man. The man unplugged his microphone cord from the amp, and she plugged in her own connection. Her voice was a muffled blast of emotion.

"I want to say this to my own kids, so I'll say it to all of you. We love you. That's why we're here."

Will heard kids start weeping and whimpering around the quad. Everyone was in shock. Will didn't know what to think of any of this, but what he did know was that wasn't his dad up there, his dad wasn't that tall.

"Bring in the food, they need to eat," the woman said to the man.

That one word, *food*, made Will's mouth well up with saliva. He knew it must have been having the same effect on every other kid. None of them had eaten in two weeks, not since they raided Varsity's food stores. The parent in the black motorcycle helmet waved his arms in a forward motion like he was directing someone into a parallel parking space.

The distant crane's motor belched to life, and then chugged along with a dull drone.

"Whoa," Will said in wonder.

A train-car-sized block of food and supplies rose into view from beyond the quad wall. Its plastic-wrapped bundles shined in the glaring sunlight. The block hung from the giant crane arm. The crane turned, swinging the block until it settled to a stop just over the center of the quad. Everyone in the quad leaned forward in anticipation. Food drops were something they understood.

The man plugged himself back into the amp with another loud squelch. "There is more than enough food for everyone. So, what I want to see, once we lower the food, is a nice, orderly line. Each box has everything one person should need for two weeks if rationed correctly. Please take one box, and move on.

Any extra can then be divided accordingly."

Everyone in the quad stared at the block of food as it was lowered, an inch a second, swinging gently from side to side on its twisted metal cable. It was almost time. Soon, the cable would detach. The block would fall.

Except it didn't. It kept on creeping down at a steady crawl. People looked at each other, confused. Geeks to Nerds. Skaters to Sluts. No one was sure what to do. Would everyone really line up and do this peacefully?

When it was fifteen feet from the ground, the Skaters broke into a run, and gathered under the hanging block. They climbed onto each other's shoulders until one of them was able to grab the edge of a pallet at the block's bottom. That Skater had long black hair on the back of his head, the rest of his scalp covered in an inch of white fuzz. He scaled up the block of supplies and climbed onto the top. He pulled out a rusted screwdriver and stabbed it through the shrink-wrap that bound a cluster of boxes together. He pulled the plastic open and tugged at the loose boxes, causing them to tumble down to the ground.

The Sluts ran next. Then Varsity. They converged in the center. They converged in the shadow of the hanging block. Kids jumped up with all their might, leaping like it was tip-off at the big basketball game. They hooked their fingers around the plastic straps binding the block together and hung off it, swinging and swaying along with the heavy block, their knees knocking into the heads of the kids on the ground. Unlucky climbers, who'd made it to the top of the block, kept falling off and crashing down on to the crowd below.

"Stop climbing on it!" The voice came from above. "Make a line! MAKE A SINGLE-FILE LINE!"

The kids on the top began to rock the block of supplies like a seesaw.

"Stop that!" the man screamed.

The crane's motor lurched. The block reversed and raised up toward the sky.

Kids below the block began to curse at the man in the sky. They clawed for the block as it rose out of reach. Most of the kids hanging off the bottom of the block were pulled off by the kids on the ground.

The higher the block rose, the more frantic the parents became. A Freak, still on top of the block, was beginning to climb the cable. When the man in the black motorcycle helmet saw the climbing Freak, he waved his arms wildly at the crane.

With a heavy click, the cable detached and the block fell. The heavy mass of food crashed to the ground, crushing the kids who couldn't get out of the way fast enough. The lashes that bound the block together snapped, and boxes went flying. The victims of the falling block who didn't die immediately wailed in vicious, broken-boned pain.

"No!" the man screamed.

Will and the small group of Loners charged toward the center. The other gangs that had held back did the same. Everyone swarmed the pile of food and fought for their share of the grub. The parents in the sky screamed at them to stop, but no one listened.

4

BLOOD PUDDLES IN THE DIRT. LUCY STARED at them as she chewed her chili. The bodies of the kids who had been killed by the falling block had just been carried away by their gangs. It should have turned her stomach to eat while watching the spilt blood of other kids slowly sink into the ground and become a red mud, but it didn't. She was that hungry.

It was hard to be moved by much of anything anymore. From the moment Lucy had seen her homeroom teacher paint the blackboard red with his lungs, it had been one tragedy after another. Kids dying. Months of misery and abuse in the Pretty Ones. Brad trying to rape her. The tunnel collapsing on David. The weeks of starvation after that. The dream of escape obliterated by a speeding school bus. And then the news from that kid, Gates, and then from these parents, that even if escape had been possible, all that waited outside was death.

Bad things would never stop happening to them. Lucy was sure of it.

She glanced up to the roof line. There were no parents standing up there watching them anymore, not that she could see. After the drop was over, they'd tried to apologize for what had happened, but kids on the quad hurled so many shards of pallet wood and small chunks of concrete up at them that they retreated out of view and hadn't made an appearance since.

Lucy sat with the Loners by the east wall. Twelve kids with white hair, sitting on the ground and eating out of cans. This was everyone, except for Leonard, who was across the quad, talking to a friend in the Geeks. The rest of the Loners had escaped. The twins were gone. Nelson, Sasha, so many more.

"We're the smallest now," Lucy said.

It was an understatement; no other gang lost more than ten members in the escape. The Loners had lost seventy-seven.

"We've been small before," Will said. He rubbed her arm. He managed a half smile. He was straining to keep his face light and breezy, but it looked drawn and malnourished. She knew he was putting on a good front for her, and it was very sweet. He had to be tired, and scared, and depressed just like she was, but still Will's eyes sparkled with defiance. She loved that about him.

Mort's twisted, ruined hand started shaking before he could get a plastic spoonful of minestrone soup to his lips.

"It's not good," he chanted. "It's not good."

"Chill, Mort," Will said. "We don't know what will happen. I sure didn't expect to be eating beef ravioli under a clear blue sky today. Tomorrow, who knows?"

"We'll be out of ravioli, I know that much," Belinda said.

"Sixteen cans," Ritchie said with disgust. "How are thirteen people supposed to survive on sixteen cans of food?" He was standing and eating, anxiously shifting his weight side to side. It made the scars on his face seem to wriggle and writhe in the sunlight.

"Calm down, ugly. We had one bad drop, it's not the end of the world," Will said.

Ritchie huffed and rolled his eyes, as he turned his back to Will.

"Look at how much extra food they all have," Mort said.

Mort was looking at the two gangs on either side of them. The Loners were sandwiched between the Skaters and the Freaks, black hair on one side, blue on the other. There were close to fifty Skaters, and roughly a hundred Freaks. Both gangs were still eating, still tearing open new loaves of bread, and opening new cans of food. The Loners couldn't afford to open any more cans until tomorrow.

Other than Ritchie and Will, they had lost all of their best fighters in the escape. Belinda was slow. Mort was half a cripple. Lucy herself was new to running in the drops, and she'd tried her best, but she'd only managed to get one can of stewed tomatoes. Even the others, like Colin and Vincent, who had fought in every drop the Loners ever took part in, they hadn't fared much better.

Belinda began to whimper beside her. Lucy hugged Belinda gently.

"It's okay, Bel," Lucy said.

"You know Freddy, that boy I told you about?"

"The Nerd you kinda sorta started dating?" Lucy said with forced levity.

"Yeah." Belinda's voice went softer. "Back in the processing facility, he said I could join the Nerds if I wanted . . . "

"He's probably just flirting with you," Will said. There was an edge of irritation in his voice. Lucy looked over and saw that Will had been listening to them.

"Sort of a weird time to flirt," Belinda said.

Two guys came walking over from the Skaters. One had his head shaved except for black polka dots of hair, and the other had the top of his head shaved like he'd gone bald. Both of them had white roots. They wore braided wire rings that Lucy had seen Skater girls selling. They'd cut V-necks into their crew neck T-shirts. They walked right up to Ritchie.

"Wassup, bruiser," one of them said.

"You were pretty impressive out there today," the other said.

"Oh, yeah? You think so?" Ritchie replied.

"What is this?" Will said to Lucy. She could hear Will's anger building.

"Listen, man, we were wondering if you ever thought about going Skater. We could use a solid fighter like you."

"We got a half-pipe, rails, we have lots of in-gang competitions, you might like that. And we have lots of girls," Polka Dots said.

"Girls?" Ritchie said. Even though Lucy didn't like the idea of losing Ritchie, she couldn't help but find it cute, the way Ritchie's voice went up when he said the word *girls*. Like a hopeful little boy.

"Oh, yeah, bro. Tons of chicks. Unless you're dating a Loner, y'know, I don't know what you got goin'. . . ."

"Fuck no," Ritchie said. Lucy went back to not finding anything about Ritchie cute.

"You've got to be kidding me," Will said. He'd gotten to his feet and strode over to Ritchie, pointing his finger in his face as he yelled. "Are you serious, Ritchie? Skaters? You don't remember our run-in with them in the commons? One of them set your arm on fire!"

"I had a jacket on," Ritchie said.

"That's not the point. You think you can trust them?"

"Hey, that was a special situation," one of the Skaters said.

"How're you gonna skate your half-pipes when we broke your boards?" Will said.

"We're making more," the other Skater said, crossing his arms.

"Get lost, garbage men," Will said.

The Skaters put up their hands and backed off.

"We're gonna bounce. Think about it, huh?" one of them said to Ritchie before they walked off.

Will focused back on Ritchie. "What do you think you're doing, man?"

"You're mad at me? Look at Leonard," Ritchie said.

He pointed across the quad to where Leonard was standing by the Geeks. Leonard had a lock of purple hair clipped into his own white hair, and he was checking himself out in a mirror shard that a Geek girl held up for him. Leonard was laughing and smiling, happier than Lucy had seen him in a while.

"I don't get it," Will said. "Does Leonard not remember Zachary holding a knife to David's throat? Belinda, did you forget that the Nerds ambushed us in the library? I feel like I'm going crazy here. You don't want to be Loners anymore, just like that?"

Silence settled on the quad, and at first, Lucy thought that Will's words were so powerful that they'd brought a hush over the crowd, but then she saw that a group of the kids from the outside had just walked onto the quad. They all had white hair, like Loners. For the first time, none of them carried any guns. They stood by the hallway, squinting up at the sky. The one with long hair and one red eye stood at the front of the rest.

"I can't believe that dude, Gates, is here," Colin said with a wet belch. Typical. Colin was the grossest.

"The one who told us about the outside?" Lucy asked. "You know him?"

"You guys don't?" Colin said with a roll of his eyes. He let the moment hang.

"Oh my god, will you just tell us?" Will said.

Colin smiled, satisfied. "My cousin went to St. Patrick's. Gates is, like, a legend there. He was wild. Didn't take any shit, not from his parents, not from teachers, not even the cops. I heard that when a cop tried to shut down one of his parties he straight punched him in the face."

"That sounds like bullshit," Ritchie said.

"Well, his parties aren't bullshit, everyone in Denton knows about 'em. I went to one. No joke. It was in an abandoned Kmart. Yeah, that's right. Fucking epic. And you know how I can barf on command?"

"Yes, we do. Please don't show us again," Lucy said.

"Yeah, well, he thought it was great. My cousin had me do it for him, and he loved it. Gates brought me around the whole store and made me do it for everybody at the party. I'd never barfed so much in my life. I had to keep chugging 7UP just to keep fuel in the tank."

Belinda sighed. "The things you're proud of, Colin, I don't, I don't understand you."

Colin made a vomiting noise and doubled over. Belinda cringed and looked away, shaking her head.

"Here's your chance to do it for him again," Mort said.

Lucy looked over to see that Gates was walking toward them.

"Saint Gates, the party king," Ritchie said sarcastically.

The outsiders had already been nicknamed the Saints. McKinley used to play St. Patrick's Academy in football, and that was their team's name, the Saints. Other names for them were floating around, but she could already tell that the Saints was the one that was going to stick. It sounded great when you said it with disgust.

Gates approached with a friendly smile. He held his hand out to shake as he neared Will.

Lucy went cold. She saw Sam out of the corner of her eye, running toward Will from the south wall, holding a chrome-plated pistol out in front of him.

"Look out," she yelled. But Sam wasn't going for Will, he was heading for Gates.

Gates whipped around fast, but it was too late. Sam was upon him. Sam pressed the gun's barrel hard into the middle of Gates's forehead. The machined lines of the gun gleamed in the sun.

"You're coming with me," Sam said. His sweaty, pale yellow hair was matted down across his forehead. His eyes were blasted wide open. He was breathing fast.

Gates's bloodshot eye blinked continuously, and it scrunched up that side of his face, but his other eye was clear and piercing. It didn't blink at all.

"We're going to go over there to your friends. And you're gonna tell them to hand over the rest of the guns to my gang," Sam said, "Or they can watch me blow your brains out."

Lucy was frozen with dread. It was a horrifying thought. Varsity with guns.

Gates busted up laughing.

"You think this is funny?" Sam said. His eyebrows bunched and he gritted his teeth.

Gates tried to stop laughing. He clamped his mouth shut, his cheeks puffed out. Lucy really wanted Gates to stop. After everything they endured, the last thing she needed was to watch Sam blow someone's head off.

"I'm sorry, I shouldn't be laughing. Go ahead. Pull the trigger," Gates said.

"What?" Sam said.

"It was super rude of me to laugh at you like that. I understand if you have to pull it."

"You don't know who you're tempting!" Sam yelled. "You think I've never killed someone? Ask anybody here."

Gates chuckled again, then he sighed.

"You don't have any bullets," Gates said.

"Yes, I do," Sam said.

"No . . . actually you don't. I recognize that gun. That's my friend, Shelly's, gun. See that little spot of pink nail polish on the trigger guard?"

"You're wrong."

"Shelly," Gates said loud and clear. "Is this your gun?"

"Yep," a sweet voice said from amid the Saints.

There were giggles from some of the girls around the quad. Sam blushed. His face shook with anger, and then he pulled the trigger.

Click.

The gun didn't go off. *Click-click-click.* Three more times, it didn't fire. Gates never flinched once.

"We ran out of bullets two weeks ago. Been looking for more though if you have any hot tips," Gates said.

Sam didn't know quite what to do now. He took his gun from Gates's head and let it hang at his side. The crowd snickered, and the laughter was spreading like an infection. Sam's cheeks went a darker shade of red. He pushed away from Gates.

Lucy saw a lopsided smile bloom on Will's face. *Oh no,* she thought, *just leave it alone. Sam's a maniac.*

Will cupped his hand beside his mouth to shout to the whole quad.

"Those aren't the only blanks he's been shooting since I kicked his balls up into his stomach."

The quad erupted in laughter. This audience was all too eager to hurt Sam's feelings, to have him put in his place. Lucy knew she was. She laughed, but it was a short laugh, because she was watching Sam's face. She saw the pain he felt when he looked back at everyone mocking him. And she saw the fury build up in him, and his eyes lock on Will.

Sam lunged for Will.

Before he could get to him, Gates jumped in front of Will, and shoved Sam back.

"I can't let you do that," Gates said. "This guy saved my life."

Will walked up and planted himself beside Gates. The two of them stood together against Sam.

"You want to fight us both?" Will said, grinning again. "Feeling confident about that?"

Sam flicked his jittering eyes back and forth between his opponents.

"Varsity, back me up!" Sam yelled.

Varsity stayed seated on the ground at the south wall. They kept their heads low, and continued to eat. Most kept their gaze trained on their food. They didn't seem eager to be a part of Sam's embarrassment. Sam getting rejected by his own gang really got the crowd laughing.

Sam screamed at Varsity, "What the hell are you doing?"

When none of them answered, Sam crossed the quad and stomped into the crowd of Varsity guys. He went berserk on them, shouting orders, all while the school laughed at him. Sam whipped his hand in the direction of the gym, and Varsity shuffled off the quad, most of them looking disgruntled and embarrassed.

"Who was that guy?" Gates said to Will.

"Some loser."

"What's your name?"

"Will."

"Well, hey, Will . . . ," Gates said and stuck out his hand again with a giant smile. "I just wanted to thank you. I don't know what to say really. I owe you my life."

Will shook his hand.

"Don't worry about it," Will said.

Will was beaming. He seemed very happy with himself for standing up to Sam. He seemed even happier that the Loners had witnessed it.

Colin walked up to Gates. "Hey, dude, remember me?"

"Oh shit. Puke guy. How's it goin'?" Gates said.

A few other Saints came rushing up to Gates.

"You good, Gates?" one of the boys said.

Lucy barely looked at the Saint boy's face. She was transfixed by what was hanging from one of the belt loops on the kid's jeans. A white leather eye patch.

"Hey!" Lucy said.

All the Loners and the outsiders looked at her. She pointed to the eye patch.

"Where did you get that?" she said.

The outsider boy held the white leather eye patch in his fingers. "Oh, this? Yeah, we were looting some houses in town. I took this off a dead kid. It's cool, right?"

5

DAVID WAS DEAD. WILL WISHED HE COULD
unknow it. But he'd seen the evidence along with everyone
else, David's eye patch, hanging off that kid's hip as a trin-
ket. They'd grilled that Saint about what the body looked
like. Apparently, it had been shot all to hell, something Will
couldn't handle thinking about. The body's description fit
David's height and build along with the white hair and the
ruined eye. Even after hearing all that, Will wanted to stay
a skeptic. And he would have if the house the body was in
hadn't matched Will and David's house, right down to the
overstuffed, blue chair in the corner of the living room. There
was no explaining it away. David was really dead. Will had
known there was a possibility his brother had died when the
tunnel collapsed, and he thought he had come to terms with it
in the last couple weeks, but it was only the possibility that he

had come to terms with. To know for sure was an entirely new level of pain, and Will wasn't sure he could take it.

He gripped a torch made from a broken metal curtain rod. The flaming part was a full roll of toilet paper that had been soaked in cooking grease. Fire was the only reliable light source since the power had gone out over a month ago. Without a torch you were stumbling through a vacuum, with nothing to remind you that you physically existed other than the hard floor pressing into your feet.

Will walked at a brisk clip, down the hallway, toward the Stairs. The Loners kept pace with Will. He must have seemed like he was taking charge, but he wasn't really, he just felt like he might start crying if he slowed down. He didn't want to fall apart in front of them. He could feel that the gang was only holding on by a string, and he didn't want to be the one to snip it. The torch flame fluttered, it was nearly out. They'd need to start a fire soon.

Will and the Loners arrived at the first floor door to the Stairs. He pushed, and the door swung open. When Will and Lucy had returned to tell the gang that the door to the outside was open, they'd run for the foyer right away. No one had locked the door to their home base on the way out, because they hadn't expected to ever return.

Will hesitated. By the torch's light, only the armory and the first flight up were revealed. Everything above was black.

"Well . . . we're home," Will said.

No one replied. It was cold silence behind him. He couldn't blame them. The Stairs didn't feel anything like home now. It only felt like a place where David used to be alive.

Will stepped inside. One by one, the Loners shuffled in behind him. They moved aimlessly around the bottom landing, like sleepwalkers. Will glanced at Ritchie and saw that tears brimmed on the edge of his eyelids, sparkling in the firelight. Ritchie loved David, everybody knew it. He was closer to David than Will had been for a while there. Ritchie stared up the staircase, into the blackness that light couldn't penetrate. It was like he was peering into his own grave.

"We should get a fire going," Will said.

Ritchie saw Will looking at him. He flinched, and shook his head, quick and violent, like a chicken.

"This table's broken," Ritchie said, moving to a tipped table in the armory. "I'll bash it up."

Will nodded. He didn't want to talk feelings with Ritchie, or anyone for that matter. If he popped the cap on his anguish, he was afraid he'd never get it back on.

Ritchie made a loud racket, stomping the table. He wasn't giving anyone an angle on his face as he beat the living hell out of that wood. Will looked around at the others. Leonard was hugging himself and refused to open his eyes. Belinda had her arms wrapped around Lucy and whispered comforting

words to her. Mort rubbed his temples like he had a bad headache. Colin was staring at Will with pity, but he looked away
as soon as Will caught his eyes.

"Okay," Will said with a clap, "let's help Ritchie out, huh?
Let's get that wood up to the lounge."

The group drifted up the stairs, trailing Will and his torch.
He stepped onto the landing where the Loners shared meals
together. It was also where David would do his speeches and
gang announcements. *Always wait till they're chewing.* That
was what David used to say about delivering bad news to the
gang. Will would never see his brother again.

He climbed up another flight, to the second landing, the
lounge. The flat-screen TV he'd stolen from the Freaks was
there, still faceup to be used as a table. The piles of library
books were there too among the mismatched chairs. Their
pages would be good kindling.

People dropped wood shards and chunks of table in the
center of the landing. They clattered onto the floor. The noise
of it was jarring in the unnatural quiet. There should've been
the sound of seventy-seven other kids there, going about
their daily tasks.

They assembled some of the wood and the crumpled-up
pages of a pirate novel into a pile, inside a disembodied sink
in the middle of the floor. Within five minutes of touching
the fading torch to the paper, the whole sink was ablaze. The

thirteen sat on the floor, in a tight circle, around it. They watched the black smoke rise up the stairwell.

The burning wood crackled. Loners stared into the flames, hoping to lose themselves in it. Now and then, they'd kick up conversation.

"Like, if I'd gone to St. Patricks, and had to go on the run . . . ," Belinda said, "I-I never would have made it. I can't run fast."

"I would have liked it," Ritchie said.

"Getting hunted sounds good to you? I'd slit my throat if I had to live like that," Mort said.

"I'm just saying I would have been good at it. I could've survived."

"Do you think the others are okay out there?" Leonard asked in a thin voice.

"They'll make it if they stay together," Will said.

No one replied. He kept his focus on tending to the fire.

"Colin, cut it out!" Ritchie said.

Colin had been scratching at the crotch of his jeans for the last few minutes.

"What? I'm just itching my dick," Colin said.

"I wish you had gotten out," Ritchie said.

Silence settled on the group again. The knowledge that David was dead hung in the air like a stench. No one wanted to talk about it. Or maybe they didn't want to talk about it around Will. He could see them looking at him with worry.

Belinda broke eye contact every time Will looked at her. Ritchie wasn't being an asshole to Will for once. Lucy was the worst; she looked at him like he was about to shatter into bits. He couldn't deal with it.

Will got up and left them all by the fire. He decided to busy himself with chores. He gathered blankets from the sleeping area one flight up, for people to have something soft to sleep on. He organized the food into neat piles in the corner. He went and opened the third floor door to the hallway so the smoke would have somewhere to go. Will kept on like that, creating little jobs for himself and completing them, while ignoring every request for him to stop and sit by the fire with the others, until the Loners had all succumbed to sleep.

The fire dwindled in the blackened sink. Will sat by his sleeping gang mates, around the fire, watching its flames shrink, and die. When the fire went out completely, it took the light with it. Will had never been afraid of the dark, but in this darkness, this cold void, he began to panic. He needed to restart the fire immediately. He needed the light. There were some matches in his backpack.

Will stumbled up the stairs, feeling his way with his hand on the handrail. He rounded the corner, waving his other hand out in front of him like a blind man. The stair he slept on, his stair bed, was six steps up the next flight. He counted until he was standing on the fifth step, then he crouched and patted his hands around until he felt the canvas material of his backpack. He picked it up. The matches were in the front pocket.

When Will's fingers touched the cool metal tab of the front pocket's zipper, his mind flashed back to the first day of school, when David drove him to McKinley in his Jeep, and Will couldn't stop nervously zipping and unzipping his bag. He remembered being scared of going to high school, but excited at the same time to be in the same school as his brother. He remembered the breeze whipping through David's messy brown hair. The ratty black hooded sweatshirt he always wore. Pale Ridge rushing past as they cruised through green lights. David teasing him, giving him advice. They had no idea that a catastrophe awaited them that morning. The brutal world they would have to endure. They had no idea that David, the depressed quarterback who had quit the team, would rise to be the savior and protector of the rejected, defenseless kids without gangs.

David could have done something great if he'd had a normal life. If none of this had ever happened, or if he had survived whatever killed him. He could have helped people. He would have been a success, Will knew it. He had more potential than Will ever would. But David would never get any of that. He'd never get to be in his twenties, or his thirties. He'd never have a wife, or kids, or a career. He'd never grow into an old man. He'd never know anything but the struggle that started that day they walked into this school, the same struggle that eventually robbed him of his life.

The grief that Will had been running from all night took hold of him, and he crumpled down onto the steps. Tears gushed from him. He couldn't control himself anymore. He sobbed, and moaned, and let the sadness pull him under.

He felt soft hands on his back, rubbing in an easy circle.

"Shhhh," Lucy said. "It's all right."

He reached out for her and they embraced. Lucy began to cry as well. She must have been holding her feelings back all night, like he had. They sat there, crying and hugging each other in the dark, for what must have been hours, before they lay down on the hard stairs and fell asleep.

6

THERE WAS A MACHETE IN LUCY'S HANDS.
David's machete. He'd made it out of a radiator shell that he
hammered until it was sharp. She'd found it dangling by a
shoe string, in the furthest corner of the armory. She pulled
out the blade and ran her fingers down the cardboard sheath.
Originally, David had simply folded a piece of cardboard into a
long rectangle and sealed it with duct tape. Lucy had removed
the tape and cut the rectangular sheath into the shape of the
machete. With great care, she'd sewn the edges back together
with spiral notebook wire.

She was nearly finished now. She twisted the excess of the
two wires together, until they were a little loop at the sheath's
tip. She took a leather cord that she'd cut from a belt and
laced it through the loop. She ran the cord to the other end
and fastened it to make a strap.

Lucy sat on David's bed, legs folded under her to the side.

She held the sheath out before her and admired it. The words "THE LONERS" were spelled across the face of it in silver thumbtacks. It was an impressive design. It would have looked great slung across David's back. That could never happen now. She sheathed the blade and set it down on the floor.

She had been spending a lot of time in David's room since the last drop, hiding away behind those heavy curtains that still hung, separating the top landing from the rest of the Stairs. It was the only place she felt safe. So many people were sure that the parents were fixing to quit after how horribly the drop had ended. And even if they stuck around and followed through on their big promises, life inside McKinley wasn't any less dismal.

David's room remained a shrine that no one felt they had the right to disturb. She was surprised there weren't bunches of flowers piled all over the floor, like a highway memorial. A single lantern was the only light source. It was a glass apple-juice bottle in the shape of an apple, filled with cooking oil. A plastic gallon jug shielded the flaming wick and gave off a frosted yellow light.

The sheets of David's bed were still rumpled and thrown about, like he had only crawled out of his bed this morning. Lucy held up his bed sheets and drew their scent in. They smelled vaguely like campfire smoke, like the rest of the room. But they still smelled like David's sheets. Detergent smell. No one had cleaner sheets than him. Still, there was more. She thought she smelled a pinch of his sweat, the pink bathroom hand soap he'd used to wash his hair, and some of the vanilla extract she used to wear as perfume. But the sum of all those ingredients would never compare to smelling the real thing, David in the flesh, holding her in his arms. Lucy felt tears warm her eyes.

Their time together, really together, had been too brief. They had kissed for the very first time at the Geek show, but that same night he'd been attacked by Hilary. After his eye had healed, they only had a few weeks before he phased out of the virus and needed to leave. The food drops had stopped in that time, and their world was falling apart, but in this room, in this bed, wrapped in these sheets, they shared a couple of peaceful mornings together, where nothing past those curtains existed. When the school was still asleep, and the day hadn't started, they had their time alone to talk, to learn about each other, or to just lay there, in the quiet, with his heavy arm laid over her, and not say anything at all. She still fantasized about going further with David. She'd wanted to lose her virginity to him, but he'd held back as if somehow he knew he wouldn't be around too long.

The lights came on.

Lucy looked up. The fluorescent ceiling panel overhead flickered back and forth from dim to bright until it finally settled on bright. Cheers echoed up the Stairs, followed by applause. Lucy stood in disbelief. The power was back on.

After a month of living in the dark. The parents had come through after all. That didn't change the fact that they were still holding McKinley prisoner.

Will popped his head through the curtains. He wore a big smile, and it was a pleasant surprise. His dirty-gray hair was swooped to the side. He held his hands out, splayed like he'd just done a magic trick.

"Eh?" he said.

"What do you mean 'eh'? You're taking credit for this?"

"I mean, I can't say it wasn't me. I have been putting out some pretty positive vibes."

Lucy laughed. "Well, now you are, at least. What's with the sunny attitude?"

"I realized we had way more weapons than we could ever use, so I traded the extra ones and got a bunch more food. And then with the lights coming on like this? I think things are going to be okay."

Lucy smiled. She wasn't going to tell Will this, but he sounded like David.

"Nice smile," Will said.

Lucy blushed and smiled wider. "Oh, you like?"

"Oh, not that one though, that one looks terrible."

She burst out laughing and hugged him. She wasn't expecting to laugh today. It blew away the gloom for a moment.

"Hey, guess what?" Will said when they separated. "You know how the Nerds have been working on getting graduation going again? They got it working. Kemper's graduating right now in the quad. Wanna go check it out?"

"Sure," Lucy said. "That sounds good."

He took her hand and they walked down all three floors of the Stairs. It was dirty and dusty and there was still a lot of work to be done, but the stairs felt positively cheerful now that the lights were on. They stepped out into the bright hallway.

"Look at it all lit up!" Lucy said. "It actually feels like daytime again."

"No more torches!" Will said at the top of his lungs. "Thank God."

Lucy laughed. "Let me never see another torch again."

They moseyed toward the quad at a pleasant pace. It was nice to just walk with Will, without any crisis hanging over their heads, without the tragedies of their lives on the front of their minds. She was able to push that all away for a bit and savor the normality of merely strolling down a hall with someone she trusted.

As they stepped around the corner into the last hall before the quad, Will held his arm out in front of Lucy and stopped her.

"Do you hear that?" Will said.

Lucy strained. She could hear something that sounded like muffled voices. They were coming from a classroom ahead.

"Is somebody arguing?" Lucy said.

"I don't think so."

Will walked ahead of her to the classroom where the noises were coming from. Lucy stayed close behind him. The door was closed, but not all the way. Will pressed his face up to the crack between the door and the frame and eased the door open a few inches.

"Holy shit," Will said.

"What?"

Will stood there, staring, seemingly unable to speak.

"Is this another joke?" she whispered, and she got her face right up next to Will's. She peered inside. Lucy's breath caught in her throat.

A boy and a girl were having sex on a teacher's desk.

The girl was a Freak and she had her legs wrapped around a bare-assed Varsity boy who lay on top of her. They were forehead to forehead, staring deep into each other's eyes. The two of them were so lost in each other that nothing else existed. The girl dragged her nails across the skin of the boy's back. His fingers were dug through the tangles of her blue hair, and he held her head with both hands as he kissed her deeply. They clung to each other. They craved each other.

Lucy's heart began to throb in her chest. The Varsity boy's pants were scrunched down around his ankles, and the girl's were on the floor. Lucy watched the boy's ass rise and fall as he pushed himself into the girl. The Freak moaned in rhythm with his movements. Her softly twisting face revealed a pleasure Lucy didn't know. Lucy's breathing sped up. She found herself wanting to feel what that Freak girl felt.

Will's cheekbone brushed against her temple, and she turned to look at him. Their faces hung inches from each other's. Intimately close. Will looked into her eyes and then down at her lips. Lucy's heart stuttered.

A flying combat boot smacked into the door next to Will's head.

"Get out of here!" the Varsity boy yelled.

Lucy screamed, and Will jumped. He grabbed her hand and tugged her forward. The two of them ran away, laughing. As they neared the doors to the quad, they slowed to a walk, but they still giggled. All the conversation they could muster was about how crazy and random that was. Lucy never mentioned the steamy moment they had shared at the door, and neither did Will. Her skin still tingled at the thought of it, but it filled her with fear at the same time. Will's friendship was the only thing that had buoyed her in the darkest weeks, when she felt certain that they would all starve to death. She couldn't shake the feeling that a single hookup with Will, as fun as it might be, could end up ruining their friendship forever.

The Nerds stood in the center of the quad. Their arms were interlocked and they formed a protective circle around Kemper in the center of the quad. It looked to Lucy that, even though they'd replaced him as leader during the coup when they'd stolen David, the Nerds still cared for the guy.

The orange crane arm towered in the sky, and a cable was extended from its tip, all the way down to Kemper who was strapped into a body harness. He held the disembodied thumb scanner from the graduation booth, and a rubber cord led from it up to the man in the motorcycle helmet, who stood behind the razor wire fence at the roof's edge.

Kemper held the thumb scanner up for the crowd of other gangs that had gathered around the perimeter to see. The thing was an awkward block of metal that had been wrapped in protective layers of duct tape.

"So, basically it works like it always did," he said with a self-satisfied giggle. "When you get a nose bleed, you test yourself on here. Hold your thumb and wait. Instead of getting a reading on a monitor, they'll get the results up there."

Kemper pointed up to the man on the roof, who had the graduation booth's screen perched on a folding chair at the ledge. It had a circuit board and bushel of stray wires on the back of it. The man tilted his helmet down at Kemper and gave him a thumbs-up.

"Okay, thumbs-up, that means you're good, and so . . . that's it. Pretty simple, right? Unless you get the thumbs-down. Then, I guess . . . I don't know, better luck next time." Kemper laughed. "I'll keep thinking on this whole setup though. Maybe . . . Maybe I'll stick around out there and noodle with some other ways to make graduation more—"

"Kemper," one of the Nerds interrupted. "You gotta go."

Kemper pursed his lips, then nodded. "Right. Okay. Well . . . Bye-bye, everybody."

Kemper gave the man a thumbs-up. The crane started and the cable jerked him upward. Kemper waved to his gang. They cheered for him. He raised his fists in victory. A little higher up, his stare became fixed on one spot. Lucy followed his gaze to Violent.

Kemper waved to Violent, and smiled at her. Violent's face was still as stone. She gave Kemper no emotion back, but it didn't seem to bother him. The two of them held eye contact for a long time, way too long for it to mean nothing. Kemper ascended by cable, smiling the whole way, cheerful until the very end. He rose twenty feet above the quad's walls, before the crane arm began to turn, and he was slowly swung out of view.

Lucy looked over at Violent again. When other people's dye jobs had faded over the hard times, Violent had maintained hers. Her hair was a deep shade of red. The rumor was that Violent soaked her hair in blood once a week. Some said she drew the blood from the boys she hooked up with. Others said that the Sluts had to donate their blood every Sunday, and Violent would boil it all in a big steel soup pot that she stirred with a rusty knife, until the blood was a dense crimson sludge that she would smear through her hair.

A year ago, Lucy probably would have believed those

rumors. But she'd seen Violent cry. She'd seen her care about her friends. Violent wasn't some vampire bathing in blood. She was another kid stuck in here like everyone else. Still, she was doing a lot better job of surviving in this place than Lucy was. Violent was the leader of her own gang of fighters, and everyone in school was scared of her.

Violent snapped her eyes over at Lucy. Lucy looked to the ground out of instinct, then felt stupid for doing it. She gradually lifted her eyes again. Violent waved her over.

Lucy looked to the Loners around her and then slipped away from Will and the others as they were starting to take bets over whether Kemper would actually stick around outside the walls like he'd said or get the hell out of Colorado and never look back.

As Lucy got closer to Violent and the Sluts, she got more uncomfortable. Violent looked so mean. Her electrical tape eyebrows were cut into particularly angry arches today. She had scabs on her knuckles. A bone in her forearm jutted out like it was broken; it must have healed that way.

"Juicy Lucy," Violent said with a smile. She fixed Lucy with a drawn-out stare. "You look scared."

"No."

"You're not hard to read. It's in the way you carry yourself. But that's fine, you should be scared." She gestured toward the Loners. "How long do you really think that's gonna last?"

Lucy looked back to Will and the tiny group. "What are you talking about?"

"It's not just me. The whole school's talking. No one thinks the Loners are gonna make it to the next food drop."

"Is that all? You want to tell me I'm ugly too?"

Violent sighed. "Look, you handled yourself well in the Nerd's hallway. That's a fact."

Lucy wasn't expecting that. It wasn't every day that the toughest girl in school gave you a compliment. Lucy was surprised at the pride she felt. She stood a little straighter. Violent looked all around Lucy's face like she was disgusted with each detail of it.

"Jesus Christ, you're not great, all right? You're shit. You got lucky. Don't start thinking you're something. But you kept your head screwed on when everybody started to die. And that's good."

"Do you have a point?" Lucy said.

Lucy swore she heard Violent growl softly.

"I already made it. Your gang's going away," Violent said.

"You're going to have to pick another team soon. Now, you can go play games with the Geeks, or hide inside books with the Nerds, you could go to any of them. But, you go Sluts? It won't be fun. I'll make you work, girl. It's gonna hurt. But I promise you this. When I'm done with you, there's nothing in this school that'll scare you anymore."

Lucy felt chills pebbling the skin up and down her body. She didn't know what to say.

"I've got one open slot. There's this Freak, she used to be a sprinter, track and field. She's fast. Could use a girl like that." Violent frowned. "If I don't hear from you by tomorrow night, I'm giving your spot to the Freak."

7

SAM GLIDED THROUGH THE POOL WITH
phenomenal speed. He was alone. A shark in a tank. Full of
power. All muscle. All instinct. Fueled by a fresh feeding. He
loved this pool. It was his place to escape, his place to sort out
the problems. There were always problems.

There was going to be a food drop today. It was Varsity's only
real shot at taking control again. The last drop had come out
of nowhere, and his gang hadn't been prepared. They'd looked
like chumps. He'd spent half of the drop having to yell at his
guys two or three times to listen to him. They acted like they
didn't know who was in charge. And then there was the whole
bullshit with them not backing him in front of that Saint.

Things had gotten so messed up somehow. No, not somehow. It was that epileptic chihuahua, Will Thorpe. One lucky
kick and that uppity Scrap knocked down everything Sam
had built. It took a year to make Varsity that strong, that tight,

that obedient. It took a year to pile up that much food. And in the end, all Sam could do was watch as the entire school stole from him, and filled their pockets with his food, right in front of his face. Buzzards. They plucked those bleachers clean.

Something plunked into the water in front of Sam and bumped into his head. It was a basketball.

Somebody threw a ball at him?! Chlorine stung his eyes, making him more agitated. He looked up, in search of the dead man that hucked a Rawlings at his head. Instead, he found a hundred of them.

All of Varsity stood at the pool's edge, lining the entire perimeter. Sam tensed up. He didn't like this.

"Free swim's not for another half hour," he said, keeping his tone restrained. "Get the hell out."

No one moved. He took slow-motion steps through the water, toward the stairs at the shallow end. The cloudy water rippled around him, and the little splashes echoed off the high ceiling.

"This water's filthy," Sam said. "I want it cleaned today."

Sam wasn't an idiot. He knew Varsity was grumbling. He knew they had grievances. He knew this was them flexing their muscles. But he wasn't about to let them complain. He told them how things were, not the other way around.

He rose out of the water, striding up the steps toward the wall of Varsity in front of him. They didn't part for him. Sam locked eyes with Anthony.

"Get me a towel," Sam said.

Anthony stayed still.

"Get your own towel, Sam," someone said. Sam knew the voice instantly. Terry Sharpe.

Sam turned around and looked from face to face until he found Terry. He was a tall bastard, but proportionate. Not skinny tall. He had caramel skin and gray eyes. A real pretty boy. Terry had been captain of the basketball team and one of the baseball team's most powerful sluggers. He'd been the key to assembling Varsity early on and keeping it intact. There was an unspoken agreement that Terry vouched for Sam with his guys, and in return, Sam let Terry live like a prince on a healthy allowance of food and perks.

"You got something to say, Sharpe?" Sam said. "'Cause I hope it's not bitching. I pray to God, it's not bitching. I'm praying that all of you didn't just come down here to piss and moan . . . " He got louder now to scare them. " . . . when I'm in the middle of working up a game plan for the drop!"

Nobody moved. They didn't shuffle. They didn't flinch. They were solid. It made Sam feel crazy.

"You're all done, man," Terry said. "Nobody wants to hear you barking anymore, and we damn sure don't need your game plans. I'll be giving the orders from here on out—"

Sam had heard enough. He pointed at Terry and screamed his words.

"What do you think this asshole's going to do for you?" he

said to the rest of Varsity. "All I've ever seen him do is sit on his ass and take. He hasn't run shit since he ran the basketball team into the ground against Fairview. And lemme tell you something, leading Varsity isn't about running a gang . . . ," Sam said, pointing his chin up toward the ceiling. "It's about running a school. And that's something you know nothing about. None of you could survive without me."

"We'll take our chances," Terry said and looked to the others. "We got nothin' to lose. Thanks to you. Isn't that right?"

"That's right," Anthony said. He was backed by more *that's rights* and *yeahs* around the circle.

"Is this about the gun incident?" Sam said. "You're gonna give up on me just 'cause of that? You can't be that stupid. Think of how it'll look to everybody. Without me, they'll know you're weak. You'll never get respect back—"

"It's not about the gun thing." Terry laughed. Others laughed too. "This has been a long time coming."

"Oh, is that right?"

Terry nodded. "Yeah, that's right. Doubt you noticed, but no other gang leader in school talks to their people the way you do. I'd even say those leaders like the people in their gang. Do you like us, Sam?"

Sam could feel his top lip tightening, pulling back to reveal his teeth in a sickened scowl. He wasn't going to honor that question with a response. It was irrelevant, exactly the kind of *Sesame Street* crap that was going make Terry fail as a leader.

"That's what I thought," Terry said. "And maybe that would've been okay, if you could've kept things going, but you lost all our food because you were too obsessed with David."

"That's not what happened," Sam said.

"It is what happened, bro. It's exactly what happened. And then you disappeared for two weeks when we needed you most. I don't know what the hell you were doing. Collecting guns with no bullets, I guess."

Laughter bounced off every wall. It went on way too long, especially when what Terry said wasn't funny.

"Then, you show up again and expect us to do what you say? You think you can swim in our pool?" Terry said. "Think again."

Sam scowled. He'd listened. Now it was his turn. He had one last weapon.

"So, you're really gonna take your chances without the Pretty Ones? 'Cause I'll tell Hilary to walk. And every one of your girls will go with her. I'll see if maybe some other gang is looking for a little pussy infusion." Sam turned away from Terry to face the rest of the gang. "Is that the kind of chance you boys are ready to take now? Losing your women just 'cause this guy's got big ideas about what he thinks should happen?"

Terry, the dumbshit, didn't have an answer for that. And Varsity was waiting. Sam had hit them where it hurt. He smiled. They still belonged to him.

"The Pretty Ones aren't going anywhere."

The Varsity line parted for Hilary. She stood beside Terry. Close enough to touch. Too close.

"What are you doing?" Sam said. He should've kept his mouth shut and stayed strong, but he couldn't help himself. Hilary had said horrible, stupid things about how much she hated him before. But he didn't think she'd ever pull this shit on him. Didn't she know what he'd do to her? Did they all forget?

"Nobody's scared of you. Not anymore," Hilary said. "So, just give it a rest."

Terry nodded at Hilary. How long had they been screwing? Sam wondered. Did Terry know that Sam had knocked her tooth out? Terry thought he had a prize, but all he had was a toothless whore. Fuck him. Fuck 'em both. He'd save that little nugget of info for the right time later, when he could make the most of it.

"You got two choices," Terry said. "You can fall in line, behind me, or you can leave. Finish up your swim, think about it. We'll be upstairs, getting ready for the drop."

Sam was so hot with rage he thought the water around him might start to boil. He stayed perfectly still, never breaking his stare from Hilary. Her eyes had drifted down. Terry waved for the gang to leave, and they all stepped away from the pool, heading for the exit.

"Oh, and don't think about stirring up shit behind my back," Terry said. "It'll just go in one ear and then into mine.

Everybody's on board with this, Sam. And none of us like you."

Terry followed Varsity out. The door swung shut and clicked. Sam stood in four feet of water, alone, with nothing. He chewed on his lip, hard enough to draw blood.

He could fix this. The slight sway of water clapped against the pool walls. Something could put everything back to normal. In McKinley, you lived and died by your reputation. If Sam was going to set things right, and take control of the school again, he had to make people forget they ever saw him fall. Only one thing worked with these animals. Danny Liner proved it. Alan Woodward backed it up. It was what Terry didn't have in him, and today Varsity would get a reminder. The whole school would see.

WILL AND NINE OTHER LONERS PEERED AT
the quad through the bent metal blinds of a first-floor class-room window. The gangs were starting to gather. They flowed in from every direction, and each gang was huge. No wonder they'd lost three Loners on the walk from the Stairs.

"Most people don't even think there's a Loner left in the school," Mort said.

"That's not true," Will said.

"I heard the Freaks have eighty-seven."

"Varsity's still got a hundred guys, easy," Ritchie said. "And they're the biggest dudes in school."

"Did you see Varsity at the last drop?" Will said. "They were totally disorganized."

"Yeah, well, they're not gonna make that mistake again," Ritchie said. "Everybody's gonna be on their A-game."

Belinda poked her finger through the blinds and tapped on

the glass softly. "Look at the Geeks, they've got a ton. So do the Skaters. Even the Saints are four times our size."

All eyes traveled to the Saints in the quad outside. They filled the wall where the Loners used to stand. They even had the white hair. This was their first food drop, and they looked uncomfortable. It reminded Will of the early days of the Loners, when they were first learning to work together as a gang.

"I'm just saying," Mort said, "maybe we're just better off being Scraps again. I mean, was it really that bad?"

"Yes," Will said. "It was that bad!"

They were all looking at him now. It was time to do his speech. He'd been practicing it in his head during the whole walk to the quad. He wasn't going to let what David built fall apart. The Loners were all that was left of David in Will's life, and if he lost that, he'd have nothing.

He cleared his throat and rubbed his hands together. His mouth was dry.

"The other gangs are bigger, and the odds are against us," Will said. "And now there's only ten of us left. But ten is all we need. We don't need the quitters. This is the core group, the originals. We did this once already. Nine Loners stood against a hundred Varsity and we won. We can do the impossible again."

The Loners seemed unmoved.

"There's no army of Scraps to help us this time," Mort said.

"And we don't have David," Ritchie said.

"We could just skip this one," Belinda said.

"Guys," Lucy said, "let Will finish."

The group hushed again. Will appreciated Lucy standing up for him, but he had nothing else planned. That was the full extent of his inspiring speech. His heart thumped in his chest. The Loners still waited for him to speak. This was far harder than David had made it look.

"Listen . . . I'm not stupid, I know you want to join other gangs," Will said.

They all looked away.

"I know we've had a lot of bad luck, and you all think we can't make it without David. But it isn't true. The Loners can go on, we can be big again. Just give me this one chance to prove to you that I can be your leader. One chance, that's all I'm asking for. If we don't get enough food to survive today, than you can all do whatever you want, go off and join another gang. If we fail today, then you'll have every reason to. I wouldn't even be mad. But that's not what's going to happen. We're going to go out there, and fight like beasts, and take our share back to the Stairs."

They were all looking at him again.

"Please. One chance. What do you say?"

The forty foot block of supplies hung from the orange crane, three stories above them. They'd lower it any moment now.

Will was filled with excitement and terror. All nine Loners

stood behind him. They'd agreed. They'd put their trust in him. He couldn't let them down.

Will's hand went to his belt and clasped the T-shirt-wrapped handle of a plastic shiv he'd made by sharpening a toothbrush. He held it just for comfort. Just to know it was there. The plan was they were going to run in pairs, one to grab, one to defend, and they'd focus on the little stuff, the stuff other gangs dropped or couldn't bother with. They'd run everything to Mort, who was stationed in a first-floor classroom with a window open. He'd stockpile everything, away from the danger of the quad. Will figured all the little grabs would add up.

Without warning, the block of food fell.

The bound pallets crashed to the ground and burst apart, flinging food and supplies everywhere. The gangs charged the mountain of supplies in the center of the quad.

"Go!" Will shouted.

The Loners ran. They broke off in twos, and joined the flow of the scavenging crowd. It wasn't safe to stand still. Will and Lucy ran side by side. The empty garbage bag Will brought with him trailed off his belt like a black snake snapping at his legs.

"You with me?" Will said in the huff of an exhale.

"With you," she said. "See anything?"

"Not yet."

Will's eyes twitched across the quad. He and Lucy sped past a strangling match between a Freak and a Varsity, a plastic tub of protein powder at their feet. He whipped his head from left to right as he wove between thrashing battles. Hair colors smeared across his vision, blue, red, orange, white, black. A stocky Slut tried to trip him. He stomped on her foot. She barked in pain.

Lucy's scream cut through the air, eclipsing the Slut's yowl. He snapped his head left in time to see a Skater throw Lucy to the ground. Lucy was clutching a pink and white box of sugar cubes. The Skater swiped the box out of Lucy's hand. Before the kid could pull the box close, Will tackled him to the ground.

Will grabbed the boy's foot and twisted it. The kid squealed and kicked Will's neck with his other foot. Will's vision went sparkly for a moment. He put his hands on the box and tried to wrestle it away.

"Mine!" the Skater shouted. That Skater was wrong.

Will yanked and yanked at the box. He felt people kick him in the back. The Skater head-butted him in the nose. Blood poured from Will's nostrils and splattered onto the kid's face, like watery ketchup. The kid yelled in disgust, and more blood drizzled into his open mouth. The boy let go of the box.

Will shoved his sweet trophy into his garbage bag and stood. His hand went to his nose and he gave it a little squeeze. It was straight, not broken. Must've been his lucky day. He looked to Lucy, who was on her feet and had four cans of beans in her arms.

"Nice!" Will yelled, and wiped his bloody nose with his forearm. Lucy cracked a quick smile at him, before switching back to being on guard. Will pointed to Mort in the classroom window, and they ran to him. Will blocked for her the whole time, making sure no one got near Lucy or her beans.

They handed the food to Mort through the window. Will peered into the classroom and saw that there was already a tub of powdered fruit punch, a family-sized box of crackers, a bag of sunflower seeds, and four Styrofoam bowls of dried ramen on the floor.

"It's working!" Will said to Lucy. His voice went embarrassingly high. Lucy giggled at him.

"We're doing it!" she said with a burst of tiny applause. He wanted to stay here in this moment forever, with Lucy proud of him, impressed with him, cheering him on. But they had to move; the mountain of food was disappearing quickly. He took her hand and led her back into the fray.

Victorious cheers, battle cries, and screams of pain mingled in Will's ears. He and Lucy sprinted by a crying Freak girl who whipped a length of chain at the crowd of Geeks that surrounded her. They all lunged for the 400-count pack of flushable moist wipes she had clutched against her belly.

Will and Lucy passed a Saint who swung the butt of her

rifle into a Skater's ribs. The Skater crumbled when the gun hit his side, and the Saint stole his bag of jerky.

"Looks like the new kids are getting the swing of things in here," Will said. Lucy nodded with a pant.

A few feet away, Will spotted a box of disposable lighters in the dirt, and he scooped them up. A Nerd was bending over to pick up a bottle of shampoo nearby. Lucy kicked her in the ass, and the girl fell forward on her face. Lucy grabbed the shampoo, and smiled at Will with pride. He felt a cool breeze all over his body.

Then knuckles cracked into the back of his head.

Will staggered forward and whipped around, pain blossoming in his skull. Sam stood opposite him, fists up in the air, lip stretched up into a snarl.

Nausea twirled in the pit of Will's gut. Just a flutter of it at first. Then, that flutter took shape and grew into solid a lump of sick. A cold stone in his belly. He'd known Sam might come looking for revenge—he'd mocked Sam in front of the whole school—but Will didn't think that he would be this afraid when it happened. Sam spat on the ground and stomped forward.

The sheet of muscles along the side of Will's neck clenched, and bent his head over. The truth chilled his blood. He wasn't paralyzed with fear. He was about to seize. Will tried to yell, but all that came out of his throat was a wet, grinding honk. His skin was pins and needles. He felt a cold rope of his own spittle drip across his fingers. The ground collapsed under his feet.

Everything became white.

Warbling laughter was the first thing Will was aware of. He opened his eyes, and the light was blinding. He saw a human shape, all out of focus, standing above him. The top of the person's head was a blurred blob of yellow. The person's hazy foot swung back and then kicked forward.

Will's balls exploded with pain. He tried to cup them with his hands and guard against another strike, but his arms flailed around like water weenies. They wouldn't work right. Another kick, and Will retched.

Will tried to scream at Sam to stop, but it was just noise with no enunciation. His tongue was a dead lump in his mouth. Will's eyes sharpened gradually. He could see the drop was over. Everyone was back on the sidelines, except for him, and Sam, and the Loners trying to pull Sam off of him.

He saw Sam knock down Leonard with an elbow to the chest. Sam shoved Mort off him like he was a paper doll. Mort got back up and came back for more punishment, throwing a crazed, ragged swing at Sam. Sam grabbed his deformed fist, mid-punch, and socked Mort in the eye with his other hand. Mort dropped to the dirt, unconscious. Ritchie limped over on a freshly twisted ankle, and Sam kicked him in it. Ritchie hollered and hit the ground, clutching his foot.

Will tried to stand, but his legs were another part of his system that had yet to come back online. He was able to get on his hands and knees in time to receive another heavy kick from Sam, in the kidney this time. Will crumpled, his face on the ground.

He saw a shiny red dot, a ladybug, moseying across ridges of dirt in front of his face. Beyond the ladybug, the crowd watched. Will could discern a mixture of pity and mockery across the different faces watching. Will felt himself urinate, he had no control over it. His bowels loosened and warm filth flooded his boxers. He saw Lucy running toward him. He shouted for her to stop.

"Agh oh shtuhh!" was the best he could muster.

Peripherally, he saw Sam punch Belinda in the stomach, and she folded over. The crowd groaned for her. Lucy rushed over to Will in a panic. Sam slapped her across the face, hard enough to knock her down. Will tried to attack Sam but he flopped around like a fish on a boat deck.

"Woh ganh fuff!" Will whelped.

Sam laughed with glee. He grabbed Will by the hair on the back of his head and twisted his head around so they could be face-to-face. Sam's eyes were crazed.

"Where's your big brother now?" Sam said, low at first. He shouted it again for the whole quad. "WHERE'S YOUR BIG BROTHER NOW?"

Sam pushed Will's face into the dirt. He dragged it back and forth. Will tried to fight. He tried. But he couldn't work his fingers well enough to grasp Sam's wrists. He had to let the dirt and rocks scrape across his face, again and again. Sam let go. Will waited for the next strike. Nothing came.

Will got himself up on one elbow. His arms were beginning to listen to his brain. He looked back. Other Loners lay on the ground, defeated. Sam was a few feet away from Will now, facing Varsity, who watched the show, as stunned as anyone else.

"Are you satisfied now? Huh? I crushed the Loners," Sam shouted at his gang. "What else do you need to see?"

All of Varsity turned and began to walk out of the quad. They shook their heads at Sam, or ignored him completely. Sam shuffled a few steps after them.

"Where are you going?" Sam said.

Other gangs like the Sluts and the Geeks began to leave as well. Sam turned his rant to everyone when Varsity stopped caring.

"You all saw that! I— I beat Will. You saw it."

The crowd hissed and tsk'd at him. They made crying baby fists by their eyes. They laughed at him, they flipped him off. Sam's face went wine red. He looked like he wanted to say something but he kept stopping. When the last Varsity stepped off the quad, there was no one left for him to shout at, and he ran for the nearest hallway. Laughter spread in his wake and stayed with the crowd even after he was gone.

As the rest of the quad cleared, the Loners got to their feet, except Ritchie, who only stood on one. They were beat up. Disrespected. The school had just seen the once mighty Loners get stomped by one guy. Will tasted mud and blood. Lucy walked toward him, a split in her lip and one red cheek. He wanted to scream at her to stay back, he didn't want her to come close enough to smell him. She couldn't know he'd just soiled himself, like an infant. She couldn't know. But she soon did. They all did, when they helped Will to his feet. They smelled his shame. None of them would look him in the eye as they helped him wobble-walk out of the quad.

He'd never wanted for this to happen, not to him, not to any of them. He'd tried so hard to not let it happen, he'd tried with everything he had in him . . . He just wasn't strong enough.

9

THE MARKET BUZZED WITH EXCITEMENT.
This was the third one since the parents' arrival. The first
two had been disorganized and halfhearted, but not this one.
This market was like Lucy remembered them, back when the
military had still been feeding them. The wide hallway bustled
with activity, with deals going down everywhere she looked.

Lucy stood with Ritchie, Mort, Leonard, Colin, and Belinda
at the edge of the market. They watched kids from other
gangs, with their hair freshly dyed, walk with their friends,
joking and laughing, from one trading room to the next.
Life was returning to normal, better than normal actually,
because there was more food to go around. Varsity hadn't
hoarded most of the food this time. They'd only taken their
share, a reasonable amount to support a gang, and didn't
try for any more. It had people talking. Had Varsity actually
dethroned Sam as their leader? It looked that way. They didn't

seem concerned with keeping a mountain of food on display behind their trading tables to taunt the rest of the school. Without Varsity hoarding the lion's share of the food, every gang ended up securing more supplies than they ever had. Every gang but the Loners.

They'd failed at the drop again. They weren't gelling as a team. Will hadn't gone because he said he had a cold, but Lucy thought that maybe he was too embarrassed to show his face in the quad. She understood, they all were embarrassed. Without Will, there were only six of them remaining, and they felt stupid standing with all the huge gangs, fully aware that everyone had seen them get trashed by Sam two weeks before. By the time this drop had started, almost every gang had sent a representative over to pitch joining their gang to the Loners. They all talked like it was an inevitability, like Violent had said, that the Loners were finished and now was the time to pick a new gang. Once the drop started, none of the Loners took the lead. Ritchie did well on his own, but all together they'd barely gathered enough stuff to trade for the eight rolls of toilet paper, two boxes of tampons, five packets of instant oatmeal, and the twelve-pack of ramen noodles that they held in their hands now.

Ritchie dropped the toilet paper rolls on the market floor.

"I'm going Skaters," Ritchie said.

"What?" Lucy said.

"You heard me."

Lucy began to panic.

"No, don't. Ritchie, we need you. You're our best fighter."

"I gotta look out for myself."

Mort stepped forward. "Lucy? Uh ... I'm really sorry, but, I'm joining the Freaks."

"So am I," Colin said.

"Guys, come on. We're just down on our luck right now," Lucy said, but she barely believed it herself. She could understand why they wanted to leave. She still felt the sting of Sam's palm on her cheek. She didn't honestly know how they would survive as a gang, but she felt an overpowering need to stop them from going.

"They said we could have our own rooms," Colin said.

"But, we're the Loners. You guys don't want to walk away from that. That means something," Lucy said.

"David was the Loners," Ritchie said, "and whatever we are right now, whatever this is? I'm not into it."

"But ... ," Lucy said.

"See you guys around," Ritchie said, unwilling or unable to look anyone in the eye. He turned and walked off.

"I guess we should . . . ," Mort said, pointing his thumb toward the Freak trading post. He attempted a smile, but it was eighty percent cringe.

Lucy couldn't summon words. What else could she say to get them to stay? She thought of Will back in the Stairs. He'd be devastated when he heard they'd lost three more. He'd never stop blaming himself.

"I'm sorry," Mort said. "I'm bad at good-byes. Take care of yourselves."

"You . . . too," Lucy said.

Mort and Colin walked off, leaving Lucy with only Leonard and Belinda on either side of her. She turned to Belinda, hoping to see the shock Lucy felt, but instead, tears were pouring down Belinda's cheek. She was trying desperately to keep from breaking apart.

"It's just—it's just that, you have somewhere to go, right Lucy?" Belinda said.

"Oh, Belinda . . . ," Lucy said. "Why?"

"Freddy. He pulled some strings. The Nerds weren't looking for new members, but he got me in. He said he'll take care of me, Lucy. I think he really loves me. You understand, don't you?"

Lucy took deep breaths, to stave off her sudden dizziness.

"I understand, Bel," Lucy said. And she did understand. She understood all the reasons the other Loners wanted to leave, and she certainly understood Belinda being unable to turn down an opportunity for love and safety.

"But I need to know you'll be okay, Lucy. I need to know that or I can't go."

"Don't worry about me, Bel," Lucy said softly. She felt the

tears coming, but she fought them back. "Go find that boy and hug him tight for me. I'm sure we'll see each other soon."

"Yeah, real soon," Belinda said.

"Leonard, we should head back," Lucy said. She had to get away from Belinda; she was going to cry.

"Geeks," Leonard said. His shoulders were slumped and he kept his eyes on the ground.

"What?"

"I want to learn to sing."

10

HE WAS LOSING HER.

Will sat on the stairs, alone in the dark. He'd traded all the lightbulbs in the Stairs for two salamis and an old matchbook. It hadn't been a popular decision with the Loners who had stuck around in the weeks since the Sam incident. Will couldn't bring himself to care though. He preferred the dark.

"Hello?"

Lucy's voice below made him sit up, but he didn't answer.

"Is anybody here?"

He couldn't see Lucy, only the white rectangle of her cell phone's screen, moving through the black. Will coughed. The white rectangle turned toward him and shined a weak, milky light in his direction.

"Hi," she said. Lucy tilted her phone's light back at her own face. She forced a slight smile, but he could tell she was sad. Join the club.

"Might want to stay back. I don't want to get you sick," Will said.

It had been going around, clogged nose, pulsing pain behind the eyeballs, exhaustion, and a sore throat. The Saints must have brought it in, because it was all over the school now.

"Here," Lucy said, and handed him her phone. He shined it on her as she put down the water jugs she'd been lugging.

"How much water have you had?" she asked.

"Not enough, probably."

She nodded and knelt down. As she poured some water into a tall thermos, she stared off at an empty wall, her brow bunched up, and her eyes too far open.

"I'll start a fire," he said.

Will rocked forward; he needed the momentum to stand. He drew the crinkled metallic fabric of an emergency fire blanket tighter around his shoulders. There was wood already piled up in the disembodied sink on the floor. He put the phone on the floor, faceup, and lit a match. Will tossed it into the sink and the book pages under the wood caught fire right away. The flames grew into a respectable campfire. Lucy hadn't said a word the whole time.

Will sat down, out of breath from the strain. Lucy walked over and handed him the thermos. He drank half of it in one gulp. Lucy sat near him. Still silent.

"Are you doing all right?" Will asked.

She nodded. He knew she was lying. She leaned toward the

flame, eyes closed. Will watched ribbons of golden light flutter across her face. Her cheekbones were round like twin scoops of butterscotch ice cream. A tear spilled from her eye. It drew a gleaming string of light down her cheek.

"Lucy?"

"They're all gone," she said.

"Who's all gone?"

"The only ones who were left. Belinda went Nerds. Ritchie went Skaters. And Mort and Colin—" She let out a breath. ". . . Leonard. All gone."

Will slumped. "Matter of time, I guess," he was barely able to say.

It was just the two of them.

Will's headache tightened like a fist inside his head. Nausea bubbled in his belly. He had failed David. The Loners had fallen apart. He took deep breaths. Lucy was staring at him, clearly concerned. He didn't want that.

"It'll be all right," Will said.

It was the most he could muster. He wanted to promise her that he'd protect her and provide for her, that was what she wanted. But, he couldn't promise what he couldn't deliver. He couldn't even protect himself. He'd proved that when Sam dug a trench in the quad with his face.

"What do you think we'd be doing right now if none of this ever happened?" Lucy said.

"For real?" he said.

"Yeah."

"You want to talk about this now."

"I see you as really fat," Lucy said.

It made Will smile.

"Out of all the possible scenarios of being outside, you're fantasizing about me gaining weight?"

She bounced as she laughed.

"I've seen you scarf cans of clam chowder with no spoon," she said. "I'm just saying. You're going to balloon. It's gonna be scary."

"Okay, you want to play like that?" he said. "Have you watched yourself chug fruit punch? You're like a pelican."

"A pelican!" Lucy said with mock outrage. "That's not the kind of thing you just make up! You've actually thought that before, haven't you!"

That made Will laugh even harder. "See, this is great. Maybe the Loners fell apart for a good reason," Will said, excited. "Who needs all them? We have each other. It can be just the two of us. We could go back to the elevator. We could be happy."

Lucy twisted her lips from side to side. Her silence made the crackling fire sound loud, like crumpling cellophane in his ear.

"Will, I'm worried about you."

Ouch. The scenario of the two of them in the elevator

had just spilled directly out of Will's heart, and it clearly did nothing for her. He felt like an idiot for blurting out his feelings.

"I'm fine," he said.

"You haven't seemed fine lately."

God, why was she saying this? She could just turn him down instead of keep reminding him that he was a broken person.

"Same as always," he said, working hard to keep a lid on any angry tone.

"Will, I think . . . We need to get realistic—"

"I am being realistic. David and me had a whole business before the Loners. We did fine as just two people."

"You barely pulled it off, and that's when things were stable. Who knows how reliable these parents will be?"

That was a bullshit excuse. If it were David asking her to go live in the elevator, just the two of them, she'd be there in a second.

"Are you joining another gang?" Will said.

Lucy opened her mouth. It hung open for a moment and then she closed it.

"I've thought about it . . . ," she said. "I mean, wasn't being in a gang the whole point of forming the Loners? Isn't that what we fought for?"

He wasn't going to beg her. He wouldn't sink that low. He really wanted to beg. He was ravenous to beg.

"... And I know you probably think that nobody wants you because of ... what happened," she said.

"You're right," Will said.

"But that's not true," Lucy said, pouncing. "I mean, okay, you've got a lot of enemies. The Freaks and Varsity. And the Skaters probably haven't forgiven you for their boards, but—I talked to some Geek who said they're desperate for people to join, and Zachary hasn't seemed to hold a grudge about the Loners putting him in a cage."

The Geeks wouldn't have Will. Not after what happened in the quad. No one would. Lucy was fooling herself. She needed to believe it. He guessed she'd never forgive herself if she bailed on poor, little, epileptic Will.

"Geeks, huh? That seems like a good gang for a coward," Will said.

Lucy stared at him, confused.

"That's not funny."

"I'm not laughing. I'm just saying, that's what you are."

"Why are you talking like this?"

"Think about it. You always hide. In the Pretty Ones. Behind David. Why not behind Zachary?"

"I'm trying to help you, Will."

"Don't strain yourself."

"Don't say this stuff. You don't mean it!"

"Why are you here?" Will said. "Why don't you just walk

to the auditorium right now? You probably have your bag packed. Am I right?"

Lucy didn't answer. She looked down.

"Then go," he said. "Get the fuck out of here. I don't want you around me."

"No!" she said. "You can't do this. I won't leave you."

She cried. She was going to hate him, but that was better. If she hated him, she might be able to forget about him.

"Do yourself a favor . . . "

She looked up, cheeks wobbling, eyelashes clumped by tears.

" . . . and fuck off," Will said.

She slapped him. She disappeared up the stairs, crying, then came back down, with a small, half-full backpack over her shoulder, and her phone lit up in her hand. She walked right past him and her phone's glow faded off down the stairs toward the ground floor exit.

If he was going to go after her, this was his chance. To take it back. There was still a window, he hadn't heard the door open or shut yet.

Will struggled to his feet. He let the crinkly blanket fall off him as he trudged to the top of the stairs. Down past the darkness of the stairwell he saw Lucy standing at the open door, her cell phone shining on her face. She looked up at him. If he persuaded her to stay, she'd only leave later. He could never be what she needed.

"Don't come back! You hear me?" Will shouted. "I don't want your pity!"

She slammed the door shut and left. Will walked back to the sink fire and sat. He tried to let the flames warm him. They wouldn't last long. The cold of the empty Stairs would win in the end. Will had better get used to it. He was alone for good.

11

"I WANT TO BE A SLUT," LUCY SAID.

Violent looked surprised. She stood in the doorway to the cafeteria, holding the door open. There was an ugly Slut beside her, who was topless. These girls were a marvel. Even their breasts were aggressive. Violent looked different in the middle of the night. Her red hair was a mess, and the stitched seam of her pillow had left its imprint across her cheek. She wore a XXL boy's black T-shirt, full of holes and rips. Without her tape eyebrows, her sinister makeup, and all the spiky armor, Violent almost looked nice, like a mom. A mom with no eyebrows.

"Violent, I know I missed the deadline on your offer, but—"

Violent raised her hand to quiet her. She pulled Lucy close and wrapped her in a sturdy hug. It took Lucy completely by surprise.

"Ssh," Violent said. "Come in. We can talk in the morning. Right now it's time to sleep."

That was good by Lucy. She'd never felt so drained. The empty cafeteria was quiet. It smelled faintly of berries. Everything was clean and organized, every weapon hanging in its place on the far wall, like the pegboard wall of tools her dad used to have in their garage. The main floor of the cafeteria had been cleared away. The dining hall tables were broken down and stashed up against one wall. The beige plastic cafeteria chairs were stacked high next to them.

"Lips, get her a mattress," Violent said to the topless girl. Lips. It was a joke of a nickname. The girl barely had any lips at all. They were just thin, flat strips of skin. It was almost like her face stopped and her mouth began without an intermediary step. Lips nodded to Violent and walked off.

Violent led Lucy toward the kitchen without a word. She stopped at the doorway and took her shoes off. Lucy figured she should do the same. She put her stuff down and slipped off her white canvas sneaks that had served her for so long. It was a lie to call them white. She couldn't wash them as well as David used to, and even he couldn't get them white. They were gray and speckled with black like an Oreo milk shake. She put them in a cabinet, next to where Violent put hers.

Lucy followed Violent into the heat of the kitchen, where Sluts lay sleeping all over the floor. They were nestled in around each other like jigsaw puzzle pieces. The only light in the room came from the oven door windows, receding rectangles of glowing red.

Violent led Lucy through the obstacle course of bodies. From what she could make out, most of them wore boxers and T-shirts with the sleeves torn off. Even that seemed too hot to sleep in. The heat from the ovens pressed in all around her like a sauna. The purr of the gas ovens softened all other sounds. Violent reached a clear spot of floor by the dishwashers, far from the ovens, but still entirely warm.

"You can sleep here tonight," Violent said in a low hush.

Lips arrived silently and dropped a man-shaped mattress on Lucy's spot of floor. The mattress was a pair of khaki pants and a long-sleeve denim shirt that had been sewn together and stuffed with pink wall insulation, which puffed out where the seams had come apart. Lucy lowered her bag to a spot right next to the mattress.

Lucy opened her arms to hug Violent again. Instead, Violent patted her shoulder and walked off with Lips.

"Okay," she said, mostly to herself. "Okay, then . . . "

She guessed that was it. This was her gang now. She lowered herself down on her headless, handless, footless mattress man. She scanned the nearby faces, trying to see if she recognized any of them. Not a one. She was sleeping with a bunch of strangers. What had she gotten herself into? Was she so desperate to prove Will wrong that she'd actually thought for a second she could be a Slut? When she knocked on the cafeteria door she felt like she knew what she was doing, she thought she wanted everything Violent had described about being a Slut. Now she feared that she was not like these girls, that she would not be accepted here, and she wouldn't have what it takes to be one of them.

You're a coward. She swore she'd never forgive Will for what he'd said. She cussed him in her mind, but no matter how many times she wrote Will off, she'd hear him say those sharp words again. She just wanted to forget about him, and the Loners and how everything had gone so wrong.

She squeezed her mattress man. The oven heat seeped into her, soothed her. It made Will's words hurt less and less. She felt sleep pull her under, into the warmth.

It was the clong of a steel ladle on an iron skillet that woke Lucy up. It took a second for her to remember where she was.

"Five more minutes for chores!"

Every light in the kitchen was on. She looked around the floor and saw that she was the only one still sleeping. The other Sluts had already risen and stored their bedding away. Lucy sat bolt upright. No, it couldn't start like this, with her looking like a big slacker. She looked over at a Slut standing by one of the stovetops. She held a huge steel pot by its towel-wrapped handles. The Slut tipped the pot and poured steaming water on the tile floor. The piping hot puddle spread fast toward Lucy. She sprung to her feet with barely enough time to keep from being scalded. She picked up her mattress man, just as the water touched it. The soaked fabric seared her fingers. She looked around for her bag, but it was gone.

Lucy tiptoed around the scalding mop water. Steam rose knee-high. Every Slut she walked past ignored her; they were completely focused on their tasks. Lucy could feel the walls they had up against her; but she was determined to break through. She approached a bony Slut pouring ash into a tall aluminum broiling pot.

"Um, can I help?" she said.

The Slut responded without looking at her. "You're supposed to be out there." She flicked her head toward the cafeteria.

"Thanks," Lucy said. *For nothing,* she thought.

Lucy made her way out of the kitchen, the same way Violent had led her in. She saw mattress men like hers stuffed into the open storage closet where she'd stowed her shoes. She wedged hers between two others, and went to grab her sneakers. Like her bag, they were gone. Maybe Violent had moved them, or sent them to be cleaned.

Lucy walked barefoot into the dining hall. In one corner Sluts worked out in pairs. One would do push-ups or deep knee bends with her partner on her back. There was sparring in the opposite corner. Girls wore oven mitts stuffed with something that made them plump like boxing gloves. Near Lucy, other girls were busy at work, clearing out the last of the breakfast. On the last uncleared table, there was a wide iron pan of scrambled eggs. A third of it was still uneaten.

Lucy's stomach woke up. She knew about the powdered eggs

in the drops but she'd never actually seen them cooked. They glistened in the pan, golden and yellow. They called out to her tongue. They must have called out to her feet too because she was drifting toward the pan.

"Not so fast."

She looked up to see a group of Sluts approaching her. They were led by Lips, who was finally fully clothed in black jeans and a black half shirt.

"Girls who sleep in don't get eggs," Lips said.

"I didn't mean to sleep in," Lucy said. "I guess I was more tired than I thought."

"Oh, you guess?"

The girls laughed. Lucy didn't know what was so funny.

"You need to shower," Lips said.

"You're dirty," another Slut said.

"Okay . . . ," Lucy said. "I didn't know you had showers."

"The Sluts are a clean gang. Don't you know nothing?" another girl said.

"You're behind schedule. Move it," Lips said to Lucy.

Lips pulled Lucy back to the kitchen. The others stayed behind. All the kitchen chores were apparently done, everything was put away neatly and there was no one else in there. Lips brought her in front of a sink with one of those high-power dishwashing hoses hanging above it. She tossed Lucy a cardboard box of powdered dishwashing detergent.

"Strip down and soap up."

"What, right here?"

"Stop being a little girl."

Lucy pointed at the sink. "This is the shower? There isn't a bathroom or something?"

"You want to put us more behind schedule? Come on!"

Lips creeped Lucy out. How did she get trapped with this chick? Was this some kind of twisted come-on?

"Where's Violent?" Lucy asked.

"She's busy. Get on with it already."

Lips squeezed the handle on the hose's nozzle and a jet of water fired out of it. The water hammered down on the metal of the sink, sounding like a drumroll on a trash can. Lucy sighed. She unzipped her dress. It was the second replacement zipper she'd salvaged from another dress and sewn in. Her fingers quivered. This didn't feel right. Maybe Lips was playing a trick on her.

"I can do this myself. I don't need you working the hose," Lucy said.

Lips smiled, but her eyes stayed mean. Lucy didn't like it.

"Fine. Be quick about it," Lips said.

Lips walked out of the kitchen. Lucy still wasn't sure she wasn't being made a fool of, but she wanted to make a good impression. And the truth was she couldn't remember the last good rinse she'd had. She was already the new girl and the slacker girl. She didn't want to be the dirty one too.

Lucy wriggled out of her dress quickly. Then her underwear.

She laid them over the counter, then poured the white powdered detergent into her hand. The detergent had little blue flecks in it that were kind of pretty. She made a mud out of it with water from the hose, and smeared it on to the important parts: pits, feet, and undercarriage. She didn't intend to linger in this "shower."

When she was sufficiently lathered up, Lucy sprayed herself with the hose to rinse off. The jet of water sprayed soap into her eyes.

"Damn it—"

She dropped the hose and rubbed her eyes. She fumbled around like a blind girl, trying to smack her hand into the hanging hose and get it again. Eventually she found it and was able to splash some water in her eyes. She could see again. She glanced down at the counter.

Her clothes were gone.

Sluts grabbed her from behind. They held her arms and pushed her toward the cafeteria. She tried to stop them but her soapy feet slid across the floor.

"Stop! What are you doing?"

They shoved her out of the kitchen and she fell on the floor, scraping her stomach and breasts. All the Sluts in the cafeteria were gathered around Lucy in a semicircle. They stared at her. Lips was in front.

"Stand up," Lips said.

Lucy stood awkwardly, trying to cover her breasts with one forearm and her privates with her other hand. She felt like a complete and total dipshit, naked in front of a smirking crowd of fully clothed bitches. She'd never felt more embarrassed in her life.

"Where is Violent?" Lucy said in a tiny voice.

"She can't save you," Lips said.

"Why are you doing this?"

"It's day one," Lips said. "You know what that makes you?"

Lucy shook her head. She tried to breathe slow; it wasn't working.

"Who is she?" Lips said to the room.

"A GOOD LITTLE GIRL," the Sluts hollered in unison.

"And how does a good girl become a Slut?"

"SHE'S GOTTA GET NAKED!"

"What's that called?" Lips said, hyping them up.

"NAKED WEEK!"

"Say it again?"

"NAKED WEEK!"

"One more time!"

"NAKED WEEK!"

The girls whooped and cheered.

Lips stepped in and got an inch from Lucy's nose.

"From here on out, you have no name. You're nothing," Lips said.

Lucy was angry. She felt duped, but she didn't know what to do. Lips reached out and pinched a strand of Lucy's long white hair between her fingers.

"Until this hair is red, any Slut can tell you what to do. You're our slave, and you do whatever we tell you to. Got it?"

Lucy was watching Lips's thin lips wrinkle as she talked. She wanted to split them.

"GOT IT?"

"I guess."

"Not 'you guess.' Do you got it?"

Lucy took a deep breath.

"Yes."

"You don't talk back, you don't resist, and you do not put your hands on anyone. You obey without question. Got it?"

"Yes," Lucy was quick to say.

"Good," Lips said. She snapped her fingers. Someone threw a scrub brush at Lucy. It bounced off her chest and fell to the ground. "Pick it up."

Lucy lowered herself slowly, and picked up the scrub brush.

"That's how you earn your keep around here, slave. You never let go of it."

Lucy stared back at Lips. She was thinking how she should demand her clothes and walk out right now, just cut her losses. *Coward.* Will's voice was in her head again.

"What are you looking at me for, white hair? Don't look at

me. Don't look at any Slut unless you are instructed to," Lips said.

Lucy looked down. She could do this. If they had all done it, then she could do it too. *They need me to prove myself,* she thought. She had to try her best. She would work hard. She'd show them that they couldn't break her.

"Give me your scrub brush," a girl said, stepping out from the circle.

Lucy extended her brush to the girl.

"What the hell are you doing?" Lips shouted.

"I— She said to . . . "

"And I said never let go of your brush! Are you thick?"

"And I said give me your brush!" the other girl said. "You gotta do what I say."

Lucy pulled the brush back. The Sluts *ooh'd* and shook their heads like Lucy had just spat in her face.

"You're gonna pay for that," the girl said.

"Damn," another Slut said. "Making enemies on your first day."

"What do you think of our new slave, ladies?" Lips clamped her hand down on the back of Lucy's neck, and the pain made her wince. "I don't think she's gonna make it."

12

HILARY SAT ON THE BLEACHERS IN THE GYM,
in the same spot she'd always sat when Sam still ran Varsity. But now Terry, the new leader of Varsity, sat by her side. She looked out at the gym, and it looked different. The mountain of food that had always cascaded down the bleachers on the other side of the room was now a neat stack of supplies that needed to be moderately rationed. With Terry in charge, the combat training areas of the gym floor had been scaled back and replaced with a lounge, and a small library of books on loan from the Nerds. The Varsity boys still played their games, there was a lively game of half court basketball across the gym from Hilary, and their sneakers squeaked like a family of chipmunks.

"Hilary, I know how much the Pretty Ones mean to my guys," Terry said. "We're all on the same team. I don't want to change anything about that."

"How come I don't believe you?" she said.

Terry shrugged. Hilary's tongue flicked over the back of her right cuspid. The superglue that held it in place was bitter. She had to stop messing with it or she risked popping it out of place. It had become a bad habit when she got anxious.

"This morning, Anthony told me that I wasn't allowed to take my regular morning swim anymore," Hilary said. "He said I needed to talk to you. And just now, I was told by three of your guys that I needed to pack up my things because my room is now a 'date' room, whatever that is."

"We have so many couples, it always seemed unfair to me that none of them got a chance to spend any time alone together," Terry said. "Now there'll be a schedule posted and anybody will be able to sign up and have it as a place to do dinner and a movie or something."

"Yes, but it's my room," Hilary said. "It's always been my room."

"It's been your room since Sam was in charge," he said, his voice staying cool. "Now that he's not in play, there's no reason why you should have anything more than any other Pretty One. There's plenty of cots open in the girls' locker room."

Hilary flicked her tongue across her tooth.

"Cots," she said.

"I'm going to need you to be a team player, all right?"

Hilary's mind was racing for an angle, but she had nothing.

"I really hate that you're gay," she finally said.

Terry chuckled. "I know you do."

Terry slapped her on the knee and walked down the bleachers.

When she'd told Terry that the Pretty Ones would back his move to take over, her plan had been to seduce him. She had no idea he would come out of the closet days later, and even less of a clue that Varsity wouldn't care one bit. It was more than they didn't care. They seemed to like him more. It was as if they wanted the polar opposite of Sam, and Terry fit that perfectly. He wanted to transform Varsity's image, to undo all the damage he said Sam had done. He said they didn't need to be hated and feared anymore. That was all Sam. Everything bad about Varsity was Sam's fault, not theirs. Now was their chance for a fresh start, to make friends with other gangs instead of enemies.

Terry just wanted a date and he couldn't get one in Varsity. She was sure that was what it was. Make friends? She'd never heard one person shovel so much shit in her life.

Hilary didn't want to make friends. She wanted her life back. She wanted private swims in the pool. She wanted her closets back. She wanted the same huge assortment of food she always had to choose from. Terry didn't even want Hilary to shave anyone's head for wig hair anymore. She hated Sam for knocking out her tooth, but sometimes she missed the crazy psycho. At least with him, she got to shower alone.

Now, not only did she have zero chance of getting Terry under her thumb, he didn't even seem concerned with keeping Varsity and the Pretty Ones number one. Hilary couldn't understand that kind of thinking. It wasn't how she'd been raised.

Her mother had been a model in the eighties, and she'd reached a certain level of local fame for being the face of Brandt's, a Colorado jewelry store chain. She'd once been stunning, but by the time Hilary had reached junior high, her mother's best years were behind her. That was around the time her mother's opinion of Hilary began to sour.

Hilary had been growing into a true beauty, blossoming more every year, and it perturbed her mother to no end. She resented the attention Hilary got for her beauty. There was only room for one beautiful person in the house. She competed with Hilary for every male's attention, even the boys Hilary would bring home from school. Hilary's mother would parade around in outfits that were too young for her, that showed too much for a woman of her age. She'd refuse to pay for Hilary to get her hair done. Hilary was allowed only the cheapest soaps and beauty products while her mother spent heaps of cash on her own beauty regimen. Then, she started buying Hilary boys' clothes. She attacked any insecurity that Hilary failed to hide from her. She offered Hilary plastic surgery for her birthday two years in a row, even though Hilary never expressed any interest in it at all.

It was only a matter of time before Hilary stopped trusting her mother altogether. In Hilary's mind, she'd lost her mother, but she'd gained her first real adversary.

Hilary's parents divorced when she was seven. For a while, there was a stream of boyfriends showing up at the house, but like her mother's face, it had dried up. Then, her mother met Gary. Gary was a venture capitalist who dressed like a ski bum. He'd taken a shine to Hilary's mother at a wedding, and they'd started dating. Her mother became obsessed with Gary because she'd decided he might be her last chance at love. All her hopes of the future were pinned on landing him as a husband.

Hilary couldn't help but seduce him. It wasn't even that hard. She walked around the house in her underwear. She flirted with him. She laughed at all his jokes. She stole moments with him when her mother was out of the room. She made him feel like she was really impressed by him, that she liked how old he was, that she was dying to sleep with him, and that a connection like theirs was rare.

Two months she kept that act up, and one afternoon when her mother was in the basement folding laundry, he kissed Lucy in her room. She had a video camera set up, and she made sure he was facing the camera when he did it. She e-mailed him that video, and told him to never contact her mother again, or answer any of her calls, or Hilary would send the tape to the cops.

Week after week Hilary relished getting to ask her mother the same question over breakfast . . .

"Hey, what ever happened to Gary? I liked him a lot."

Hilary smiled at the memory. In her peripheral vision Hilary saw ten white dresses moving across the polished gym floor. Pretty Ones settled on the bleacher rows below her. Linda, the tallest girl in the gang, climbed up to Hilary. She'd been giving Hilary the most attitude of all the girls, and now she stood in front of Hilary with a wide stance, her hip cocked, and her yellow hair over one eye. The other Pretty Ones watched, eager to see what was about to happen.

"We've been talking," Linda said. "We don't want to be expected to date Varsity anymore. We're sick of it, we want to date Skaters, or passionate artist boys from the Geeks, or whoever we want. And it's not up for discussion."

Hilary narrowed her eyes at Linda. That was a threat. Hilary looked around the room. Every Pretty One was fixing her with slitty bitch eyes.

"Why don't you go help Suzanne make the soap."

"I don't feel like it."

"Do it."

Linda held the stare. She was testing Hilary. The root of Hilary's tooth ached in her gums. She had to shut Linda down right away. She needed something that would break her. Hilary reached down into the dark of her mind for something cold and sharp.

"Didn't your last two boyfriends die?"

"Wh— what? What does that have to do with anything?"

Linda's face sank. It was true, her last two boyfriends had died. The first, Dennis, got drunk and drowned in the pool over a year ago. The second, Antonio, the one she really liked, he was killed by the falling block of supplies at the parents' first food drop.

"You really think you should be looking for another? How much blood do you want on your dress?"

Linda's bit her lip. She cried.

"Linda," Hilary whispered. Linda looked up at her like child who had just been spanked. "Soap."

If Linda wanted to say something back to Hilary, the words weren't coming. She shuffled off, confused. The other Pretty Ones drifted away, her leadership reasserted for another day.

Hilary had eagle eyes when it came to spotting someone's weakness. She knew the brittle spot of every girl in her gang. Everyone had that thin part of them, where they were defenseless, a spot you only needed to push, and it would break them open. Cindy got a lazy eye when she was tired. Britt was dyslexic and was always trying to prove she wasn't stupid. Megan's father walked out on her family when she was ten. Maria had no waist.

Hilary tongued her tooth. It didn't budge. The glue was holding. So far, no one knew that it had been knocked out, except David and Sam. But one was gone, and no one wanted anything to do with the other. In her drunken stupor she still had the awareness that night to grab the tooth and put it in her pocket. She'd spent the next hour, while Sam was having his fight in the quad, swaying drunk in front of a mirror, fingers fumbling to stick her tooth back into her gums. She'd worn layers of duct tape on the back of her top teeth in the beginning. She might have to start doing that again, because she was running out of superglue. Hilary lived in constant fear that the glue would snap. That she would smile too wide and the pressure of her lips stretching around her teeth would pop the tooth right onto her tongue. She could hear the *click* of it displacing in her mind. What if a boy kissed her aggressively? He might kiss her tooth out.

She needed a new boyfriend. Someone to raise her back up to her rightful position at the top. But no one could know her secret. The leader of the Pretty Ones was not missing a tooth.

13

WILL SUCKED ON A MUSTARD PACKET. THE
traces of yellow he could get out would be the only meal
he'd had in two days. He'd already traded everything that
remained in the Stairs, and the only things he had left were
items no one wanted. He had a belt buckle that was missing,
the part that goes through the belt holes. He'd found some
three-ring binders, but the paper-holding mechanisms had
been ripped out. He had a plastic bag full of discarded sunflower seed shells. He'd already tried to get a Geek to buy it
for an art project, but none of them went for it. His only hope
was a half-full package of toilet seat covers he'd found the
night before.

Will sat down on the elevator floor. He had moved back to
the elevator after Lucy had left. He wanted to be where no
one could find him. The elevator was secret. No one except
for him and Lucy knew about it. It was where he spent all of

his days, and he went scavenging for food at night.

If Will had been willing to show his face at the food drop or the market, he might have been able to get more to eat, but he couldn't do it. He was far too ashamed. Everyone had seen his body give out on him in the quad. They'd seen Sam decimate him, humiliate him. They knew he had a glitch in his brain that could hit at any time, and when it did, you couldn't depend on him, and he couldn't defend himself. They'd seen his flaw, and now the flaw was all they would ever see.

Will laced up his black Converse high-tops. He'd inked in the white rubber toe caps with blue ballpoint pen scribbles forever ago. One shoe had dirty white laces. The other had the cord of a broken pair of earbud headphones woven through the aluminum eyelets. He had to quadruple knot it to make it hold. The shoes hugged his feet. They had good cushioning. It was a sad fact that the soles of his shoes were the only thing supporting Will anymore.

His sneakers were his only truly valuable item, and he didn't want to lose them, but he couldn't go another whole day without eating. If he didn't scrounge up food tonight, he'd have to bear his shame and go sell his shoes at the market tomorrow. It made him sick. He'd be walking into the market as a Scrap again, back on the bottom. If Sam had failed to murder his reputation in the quad, then Will walking out of the market barefoot would be the killing blow.

Will pulled his backpack off a high hook and stepped onto

an upside-down bucket on the floor. He hoisted himself out of the hatch in the ceiling, onto the roof of the elevator car. The shaft was dark, as usual, except for the dim glow of the maintenance light that escaped from the elevator. David's laundry lines still crisscrossed their way all up and down the shaft. Nothing hung from them anymore, except for one magenta satin bra with a broken strap, dangling from the highest laundry lines, nearly thirty feet up.

Will approached the maintenance ladder on the wall of the shaft. Each rung was visible only as a single horizontal glint in the darkness. Will crouched to jump but hesitated. Hesitation was a new thing for Will, and he resented it bitterly. He'd jumped the gap from the elevator edge to the ladder a million times, but lately, each time he got here, it felt like the first. The threat of a seizure was ever-present. It could drop him at any moment, and he would plummet down the shaft. Death was everywhere, and he'd lost the urge to tempt it.

Still, life had this nasty habit of going on. Will took a quick breath and jumped for the ladder. His hands struck the cold metal bar. His full bodyweight pulled against the grip of his fingers. His right foot slipped off its rung but the left landed solid. Will climbed quickly. He wanted this over with. When he pulled himself into the air duct in the wall, he was hyperventilating. His fear sickened him. He couldn't even climb a ladder without falling apart.

For all the complaining he'd done last year, the amount of

times he'd told David that he didn't need him, that he'd be fine without him, what a crock of shit. He had needed David there, every minute, and he still did. Will needed someone to look out for him all the time, in case he seized. He'd always denied it, and wanted to disprove it, but now he knew it was a fact. And he'd either lost or driven away all the people who might even consider looking out for him.

Will stepped into the hall. He tightened the straps of his backpack, and ran.

If Smudge had been around, maybe Will would have had an easier time with living on the fringe, but there was no sense in wishing for things that couldn't come true. Smudge was rotting under a pile of rubble in the East Wing ruins.

Will had heard about a trader that had filled the void left behind by Smudge, someone who would buy your stolen goods. The rumor was that he could be found somewhere on the third floor for an hour after midnight. Will had spent most of that hour trudging the halls in search of this mysterious, maybe mythical, character.

"This is stupid," Will mumbled to himself.

He dragged his hand along the wall, coating his fingertips with char. The lights coming back on had revealed the scars left behind by weeks of hopelessness. A lot of walls were black and gray from torch soot, and some walls had been torn open and gutted by people looking for wood to burn for campfires.

The entire school was starting to look like the ruins.

The hall Will was in ended with a circular space that people called the Lighthouse. It had been built to be a student reading nook, and it supposedly had a panoramic view of Pale Ridge and the mountains. Now, it was just a steeled-in cul-de-sac. He was about to bail when he saw a long, thin shadow stretching out in the flickering fluorescent light ahead. Then, it vanished.

Will approached cautiously, moving his hand to the toothbrush shiv tucked in his belt. As he got closer to the end of the hall, Will could see somebody leaning against one of the steeled-up windows. The guy had shoulder-length, black hair and a ripped-up, vintage, heavy metal T-shirt. He looked like a Skater. That would have been just Will's luck, trading with some dude he'd probably punched before.

The Skater kid locked eyes with Will and pushed away from the window.

"'S up," the kid said with a nod.

Will kept his distance. "Are you Heath?" he asked.

"Totes ma'gotes."

"I'm looking for food," Will said.

"Let's see what you got."

Will was about to unshoulder his backpack, but he paused when he noticed that Heath didn't have a bag or any goods around him.

"Where's your stuff?" Will said.

Heath shook his head. "Number one rule of doing sketchy shit, never keep your stash on-site. I'll see what you got, then we'll talk for real."

That seemed reasonable enough, and Will wasn't in a position to argue anyway. He unzipped his backpack and held it open for Heath to inspect.

"What am I looking at?" Heath said.

"Three pieces of mirror and some paper toilet seat covers, fifty count."

"You got a sock in there too."

Will glanced in the bag. Sure enough, there was a lone sock in there. He'd never seen it before and had no idea where it came from.

"What's the story on the toilet seat covers? Used, unused? What's the deal?"

"Unused."

"Interesting."

Heath pursed his lips while he considered the goods. This guy hadn't acknowledged that he knew Will, but how could he not? Will didn't want to lose out on this deal, he couldn't.

"I like that shirt . . . ," Will said.

Heath looked down at his black-and-red logo'd T-shirt.

"Yeah? You like Fastway?"

"Sure," Will said. Who knew, maybe if he'd ever heard one of their songs, he actually would like them.

"Rad," Heath said. "What's your top track?"

"All of 'em, dude. I mean, come on," Will said. Heath smiled. He seemed to like that. Will moved on fast. "So, you're a Skater, right?"

"Yeah, I roll with P-Nut, but a guy needs a little money in the bank these days. Not like it used to be. Nothing's set in stone-henge y'know. Who knows what will happen next week?"

"Sure, right," Will said, nodding along.

"You know better than anyone. One day your gang could be on top, the next it could be Cinnamon Toast Crunch."

"Yeah," Will said. What else could he say? It was true.

"I mean . . . no disrespect," Heath said.

Will gave him a shrug that must have looked pathetic.

"So, anyway . . . I'm gonna pass."

Will stared at Heath. "Wait . . . What do you mean 'pass'?"

"Pass," Heath said and stepped away from Will's backpack, "like not interested. Like no dice. I just can't unload this stuff."

"Yeah, but . . . come on, man. I gotta eat. The guy I dealt with before, he—he woulda given me five cans, at least, for just those seat covers."

"So, take 'em to him."

"He's dead."

"Sucks," Heath said. "But like I said, it's just the way things are now. Even though the drops started up, people are still saving for a rainy day, know what I mean? They don't want mirrors. They want food. They want batteries. And if they gotta sit on a toilet, they suck it up and hover. 'Cause who knows, man, those parents could split tomorrow. Then what?"

Will had stopped listening. "Is this because of that battle in the commons? Did I break your board too? Because if that's what—"

"No, man, I'm professional here," Heath said, offended. "Uncool."

"I'm sorry . . . ," Will said, his voice choked with worry. "I'm sorry. I just don't know what I'm gonna do."

The Skater gave him a sympathetic look, the kind that usually made Will cringe, but at the moment, he'd take it.

"Tell you what," Heath said. "It's too bad you don't have the other sock, but . . . I'll give you a can of green beans for those shoes."

Will looked down at his Converse. He was so damn hungry.

"It'll save you a trip to the market," Heath said.

He wasn't that low yet. He refused to believe it.

"No," Will said. "Forget it."

He zipped his backpack, turned, and walked away. The night wasn't over yet.

"Hey, if you every wanna just hang and crank tunes, lemme know!" Heath called out after him.

Will didn't answer.

"All right," Heath said, unaffected. "Later, man,"

Will searched for hours without finding anything of value, but when he did find something, it was a doozy. He was scouring the lover's chapel at the time. The chapel was a second-floor classroom that looked out to the quad where two McKinley students, a Geek and a Freak, had once gotten married. Girls liked to talk about them, because they'd never broken up, and they'd both graduated on the same day. A lot of couples would come to this room on dates and carve their initials into the wall, and hope some of the married couple's luck would rub off on them. The walls were covered in initials, written in pen, or carved in with a knife. The entire surface of the black-board was scratched-in names inside scratched-in hearts.

He'd been searching the room for ten minutes before he found a plastic squeeze bottle of honey hidden above one of the dormant ceiling light panels. Most of the things Will had been finding on his night trips were things people were hiding from their own gangs. When someone snatched up something really nice, like sixteen ounces of honey, they'd pocket it, not tell their gang, and then keep it somewhere away from home.

Whoever's honey it was, Will was thankful for their greed. He brushed shards of glass off the windowsill, and sat by one of the shattered windows that overlooked the quad. Will squeezed honey into his mouth, piling it high on his tongue.

He heard a voice through the open window.

"It's me, Sam."

Will swallowed the pile of honey, and nearly inhaled it. He looked down to the quad and saw Sam standing underneath the window, about fifteen feet from the wall. His first thought was that Sam was talking to him, but that made no sense. Sam was looking higher than Will's window.

As Will watched Sam, his emotional wounds from three weeks ago reopened. Will wanted to hurt Sam. To make him cry. He wanted to humiliate Sam in front of everyone, and break him so completely that he would never believe in himself again. Will wanted Sam to feel everything that he felt.

"I kept looking at that amp that's up there," Sam continued on from outside. Sam's head was craned back, and he was staring to about the height of the roof. Will was careful to keep out of the moonlight.

"I couldn't stop thinking about it, then I realized I knew it. The stickers that are on it. The colors, the way they're placed. It's yours. I mean, it is you, isn't it?"

Will wanted to drop a desk on Sam, but not before he understood what was happening. The only amp Will knew of belonged to the man in the motorcycle helmet.

"Just give me a sign," Sam called up. "I know I'm making a scene, I shouldn't be doing this. Just one sign and I'll go. I just need to know I'm not crazy. Please," he said, his voice drenched in a level of emotion Will never knew Sam was capable of.

A glittering object fell from the sky, jingling as it went. Sam reached out and caught it. His face lit up as he looked into his hand. It was a key chain in the shape of Notre Dame's mascot, the Fighting Irish leprechaun.

Sam's head rose slowly, and it appeared that the psycho was feeling some form of love, but somehow Sam made love look angry.

"I knew it was you, Dad!" Sam said. "I knew it."

Sam dashed out of the quad, clutching the key chain with both hands.

Will slowly shook his head. No. It couldn't be true. The man in the motorcycle helmet couldn't be Sam's father. Life couldn't be that unfair. How did the tyrant of the school, the kid who beat up people having seizures, get to have his father back, while Will would never see David again?

Will grabbed a desk and hurled it across the room. It spun through the air and crashed into other desks, making a loud clattering noise. Will refused to accept that this was how things would turn out. He'd make sure things didn't work out for Sam in the end. There had to be a way.

"Give us that honey," a voice said.

Will looked to the door to see three huff-heads from the ruins walking into the room. Burnouts. David had always been paranoid about getting mugged by burnouts and it never happened. Will had come to assume it never would. Whoops.

There was a big guy, a little guy, and a girl. The three of them seemed both exhausted and wired at the same time. Giant dark circles under their eyes. The big guy wore a dead teacher's suit, with a brown bloodstain that covered the front of the dress shirt. The suit fabric was thoroughly soiled, and ripping at the seams, like the kid had lived in it for months. The little guy wore a heavy chain of combination locks as a necklace. No shirt, no pants, just loose boxers, black leather gloves, and tennis shoes. The girl wore two large mens sweatshirts, one like a normal human being would, and the other as pants. Her ankles came out of the sweatshirt's wrist holes and she'd made suspenders out of backpack straps to keep her sweatshirt-pants from falling down. She had dirty gray dreadlocks that hung over her face.

From out of his inside jacket pocket, the big one pulled a short section of broom handle wood, with a four-inch screw driven through the center of it, like a basic corkscrew for wine bottles. He closed his fist over the broom handle part, and the long gold screw stuck out from between his fingers.

You could generally gauge how scared you should be of someone in McKinley by what kind of weapon they brandished. Knives and baseball bats were normal, but Will didn't want anything to do with a dude who carried a punching spike.

They came at him. Will jumped out the window.

Right after his heels hit the ground, his knees hit his chin. His teeth clapped together, he fell on his side. He got to his feet and ran, stumbling and weaving, with a sore chin and aching teeth, still entirely disoriented from his fall. But he'd gotten away with it. The honey was his, and he could already feel his stomach churning through what he'd eaten.

A loud thump behind him. Will looked back. The big one was getting up and dusting his suit off. He saw the girl land on the ground, while the little guy in his boxers jumped from the second-floor window.

"Kill me now," Will said to himself.

He bolted into the nearest hallway and ran all the way to the front foyer, honey in hand. Will could hear their footsteps closing in on him, and he was getting out of breath. He ran through the front foyer's steel graduation doors, to hide in the white room and hope the burnouts ran past. The white room was glaringly bright, as before, and it was empty except for shiny, plump, black trash bags piled up by the walls. He turned to face the doors and walked backward through the white room, watching the steel graduation doors, and praying that no one came through.

The three burnouts entered. The big one in the dead teacher's suit was coughing, with veins puffing out from his neck and forehead. He glared at Will. The little one had lost one of his leather gloves and the skin of his hand was badly burned. He was laughing like a panting dog. The girl with the gray dreads in her face held a permanent marker in her hand, and she had the uncapped marker stuck up her nose. Her nostrils were stained with blue. She held her other nostril closed with her finger and took long, slow inhales of the marker fumes. He could see one of her eyes. It was green, but it was so dilated that it was mostly black.

"Last chance," the big one said. "Honey. Now."

His teeth were brown. He brandished his punching spike in his fist, and the gold-plated screw gleamed in the stark light. The girl began to dance with herself, as if no one else was there. The little one took off his combination lock necklace. He let the heavy chain hang at his hip, in his gloved hand.

Will looked at his honey. He hesitated. The big one walked toward him and cocked his spiked fist back.

SSHTUHH

Will felt a door slide open behind him. He ran through the open doorway without looking and collided with a barrel-chested Saint who was trying to exit. Will saw a red button on the wall by the door and he smashed his palm onto it.

"No, wait," the Saint said from behind him.

The big burnout was dashing toward Will, but the metal door slid out of the wall and slammed shut between them. Will heard the dull thump of the burnout's fist hitting the door and a muffled whelp of pain afterward.

Adrenaline buzzed through Will's body. He turned to the Saint, to thank him for saving his life. The Saint vomited all down the front of Will's shirt.

14

"WHY'D YOU CLOSE THE DOOR?"

"Why'd you throw up on me?!" Will said. He held his puke-soaked T-shirt away from his body with pinched fingers.

"Oh, shit, look at you."

The Saint wiped the vomit off his mouth. He was a bleary-eyed guy with a moon face, sitting on his ass in the middle of the hall. "Party foul. My bad, dude. I'm so fucked up right now."

"Are you?" Will said, with maximum sarcasm.

The hallway was dim and its shadows were deep. The burnouts thumped on the metal door from the other side.

"I gotta get you a new shirt," the Saint said. He crawled on his hands and knees into one of the open containment cells that lined the hall. Half a minute later, he came stumbling back out of the cell on his feet, with a yellow shirt over his shoulder, a towel in one hand, and a bottle of water in the other. He tried to pour the water on the towel, but he missed and most of it splattered on the floor. Will managed to wriggle out of his soiled shirt. He took the towel and water and wiped the puke moisture off his body.

"Thanks," Will said.

"Here, take this." The kid held up the bright yellow shirt. It was a short-sleeve, collared, Izod golf shirt. Will pulled it on. It was brand-new. Fabric this clean and fresh and unblemished didn't exist in McKinley, and wearing it now made Will feel like it was the first day of school.

"Lemme getchoo a drink," the Saint slurred. "Come on."

The Saint weaved down the hall, away from Will, clearly drunk. Will didn't know what he was walking into, but it had to be better than the honey-hungry burnouts waiting for Will in the white room.

"Yeah, all right," Will said.

He caught up with the Saint.

"I'm so sorry, dude. Name's Fowler," the guy said. They shook hands.

"Will."

As Fowler led him through the hallway of containment cells, and through the room with the airtight doors, Will heard the sound of people laughing. Lots of people. He heard sing-alongs. Happy shouts. Will followed him into the room where the ruined school bus protruded from the wall of rubble. The giant slabs of concrete had been wrestled away from the bus and now you could clearly see the front cab of the bus extending out from the wreckage of the wall. The bus's yellow metal was bent and battered, the windshield was smashed out, the grille was crumpled. The front left wheel had come completely off so the whole thing tilted at an odd angle. Saints sat on the bent hood of the bus, joking with each other and drinking from disposable plastic cups.

"Check this out," Fowler said.

Fowler led Will to the bus, to the misshapen hole that used to be the door. They went through the bent hole and up the three stairs into the bus. It was lit only by two camping lanterns. The inside was busy with activity. Saints were tearing out the seats and passing them up front to be removed entirely.

"It's being turned into Gates's room," Fowler said.

Fowler led Will further in, past the Saints at work, to the back of the bus, where the lantern light barely reached. Every window was blacked out. Will clicked on his phone and shined its light to see why. On the other side of the glass was gray cement. He swung the phone around to see that it was true for every window.

"Whoa," Will said. "Did the parents do this?"

Fowler nodded. "Yep. It was like this when we finally got inside. They sealed the whole thing in cement. Guess they mean business."

"Guess so," Will said, marveling at it all.

"You have any cigarettes?" Fowler said.

"Cigarettes? Are you serious?"

"Figured it was worth asking. I didn't know if you had them here or not. I'm dying for one, Dill."

"Will."

"I said Will, man. Pull it together."

Fowler slapped Will in the chest and led him back out of the bus. They went to the room that was the source of most of the noise in the processing facility, the soldiers' mess hall.

It was a party. Most of the Saints were packed into this large room, plastic cups in hand. Rows of long metal tables dominated the space and Saints lounged atop them. There was slurred speech, and eyelids at half mast all around Will. So many drunk people, telling each other how much they loved each other, and thinking things were funnier than they were. A short Saint boy ran down the length of one of the long metal tables, and his friends chased him. Their footfalls sounded like someone punching a steel drum. The kids leapt from table to table, and the Saints who sat at those tables would yell in protest but almost immediately return to their sloppy conversations and be laughing moments later.

"Get this guy a drink!" Fowler said to the room.

A cute Saint girl in a sweater and tights sauntered up to Will with a bottle of vodka in her hand. She had dark eyes and short, white, wispy hair, like a baby chick. She smiled and tilted the bottle toward his lips.

"Open wide," she said.

Will parted his lips and let her pour vodka into his mouth. She winked at him and continued on her way, sharing her bottle with others.

"Where did this vodka come from?" Will said.

"Tiffy found two crates in a locked closet off the soldiers' infirmary," Fowler said.

"Man, what a score," Will said. His bottle of honey didn't seem so impressive anymore.

"Hey, let me introduce you around."

Fowler pulled Will over to a group of people standing in a circle. "This is Beaumont, Robert, Preston, Beatrice, Matt, Chauncey, Babs, Stewart, Dianne, and Fisk. Everybody, this is . . . What was your name again, man?"

"Will."

"Right. Everybody, this is Will."

"Out of the way!" someone screamed from behind Will.

He turned to see Gates, on all fours, atop a moving tower of three, precariously stacked, hospital gurneys. Two other Saints pushed the wobbling stack of gurneys, running at a full clip.

"Faster!" Gates yelled. "Faster!"

The Saints smiled like fools as they poured on the speed, and the unstable gurney-tower sped into the crowded mess hall. Gates stood and spread his arms wide, with a bottle of vodka in one hand, and his long hair flapping behind him.

"I am the party God. Hear my—oh shit!"

The gurney tower tipped, and came crashing down. Gates flew over the heads of some Saints sitting at one of the metal tables, and slammed to the floor where Will couldn't see.

Five seconds later, he popped up to his feet, grinning madly. He tried to take a swig off his vodka bottle, only to discover that he held only the bottle's neck and the rest of it had shattered in the fall. He laughed, and held his fists over his head in victory anyway. The crowd went nuts for it. Best party entrance Will had ever seen. Of course, he'd never gotten the chance to go to a real high school party before the quarantine. In a way, this was his first.

"That was insane!" Fowler shouted.

Gates looked over at Fowler, still riding the high of his stunt, and his clear eye locked onto Will. His other eye was shut.

"I know this guy," Gates said, smiling. He walked over. "How are you here?"

"I puked on him so I invited him to the party," Fowler said.

Gates busted up, laughing. "Aw, shit. I wasn't expecting that. Well, that's the price of admission, I guess. What do you say, Will, was it worth it?"

"Believe it or not, the puke was one of the better parts of my day."

"Ha-ha, nice. Well, you're here now," Gates said, finally opening his other eye. It was still red. "Welcome to our party."

"What's the occasion?"

"We found vodka."

"That's it?"

"You need more of a reason than that?"

"I guess not."

"Come sit with us."

Will followed Gates and the others to a nearby metal table and they all sat down. Will couldn't stop looking at his red eye. A pale boy in a purple Patagonia fleece came running up to Gates.

"You are a madman, I can't believe you just did that!" the boy said.

"It was fun," Gates said.

"Fuckin' maniac, this guy," the boy said.

"We got a lot of 'em around here," Will said.

"Shit, I'm no maniac," Gates said. "I'm a regular guy."

"Liar!" a smiling Saint girl with a missing pinkie finger said. "Gates, you are a lunatic, and you know it. You filled a water gun with your own blood to spray on soldiers to see if they would die."

"That was an experiment!" Gates said, clearly enjoying the attention. "Hey, if that'd worked we could have made poisoned arrows and all sorts of stuff. How sweet would that'a been?"

Kids nodded and laughed. Evidently, it would've been sweet.

"Remember the time you talked those soldiers out of searching the barn we were hiding in?" a curvy girl in long underwear said. She turned and spoke directly to Will. "He had his hair dyed brown at the time, right, and when he sees them coming he puts on this old haz-mat suit we found, then goes out there and feeds these soldiers a line of bs about him being some college kid—"

"Randall Beckwith," Gates said, and clapped. "I went to Princeton!"

The girl nodded. "Right, he said he was the son of the man who owned the farm, who said he flunked out and was back home to tend to things—"

"While I went to community college," Gates interrupted again. "That was my favorite part. Randall was a real fuck-up."

"So, the whole time he's talking to him, he's trying to keep his back to them, 'cause the ass of the haz-mat suit was ripped out. I mean, if they saw that, the jig was up."

"Did they?" Will said, cracking a smile.

The girl shook her head. "He talked to those guys for twenty minutes, never broke a sweat! One of the zillion times this guy saved our lives."

"That's nothing," a boy with a bottle of vodka duct-taped to his hand said. "I'll take it back further than that. What about at St. Patrick's?" The Saints all around the table began to smile and lean forward at the mention of their old school. "Your parents made you get braces—"

Everyone started to laugh. Gates laughed and nodded his head like he was used to hearing about this. Another girl chimed in, "He hated those braces."

The boy pointed at Gates. "Hate is not a strong enough word! You reviled them."

"Ooo, what's up, Vocab!" someone said.

The boy laughed. "Any sane human being woulda complained about them, maybe searched out alternatives to braces on the Internet. This guy tore his braces off with pliers, and he wants to say he's not a maniac? Fuck you, dude!"

The rest of the Saints burst with laughter. Gates slammed his fist down on the table repeatedly, laughing so hard he nearly fell off the bench. "I did do that," he said.

Tearing off your own braces was one of the most badass things Will had ever heard.

"How bad did that hurt?" Will said.

Gates looked at him with tears in the corners of his eyes, still red in the face from laughing. "To tell you the truth, I was on so much Ecstasy at the time, and I was doing it in a hot tub, so that part of my body was feeling really good, and the mix of the two feelings . . . didn't feel that bad."

"That's pretty weird, man," Will said. "I heard you partied hard, but that's out there."

As soon as Will said it, he regretted it. Had he just insulted his host? He didn't even mean anything bad by it. In truth, he was more in awe.

"I guess it is," Gates said with a chuckle. "But it was a once-in-a-lifetime situation, a new experience. Like getting trapped in this place. I don't know what it means yet, or what we can do about it, but it's new, it's different, and it's definitely not at all what we thought it would be—"

"You really thought we had it made in here?" Will said, recalling Gates' story the day the parents had sealed them back in.

"Totally. We thought it was like summer camp here, and you all were chilling in a safe, clean school. Then, we get here and it's like one big battlefield, you guys all hate each other, the whole place is trashed! I mean, what the hell happened, how did it get like this?"

The other Saints in the room halted their conversations and looked over at Will. For a moment he didn't know what to say, it had been bad for so long. He had a stab of doubt that maybe it was their own fault that things had gotten so bad in McKinley, like maybe if St. Patrick's Academy had been quarantined, they all would have gotten along fine, and filled their time with happy parties like this one. The Saints were still staring, and waiting for Will to speak.

He started at the beginning. He told them about the first day of school. He told them about David. He told them about the seniors losing their minds before the graduations started. He told them about Danny Liner and how Sam had murdered him in front of the whole school with a spike to the neck. He told them how the other gangs came quickly after Sam formed Varsity, just to have a shot in the drops.

The more he talked, the more the Saints from other

tables drifted over, until they all crowded around his table, listening. Will felt like a fireman visiting a kindergarten class. One by one, they asked him everything about life in the school: what a Geek show was, what the deal was with Jackal, what was in the ruins, what Varsity and the Pretty Ones' pool was like, how the market worked. No matter how many questions he answered, they had more. He grew to like the Saints across their Q&A. They were normal kids who'd been through hell, just like McKinley kids had. And they were scared about their new life here. That was something Will could relate to.

"Can I ask you a question? It might be a not that cool thing to ask," Will said to Gates, once the Q&A had died down.

"I bet I can take it."

"What's going on there with your eye?"

Gates sighed. "I don't know. Been like this for months. It stings all the time."

"Huh," Will said. "That blows."

"You're telling me."

Saints at the table next to them stood on the metal benches, and did shots of vodka together.

"Do you guys not know how valuable that vodka is?" Will said to Gates. "You could have traded those bottles for anything in the market."

"We'd rather drink it."

"Yeah, but, all of it in one night? You could have stretched it out for a few months."

"That's no way to live, Will," Gates said. "Right, guys?"

The nearby Saints cheered in response.

"Usually I'm the reckless one, but you all make me feel like a librarian," Will said.

"No, you've got it wrong," Gates said. "We believe that when good fortune comes our way, that we have a responsibility to enjoy it as much as possible."

"Responsibility to what?"

"Not to what, to who. To our friends that didn't make it this far. All of us have lost people that were close to us. Boyfriends, girlfriends . . . " Saints around the table nodded in solemn confirmation. "I had two brothers and three sisters when this all started, and now, y'know, it's just me," Gates said.

Gates rubbed his eyes, like the memory had just given him a headache. Poor bastard, Will thought, Gates probably had to watch it happen too. He couldn't imagine how terrible that was. The image of David's corpse drying up in their living room popped into Will's head and his mood sank.

"You have to enjoy life for them," Gates said. "Out there, any day could be your last. Hell, it's no different in here. You gotta enjoy the good times while you still have the chance. Like tonight. We have each other, no one is shooting at us, and we have some vodka. I want to have a good time!"

More cheers through the room.

"My brother died," Will said. He was surprised how the words fell so easily out of his mouth. He hadn't said it out loud before.

Gates's demeanor grew more serious. "That was David? The one from your story?"

Will nodded.

"Somebody pour Will another drink."

A Saint girl placed collapsible camping cups in front of Will and Gates, with an inch of vodka at the bottom of each. Gates raised his cup.

"To David," Gates said to the room. The room said it back, and the sound of thirty-odd strangers saying David's name together took Will's breath away. All the sadness, all the love Will felt for his brother came rushing to the surface. Gates saw the effect the toast had on Will. He gripped Will's shoulder firmly and stared at him, his red eye unblinking.

"You're all right man, you're good," Gates said.

Gates's encouragement actually helped to steady Will.

"You mind giving me a minute?" Will said.

"Sure, man. Of course."

Gates got up and walked off. Will picked up his cup. The idea that the best way he could mourn David was to enjoy his life as much as he could was intoxicating, and he really hoped was true. He raised his cup into the air.

"This one's for you, David," Will said to himself. He downed his drink.

As the night continued, they fed him more vodka. Someone gave him a pill and said it was a muscle relaxant. He ate three peanut butter and jelly sandwiches, and a whole sleeve of water crackers. Will's world began to blur and lose shape. He remembered playing a game of monkey-in-the-middle with an empty pistol, where it was him and Gates tossing the gun over Fowler's head. He remembered talking a lot of shit, to a lot of people. He ran his mouth about how they shouldn't trust Zachary. He told them about P-Nut's weakness for girls, how he was a fiend for them. He told them all sorts of stuff. It was nice to talk to anyone at all, and he didn't give a damn what he was saying. Life had been so shitty to him lately that he felt he'd earned this night of drinking and partying and not giving a fuck.

At some point near the end of the night, the girl with the baby chick hair was sitting in his lap. He couldn't remember when she had sat down, how long she had been there, or what they had been talking about so far. But her warm weight felt good on his leg, and he wanted to keep squeezing the softness of her waist forever. The party was still in full swing, but Gates wasn't with him anymore.

"I have another McKinley question," baby chick said.

"Lay it on me," Will said.

Baby chick looked around with a hint of mischief in her eyes.

She leaned in close, and for a moment Will thought she was going to kiss him, but she leaned further in until her mouth was by his ear, and whispered, "Where do you get condoms?"

He turned his head until his lips grazed the tender skin of her earlobe. She smelled like baby shampoo.

"The Sluts trading post is the easiest place," Will whispered.

She drew her head back and smiled.

"You want to see my room?"

"Yes," he said.

The baby chick girl took his hand and pulled him away from the table. He fell on his face immediately. The world had tilted and no one had told him. He heard her laughing, at least he thought it was her. The cool concrete floor felt amazing against his cheek.

Somewhere, in a dark room, the baby chick kissed him. She pushed him onto a bed and laid herself onto his body. Her tongue met his. Salty-sweet lips.

"Take off my shirt," she whispered.

He went for it. His hands grabbed cotton and he pulled. With the room spinning all around him, it was far more difficult than he thought, but he managed to get that shirt off of her. What was underneath her shirt was so much softer than cotton. He wished he could see it straight.

"You're fun," she whispered in his ear. And that was the last thing Will remembered.

15

LUCY STARED AT A PILE OF BROKEN GLASS

on the floor below her. She was in a push-up position, and she was naked. A circle of Sluts stood around her, shouting.

"Fifteen . . . ," Lucy said as she lowered herself toward the glass. She barely pushed her way back up. Her fully extended arms quaked.

"Again! Push, you little bitch!" someone shouted at her.

It was day seven of Naked Week. The Sluts had told her for days that she didn't stand a chance, that she'd never make it this far. They said eleven girls had died during Naked Week, and they were now stuffed in random locker graves through the school. It was all Lucy had been thinking about for days, her naked body hanging dead in a five-by-one metal box.

Half of her had thought about running. No, most of her had. She was sick of living like this. It had been endless, point- less abuse. She was Cinderella to sixty-three evil stepsisters.

They all picked on her. She survived on only oatmeal which, most of the time, they threw at her. They slapped her, tripped her, purposefully spilled shit on floors she'd just cleaned and made her clean it again. There wasn't a day where they hadn't mocked her naked body, poured cold water on her, or flicked her nipples when they caught her off guard.

She'd told herself all kinds of excuses to stay along the way, but the one she repeated the most was that she'd wanted this. She'd signed up of her own free will because she'd wanted to be like these girls. Tough. Unafraid. Sluts all had this odd way of smiling, like they were wearing an invisible suit of armor that made them invincible, and they were amused that you didn't know about it. Actually, it was Violent's smile. Everyone else just seemed to copy her.

Lips wore it too. She crouched in front of Lucy, planting her hands on her knees and shoving her face forward like a lip-less gargoyle.

"You better start pushing or I'm gonna shove your face in that glass," she said.

"No boys will smile at you then," another Slut said.

"You better hit sixteen! I've been dealing with this 'fifteen' bullshit for a week now!" Lips screamed.

Lucy's arms were blazing with pain. Her waist was rapidly sagging down.

Lips stood up. "Pathetic!"

She wasn't going to give Lips the satisfaction of giving up.

The pile of clear glass shards glinted underneath her. Jagged spires pointed up at her eyes. Curved shards from broken bottles waited for her face, ready to plunge through her cheeks if her head were to come crashing down.

Lucy bent her elbows. She felt her chest muscles pull tight and blossom with pain. She tried to stop her descent, but realized immediately that she could only push hard enough to slow it, not stop it. Blades of glass crept toward her face.

All of a sudden, Lucy's muscles shut down. Her smooth cheeks, the tender skin of her lips, the thin membrane of her eyelids, it all plummeted toward the mound of glass knives.

She felt something yank on the back of her hair. Her naked body slapped down onto the floor, but the hair-puller kept Lucy's head cocked all the way back, and Lucy's face stayed out of the glass pile except for a single shard that pricked the skin of her chin.

She was able to do half a push-up, enough to get a knee under her and get on all fours. She rolled to the side and saw that it was Lips who had held her hair.

"You'll never get any stronger, will you?" Lips said, disgusted.

Lips kicked the shard pile at her. Lucy barely had time to cover her face. She felt stings of pain all over her forearms, stomach, and thighs. She lowered her arms from her face. Glass shards were all around her. Dots of blood popped up all over her bare body, and those dots began to swell into little round berries of blood, before succumbing to gravity, and dripping down her skin.

"Take her to the freezer," Lips said to the other Sluts.

Lucy could see her breath. It came out in foggy huffs, lit blue by the single bare bulb above her. Her body hadn't stopped shaking for the entire four hours that she'd been locked in the kitchen's walk-in freezer. She knew why Lips had locked her in there. It was the last day of Naked Week, and that vindictive cow wanted to squeeze as much suffering into the remaining hours as she could.

This was almost the end. As soon as they let her out of this ice box, it would all be over. Lips would have to eat her words. She will have proved herself. All Lucy had done in the past week was work, get yelled at, get pushed around, flinch about every five minutes, and eat oats off the floor. She couldn't believe she'd endured it all. They had to respect her after this, she'd taken all they could dish out. As miserable as she felt now, with her blood running cold, and her teeth chattering uncontrollably, she was impressed with herself. She never would have imagined she could handle all this.

Lucy heard a metal *plink* and looked up. The freezer door opened, and Violent stepped in. Lucy's eyes widened with hope. She hadn't seen Violent since her first night in the cafeteria, and she'd been getting more and more upset about it. She felt in her heart that if she could just talk to Violent, she could cut this whole Naked Week thing short. They had history together. The other Sluts never would have been so bold with their abuse if Violent had been there to see.

"Where have you been?" Lucy said through clacking teeth.

"None of your business, is it?" She shook her head at Lucy. "I hear you haven't been doing well."

"What? That's not true. I've been doing everything anybody's asked."

"People have been saying that they don't think you want to be here."

"I—I don't want to be cleaning people's feet and getting kicked in the ribs and scrubbing ovens if that's what you mean," Lucy said.

"Lips told me about your attitude. Your lack of obedience. This is your chance to show us you're Slut material, and you haven't shown us anything yet." Violent sighed. "You're going to have start Naked Week over."

"No," Lucy muttered. "You're joking."

"I'm not. It starts over now. This is day one."

Violent turned and walked to the door. She stopped in the doorway, with her back to Lucy.

"First task," Violent said. "Get out to the cafeteria and bring a mop. Someone threw up."

Violent left, leaving the door open behind her. Lucy stood trembling. Whatever semblance of friendship she thought she'd had with Violent had been an illusion. She'd made an awful mistake joining this gang. The Sluts weren't tough, they were sadists.

Lucy didn't follow Violent out of the freezer. She began to pace again, much faster this time. Another week of being treated like she was subhuman? And what would happen at the end of that week? A third week? How about a month of being blindfolded and hit with sticks? She wasn't cold anymore. She was sweating.

Fuck these girls, Lucy thought, *I'm out.*

She charged into the warmth of the dark kitchen, and out into the light of the cafeteria, which was filled with boisterous conversation, and the *chock-ch-chock-chock* of Sluts slamming their knives down into the long cafeteria table before sitting down to eat. Lucy didn't slow a bit, she walked straight for the exit, on the other end of the dining room. The further into the room Lucy got, the quieter it became. She could feel all eyes on her, and although a growing fear was beginning to accompany her boiling anger, for the first time, she didn't care one bit that she was naked.

"Where the hell do you think you're going, slave?" she heard Lips say.

Lucy kept walking. Something hard whacked her in the ear. Lucy stumbled left as pain stabbed into the side of her head. Her filthy, blackened scrub brush fell to the floor in front of her filthier toes.

"Oh! Direct hit!"

Lucy turned to see Lips stand up from the table, about ten feet from her. Lips smiled until her eyes were little knife wounds and her mouth looked like someone had placed a small shovel on Lips's face and stomped on it. Lucy pulled her hand away from her ear. Fury electrified her at the sight of her own blood.

She dashed at Lips. Lucy saw the surprise flash across her ugly face. Lucy punched her in the tit. Lips wasn't expecting it, and she wasn't blocking for it. Lucy hadn't really been aiming for it either, she'd swung wild, and that was just where her fist hit. Lips winced, and Lucy was able to shove her to the ground. Lucy pounced on her, ready to beat her face in, but the other Sluts pulled Lucy off.

Then they did something unexpected. The Sluts started to cheer. The whole gang converged on her. They were smiling. They hugged her, they patted her on the back, and mussed her hair. They told her how great she did, how awesome that was.

"What's going on?" Lucy said to them.

"Congratulations," Violent said in a big voice, as she came weaving through the crowd. She wrapped Lucy in a heavy quilted blanket and pulled her close.

"Ladies! We've got ourselves a Slut!"

"I don't understand," Lucy said.

"I knew you had the killer instinct somewhere in there," Violent said. "I just didn't think it would take you so long."

"What do you mean?" Lucy asked.

"Naked Week ends when you fight back. Naked Week could've been Naked Afternoon, if you had fought back that first day."

Lucy furrowed her brow. She couldn't help the flush of embarrassment.

"Some girls just need a little more time than others. But in the end every Slut gets tough. That's what binds us, right, girls?" Violent said, and the Sluts nodded. "We don't wait for permission, we don't take any shit."

Lips came walking up, smiling like a proud parent. She held a plastic salad bowl full of bloodred water.

"Not bad, girl," Lips said. "Now, let's get that white out of your hair."

16

WILL OPENED HIS EYES. A WAVE OF NAUSEA
rolled down from his forehead and plopped into his stomach.
His temples throbbed with dull pain and his mouth felt like
he'd been chewing on socks. He wasn't in the elevator, and it
took him a few seconds to remember why. He was lying on his
side, on a bed in one of the processing facility's containment
cells. The baby chick girl from the party was standing over
him, next to the bed. He watched her slip into a pair of black
tights. She pulled on a gray cashmere sweater. Her wispy,
white-haired head popped through, and when she saw him
awake, she smiled.

"See ya around," she said, and turned for the cell's clear
door, which was open to the hallway.

"Hey, wait," Will said. He looked down at himself. All of his
clothes were still on, even his shoes. "What, uh . . . what happened last night?"

"You don't remember?"

Will shook his head. His brain felt like liquid sloshing up on the sides of his skull. "Parts, I guess. What did you and me, uh, do . . . ?"

"Nothing X-rated. You feel asleep," she said. Will was relieved in a way. He'd hate to have missed his first time. The girl laughed and skipped out of the cell. "Don't forget your bag. It's in the hall."

Oh, no, the honey. Will sat up suddenly and he nearly vomited. Too fast, too soon. His body despised him. He stood and a head rush made him stumble one step sideways. He swore his head was about to collapse as he walked out of the cell.

Will's backpack sat on the floor, just outside in the hall. He bent down, and the blood flowed to his head. His headache pulsed. He unzipped his bag fast. He was shocked to find his bottle of honey was still inside. He reached in and gave it a satisfying squeeze. He didn't understand. How had no one taken it? They could have gotten away with it for sure.

Will looked down the hall to where some Saints were hanging out, beyond the airtight doors in the front room where the bus had crashed through. They were doing a massage train. The kid in front told an animated story and used his hands a lot because he didn't have anyone's shoulders to lay them on.

Will wished the party didn't have to end. He thought about the life waiting for him in the elevator. Hungry, cold, and alone. Only going out at night. Trusting no one. He'd seen the love between the Saints last night. They worked together, had fun together, and watched each other's backs. Will remembered what that used to feel like.

But he felt out of place. This wasn't his gang. He didn't want to push his luck by hanging out any longer and turning into the annoying house guest who wouldn't leave. Will zipped up his bag and shouldered it. He headed for the exit.

"Where you going?"

Will turned to see Gates; he was disheveled and shuffling into the hallway behind Will. His eyes were barely open and he looked like he was in just as much pain as Will.

"Figured I should get going," Will said.

Gates wiped his hand down his face. "Huh? Where?"

"Back home," Will said. "I really appreciate you letting me hang out last night—"

"Home? I thought your whole gang bailed on you."

Will didn't like hearing his situation put so bluntly, but he couldn't deny that it was pretty much true.

"I've got a smaller place now."

"The elevator?" Gates said. "You're not going back there. That's depressing."

"How do you know where I . . . "

"You mentioned it last night."

Will groaned softly. He didn't remember doing that. What had he been thinking?

"Look," Gates said. "I know we haven't known each other

long, but, I'm not really one for waiting, in general. We need someone like you, someone who knows this school."

"You want me to be a Saint?"

"I guess we're stuck with that name, huh?" Gates said. "Anyway, yeah, that's what I'm saying. I think you should run with us in the food drop today."

Just the thought of being on the quad again, in front of everyone, made Will's hangover double in intensity.

"You don't want me in your gang."

"I do actually, that's why I'm fuckin' asking," Gates said sharply. "We're the new kids, there's no hiding it. I can't lead my people if I don't know how things work, or if I don't know who I can trust and who's trying to hustle us in the market . . . I don't know all that stuff. But you do."

The picture was clear in Will's head. He was seizing in the middle of the quad, everyone was laughing, and the Saints were walking away from him. It would happen all over again.

"I don't get it," Gates said when Will didn't answer. "You don't want forty pairs of eyes watching your back from now on? You don't want to get your respect back? Walk out there with us and you could show all of them that they can't keep you down."

"I don't run in drops anymore," Will said, breaking eye contact.

Gates threw his Nalgene bottle onto the ground, spiking it like a football. Water sprayed up on the door of a neighboring cell. The bottle clattered on the hard floor. Will looked at Gates, confused.

"Dude, what's your problem?" Will said, throwing up his hands.

"You're epileptic and it sucks. I get it. I got an earful of it last night. But, you want to hide? That's what you want to do about it? I know I'm hungover, and my head is fucking killing me, and maybe I'm out of line in saying this, but grow the fuck up. You get seizures. That's your deal. You have to accept it." He massaged his temples, clearly in pain. "I'm sorry I'm yelling, but . . . don't you want someone there to help you up next time?"

Will stared at Gates. He couldn't believe what he'd just said, but what surprised Will more was that it didn't hurt so bad to hear. Everybody usually skirted around the issue of his epilepsy, or tried to make it out to be not that bad. That always bugged him. Nobody had talked to him so plainly about his problem since David.

"All right," Will said.

"Yeah?" Gates said, his eyebrows rising high. "Fantastic!"

They shook hands, and Gates's grip was strong.

"You'll love it. We have a lot of fun," Gates said.

"I get one of those rooms, right?"

Will remembered a time when he wished everybody in McKinley knew his name. Things change. Will's head tingled. His sweat was cold. His stomach felt ready to erupt.

He stepped onto the quad with his new gang.

The quad quieted as more people became aware of Will walking with the Saints. Whispered conversations sprung up all around. There was Will, not a Loner, not a Scrap, but a Saint. He locked eyes with former Loners—Ritchie in the Skaters, Mort with the Freaks, they looked stunned. He scanned the Geeks for Lucy, but came up empty. It was almost a relief. He was more afraid to know what she thought than anyone else.

The Saints took their place against the wall where the Loners used to stand. Will was suddenly outside of himself, seeing what everyone on the quad was seeing. A desperate person throwing in with the new kids, who didn't know any better.

Will glanced at Gates, looking for that same confidence and belief that got him to step foot out here, but Gates's focus was on the quad, not Will. All of the sudden, Will's logic was melting away. He wondered if he'd just been talked into something totally idiotic by a dude who didn't really care if Will lived or died. Maybe Gates rattled off this kind of hype at everybody he came across.

Across the quad, he saw Bobby in front of the Freaks. Bobby mimed having a seizure. He went stiff as a board, then dropped to the ground, and flopped around. The blue-hairs around him laughed and pointed at Will. Colin and Mort were the only ones who didn't. They covered their faces and turned away instead.

"Try breathing. It makes you look less like a corpse," Gates said with a smile.

"Ha, right."

Will breathed out in a long, anxious exhale. It made him feel a tiny bit better. He was with the Saints now, and he had to play it out and hope for the best. There was no backing out without looking like a bigger fool. Will looked up to the empty sky.

"When's this damn thing gonna start already?" Will said.

A hubbub over by Varsity drew the attention of the quad away from Will. It was strange that they stood at the neighboring wall, rather than their usual post, across from the old Loners' spot. Sam was strangling Terry on the ground. Varsity guys converged on Sam and pulled him off. They restrained him, and he thrashed in their grip, as Terry got back to his feet.

"That's the last straw, Sam!" Terry shouted. "You're done!"

"You can't kick me out of Varsity!" Sam said. "I made Varsity!"

Terry ignored Sam and turned to face the entire school. "I want everybody to know, Varsity is heading in a new direction, and it's away from Sam Howard."

"You're losers!" Sam said. "You all just made the worst decision of your life."

Sam's words lost their power in the wide open quad, with a

wall of Varsity staring back at him, unmoved. Sam frantically rubbed his hands through his hair; he snapped his gaze up to the roofline.

It felt monumental to Will. Sam was officially alone. Gangless. Powerless. And Will had the Saints. In an instant, the tables had turned. His hangover nausea started to fade as Will's heart pumped with excitement. He zeroed in on Sam's face, which was defined by a new frantic quality. As soon as the food dropped, Will would rush Sam. He didn't have a plan other than that he had a gang behind him now, and Sam couldn't do what he did to Will last time. He felt an overwhelming craving to hear Sam cry in pain.

Will watched Sam's eyes flit across the quad, looking for an angle, some way to right his situation. He heard the squelch of the guitar amp.

"We have an announcement."

All heads looked up to see the man in the motorcycle helmet standing behind the razor wire fence.

"We've had a setback," he said. "We were counting on a shipment, but the truck never arrived. We just got word that the driver was arrested and his load was confiscated. It's . . . it's not great news. Because of this setback, there will be no food today."

Everyone flipped out. People started screaming at the man in the motorcycle helmet.

"Are they serious?!" Will said to Gates, but Gates didn't look his way.

While everyone else shouted up at the roofline, Gates started walking across the quad.

"Where's he going?" Will said to no one in particular.

"Settle down!" the man in the motorcycle helmet said, splaying his hands out. "We're working on an alternate plan . . . ."

Will kept his eyes on Gates, fascinated. Something slid out from the sleeve of Gates's jacket and he caught it by its black rubber handle. It was a hammer. Gates walked across the quad at a hurried pace. Will realized he was headed straight toward Sam, whose back was to Gates.

Gates raised his hammer up over his head and he struck Sam in the shoulder. Sam made a noise like a dog being kicked.

"Whoa," Will said softly.

Sam struggled to get away, but Gates was faster. He swung his hammer into Sam's kidney as he ran. Sam's body crimped sideways, and he belly flopped onto the ground. Gates grabbed him by the hair and lifted him to his feet. Sam was moaning. He swayed and stumbled, and probably would have fallen if Gates wasn't holding him up like a marionette. Varsity didn't budge to help him; they stood firm on their earlier declaration. Sam was on his own.

"YOU!" the man in the motorcycle helmet said. He was pointing at Gates. "STOP THAT! STOP IT!"

People in the quad watched Gates jerk Sam around like a mutt with a steak. The angry shouting from above began to settle, until the only thing that could be heard were Sam's desperate yelps for help.

Fowler slapped Will on the back. "New guy," he said. "You want a piece of this action, right?" Fowler clutched a roll of brown packing tape in his hand, and started a hurried walk toward Gates and Sam.

Will ran to catch up with Fowler. He didn't know what the hell this was about, but if it meant making Sam hurt, he was first in line. As Will got closer to Sam, he became acutely aware that he was putting himself in the spotlight again. All eyes would be on him. If there was a time to turn back, it was now. Will's gaze traveled to the Geeks again. He knew whose face he was searching for, but he couldn't find her. A few seconds later, Will and Fowler reached Gates's side. Gates was wired. Sam flailed in his grip.

"Take his arms," Gates said to Fowler and Will.

Fowler grabbed one of Sam's arms. Sam twisted his head to look at Will. He seemed rattled, but still he looked at Will like Will was an ant. "Touch my arm, Thorpe, and I'll beat you till you shit yourself again. I'll kill you this time, I swear."

Will grabbed Sam's other arm and wrenched it. Sam grunted. Gates raised his eyebrows at Will, as if to say, "Fun, huh?"

Better than fun, it felt incredible. Sam was at his mercy. He twisted his arm more, and Sam's cry of pain was melodic. He hoped Sam was scared. He wanted this to be a level of help-lessness unlike anything Sam had ever known.

Fowler passed the packing tape roll to Gates, who let go of Sam's yellow hair to peel off three feet of brown tape. Will looked up toward the roof where a group of five parents, all wearing scuba tanks and bandanas over their faces, had gathered with the motorcycle man. They shouted at Gates to stop.

"What, uh . . . What are we doing?" Will whispered to Gates.

"You said motorcycle man up there is Sam's dad, right?" Gates said.

Oh, God. He didn't remember telling him that. Will's blood went cold. He felt Sam go rigid at Gates's words.

"Yeah," Will said. He'd never actually seen who Sam was talking to up there, but now didn't seem like the time to split hairs. Sam looked up to the sky, and for the first time, Will saw the fear in his face that he'd been hunting for. Eyes opened so wide, they were nearly lidless. A tremor in his lip.

Sam got ahold of himself, put his angry face back on, and shouted at the crowd that stood on the sidelines. "You think any of you can stop me? You know what I'm capable of! Well, last year was nothing! I'll make every one of you regret ever letting this happen if you don't—"

Brown plastic tape muffled the rest of his words. Gates pulled it tight around Sam's head until it was a plastic gag. He kept looping it around, holding Sam's jaw shut, and layering tape around his mouth. That was enough to keep Sam quiet, but it wasn't enough for Gates. He taped over Sam's eyes, over his hair, he emptied the roll and turned Sam into a crinkled and shiny brown cellophane mummy, with patches of skin, and tufts of yellow hair poking through. His nostrils were left uncovered so he could still breathe. Sam's attempts to keep talking through his tape gag were unintelligible blasts of diluted noise, like underwater shouts.

The quad was captivated. Will was dying to know what was going to happen just as much as they were. Gates looked up to the sky.

"Hey," he said. "I've got your little boy."

"We don't know what you are talking about," the motorcycle man's muffled voice boomed. "Just let the kid go. This is uncalled for. We understand you're upset, but this is only a temporary interruption, we have no intention of letting you go hungry."

"Oh, thanks so much, really," Gates said. "But you're gonna have to do better than that, if you want to keep us locked up here like zoo animals. We're done jumping when you say jump. You're going to give me everything that I ask you for. Because I know that Sam here is your son."

That idea hit the quad like a bomb. All eyes zeroed in on the man in the motorcycle helmet. The black face shield of his helmet revealed nothing. He didn't move.

"Someone has been lying to you," the man in the motorcycle helmet said.

"Really?" Gates said, swinging the hammer lazily.

"Yes," the man said.

"Then you won't mind if I give Sam's face a little character."

Gates flipped the hammer over in his hand, and struck Sam in the forehead with its claw teeth.

Will felt Sam's whole body jolt and then sink against his grip. Sam made terrible grunts and yelps. Blood drizzled down from the twin triangular gouges above his left brow. It streamed over the folds and down the twists of tape that swaddled his face. He looked like a mail order jock that had been damaged in shipping.

The woman in the lilac motorcycle helmet yanked out the man's microphone cord and plugged herself into the amp.

"Stop, please! Yes, he's our son, Sam is our son. I'm beggi—" the woman said, before the man unplugged her and plugged himself back in.

There was an excruciating pause.

"What do you want?" the man said.

The crowd's eyes switched to Gates now. So did Will's. He had them in the palm of his hand, and he could ask for anything. The moment stretched.

"Pizza," Gates replied.

The quad erupted with cheers and applause. Will marveled at Gates.

"And microwaves. You hear me? I want Kraft macaroni and cheese. Pop-Tarts. I don't want canned beans, you'll give us

Frosted Flakes. The real kind. Waffles and whipped cream. Fresh meat we can grill. And grills!"

With every item Gates named the crowd's cheers grew louder and more fervent. Just saying the names of those foods placed a sucking black hole in the belly of every kid on the quad.

"And porn. And video games," he said.

Boys in the crowd hollered low.

"And raid every clothing store in this deserted town. Every closet. We want new clothes."

Female cheers soared high. Gates looked around at the girls in the crowd and smiled. He might have winked at them too, but Will couldn't see.

"What do you say, ladies, makeup? Bath products?"

The girls went a little crazy, like they were twelve again and at their first boy band concert. Gates beamed, soaking up every second of female adoration.

"And forty cases of liquor. Tequila. Bourbon. We're gonna have a party!"

The quad went nuts. Will could see the whole range of reactions. Some thought the whole spectacle was hilarious, others lusted after Gates's demands and relished the opportunity to stick it to the parents. But what seemed to get everyone in the spirit of things was that it was all at Sam Howard's expense. Sam, who had hoarded everything for himself. Sam, who had terrorized everyone. Sam, who hated all of them.

"You hear that?" Will shouted into Sam's taped-over ear. He wanted to make sure Sam knew it was him. "That's how much they want you to pay. Nobody's saving you."

Sam's head turned toward Will's voice. Will couldn't see his eyes, but he could feel his arm shaking. Will felt strong, in control.

"You're going to give me what I want!" Gates shouted at the man on the roof. "You're going to give my friend Will here what he wants. You're going to give all of us what we want."

There were shouts of joy. Will gave Gates a surprised look.

"Will, tell Sam's daddy what you want!" Gates shouted over the crowd. The shouts subsided.

The sudden wide broadcast of Will's name, the full focus on him, was more than he thought he was signing on for. He was undeniably a part of this now, people wouldn't think of this event without thinking of him, and what his answer was.

The crowd listened. Gates listened. The parents on the roof listened.

Will knew what he wanted. It was only one thing. But the idea of asking for it mortified him. He didn't want to say. Not here, not where his face had been dragged through the dirt, not where they'd all seen him fail and would never forget it. Not while he held Sam's arm. This was the worst time, worst place to say it. But, he needed them.

"Carbatrol. Extended release. Chewable if possible. Or

Klonopin. And if not that than Lyrica. They're—They're epilepsy medications."

Will received no cheers. He'd killed their fun. He'd called the cops on the party. He could feel Gates's eyes on him more intensely than any others. It made the skin on his cheekbone prickle. He glanced over.

Gates nodded at him slowly. His expression had gone grim, his eyes sorrowful, but he thought there was respect there as well. Gates craned his head back up to the roof parents. He rose his hammer over Sam's head again and froze it there.

"You heard us," he said.

"You don't understand," the man shouted. His voice was an angry, distorted blast. "Our resources are limited until we get this truck situation resolved. What you're asking is only going to make it harder. You have to be reasonable."

Birds chirped in the distance.

"Have it all by next week, or I'll cut off your son's head."

17

KIDS FROM ALL GANGS LINED THE HALLS ON
both sides. It was like they'd come for a parade, but there was
no confetti in the air here, no music, no street food. These
kids had come for the chance to see Sam's walk of shame as
the Saints brought him back to the processing facility. Gates
was just ahead of Will, and giving Sam shoves when he wasn't
walking fast enough. A few Saints walked ten feet in front of
Sam so that he'd have nowhere to go if he tried to run. Not
that he could see where he was going with tape over his eyes.

As they passed the onlookers, Gates encouraged everybody
to take a free shot at Sam if they wanted one, which most of
them did. He was shoved, punched, and slapped. His shins
were kicked, he was tripped, and stepped on. With his hands
bound behind his back, he couldn't defend himself.

"You're not a very nice person!" a Nerd girl yelled. It seemed
to be the worst she'd let herself muster, but her friend did one

better when he stepped forward and emptied a full trash can onto Sam's head. When the trash was all out, he slipped the plastic bin over Sam and left it there. Big laughs ricocheted down the hall. Sam kept walking, unable to say anything or fight back or get the thing off him. He was just a dark gray trash can with legs.

Will should have been laughing the hardest, except he wasn't.

"This made it all worthwhile, didn't it?" Gates said, slowing to sidle up to Will.

"It's pretty good," Will said, raising his voice over the noise in the hall. He was holding back, and it probably wasn't difficult to tell. Now that they were off the quad and out of the moment, now that Sam wasn't literally in Will's hands, something about the extremity of all this made him uncomfortable. Without adrenaline to keep him high, his mind kept wandering to the long list of consequences that were bound to come from this.

"Hell yes, it's pretty good," Gates said.

Will lowered his voice. "You're not really going to cut his head off, right?"

Gates let out a surprised laugh. "Dude. I'm not crazy. Give me some credit here."

Will relaxed a little, but still something nagged at him. Gates clapped his hand on Will's shoulder.

"Okay, so you're my inside man, what are the odds one of these gangs is gonna try and snatch Sam? How much do we have to be on guard here?"

Will eyed the gawkers along the lockers. He didn't see a single Varsity in the bunch.

"You're not going to hear from Varsity," Will said. "I don't think Terry was bullshitting. If they're trying to put distance between them and Sam, you just did them a huge solid. I guess as far as everybody else goes, nobody's going to want anything to do with Sam either, because on the off chance he escapes? Who knows what that psycho will do for revenge. So . . . whatever you do, don't let him get away."

"Hey, man." Gates smiled. "You're part of this too."

Will gave Gates an uneasy nod.

Will said, "I think we're good for now, 'cause who knows if this will work. But if the parents deliver, then, everybody might come gunnin' for him."

"Okay, perfect, we'll cross that bridge when we come to it," Gates said. "And I don't know what this 'might' stuff is, those assholes are gonna deliver. Have a little faith, man."

"Yeah, well, right," Will said. "That's what I wanted to ask you . . . What's the plan here? I mean, if they don't deliver—"

"They will."

"Okay then, say they do. Then what? Like I said, we can't just cut Sam loose. He'll—"

"Will—" Gates said, giving Will a shake. "One step at a time, man. Look around, they all love us. You won on the quad today. This morning, you were bitching about how worthless you were." Gates furrowed his brow. "You're not one of these whiners that can't ever lighten up, are you? Please, tell me you're not. That shit drives me nuts."

Will shook his head. "I'm not." He didn't think he was. But right now, he couldn't help but hear David's voice in his head telling him to understand all the angles. Be sure, David might have said.

"So, do me a favor," Gates said, "and start enjoying yourself."

The crowd sounded like a chorus, letting a harmonious *OH!* fly when Sam tripped over his own feet and went trash can-first into the floor. Gates clapped at the pratfall and ran to Sam to jerk him back up and milk the crowd for laughs.

Gates had a true talent with people. Will could see why he was a legend at St. Patrick's. His moves were big, he knew what people liked to see, and he made them feel like they were a part of his one-man show. Kids looked at Gates the way Will had always hoped people would look at him, back before all this, when he'd had daydreams about walking the halls of McKinley High, being on top like his star quarterback brother.

"How're you holding up, Sleepy?"

Will looked over to see the baby chick girl arching her eyebrow at him. She looked like a little elf next to the biggest kid in the Saints, Pruitt, and he was a giant. He walked beside her, pensively twisting the bottom of his white beard between his huge thumb and forefinger. She looked eternally comfy in her cashmere sweater, and he looked the opposite in his tattered corduroy blazer and wool slacks tucked into unlaced duck boots. But Pruitt seemed like the kind of guy who didn't give a shit whether he was comfortable or not. Maybe it was the way his beard hid his mouth, but none of this seemed to impress him much.

"You look lost," the baby chick girl said to Will.

"I, uh, I know this sounds bad," Will said, "but tell me your name again?"

"Classy," Pruitt said in a flat tone.

The baby chick girl shoved Pruitt; it had zero impact on his cinderblock frame. She smiled at Will and extended her hand.

"Lark," she said. "Nice to meet you. Officially."

"I'm Will," he said to both of them.

"Yeah," Pruitt said. "Got that. You talked to me for, like, a half hour last night."

"Right," Will said, and they walked without talking for a little bit. The silence between them unsettled Will. He'd just played a key role in something massive. Sam Howard was somebody's prisoner, it was a McKinley first. Gangs on the quad and now in the hall looked at the Saints the way they had looked at the Loners that first day they rose up and defied Varsity. Will could see awe at the Saints' boldness in every face he passed.

He sometimes saw a note of respect, but at the same time there was always a hint of skepticism. Nobody knew these new kids really. Nobody knew if this was one in a series of victories, or if they wouldn't fumble the ball the next time they tried something this big again. When it had been the Loners, Will had held on to a naive confidence that everything would turn out all right, but he didn't feel that now. Gates wasn't his brother, whom he'd known all his life; Will hadn't lived in the dump with these kids for weeks, he'd only partied with them for one night. Sure, he'd had a good time, but who knew if he actually got along with them without liquor to lubricate things? Will didn't know the Saints any better than the rest of the school did. And yet, as far as McKinley and the parents and Sam could see, Will was one of them.

Ahead of them, Gates had taken to shaking people's hands after they sucker punched Sam.

"He's always on like this, huh?" Will said.

"Pretty much," Pruitt said.

"You don't seem impressed."

"Pruitt always looks like that," Lark said.

Pruitt didn't say anything. He stayed unreadable. Lark shrugged.

"Here's what you need to know about Gates," she said. "You can count on him. He's always found a way for us to be happy. Look at him, he's fun! And he's got so much love to give."

"Until he crashes," Pruitt said.

Will homed in on Pruitt. "What do you mean?" Will said.

Lark rolled her eyes and waved Pruitt off. "Sometimes, Gates gets in these moods, and he just has to be alone and kind of refuel. I mean, he's only human. You'd need some downtime too if you gave two hundred percent all the time, right?"

Will nodded. Not being in control of your brain was something he could understand.

"If that's what it takes for him to do the amazing stuff he does, then that's fine by me. I know I might not be alive right now if it wasn't for him," Lark said.

Will studied Lark. She believed what she said. Her love for Gates seemed irrepressible. Will looked over at Pruitt for one last try at spotting some emotion in the guy.

"Did Gates know he was going to pull this move today?" Will said. "Did he actually have a plan?"

Pruitt glanced Will's way.

"Gates doesn't like people telling him what to do," Pruitt said. "Especially adults."

The crowd ahead began to dissipate as they neared the graduation doors and the white room beyond it.

"I don't know if he had a plan today or not," Pruitt said.

"Of course he had a plan," Lark said. "Pru's just a stick-in-the-mud."

Pruitt didn't answer, he only lumbered on.

When the Saints entered the white room, someone behind the observation window high on the right wall waved to them.

A moment later, the door to the containment cell hall slid open. The gang started to enter the processing facility, and Gates pushed Sam inside. Will slowed the closer he got to the door, forcing Saints behind him to go around him in order to enter.

This was it. If Will walked away, back to the elevator, he knew Gates wouldn't welcome him back.

"Will!" Gates said, standing just inside the doorway of the containment cell hall. "Come on."

Will looked back in the direction of the school. Beyond the glaring brightness of the white room, the gangs in the foyer were turning away, all going back home. Will turned to Gates, who put up his hands and looked at Will like "what gives?"

Will walked to the door and stepped inside the processing facility.

18

A PACK OF GEEKS PARTED FOR THE SLUTS AS
they walked out of the market. Lucy looked each one in the
eye as she passed, and each of them looked away. They didn't
want a piece of her or the girls that walked with her. She
could honestly say that had never happened to her before.
The feeling was exhilarating. But she kept her face steeled,
like the rest of her gang.

"Yeah, that's right," a spiky-hair Slut named Raunch said to
one of the Geeks, then raised her voice for the whole market
to hear. "You steal from us? You got a whuppin' coming your
way!"

Blood streamed down Lucy's forearm; it matched the color
of her hair. It flowed from a three inch gash she'd gotten from
a Skater girl, who'd tried to shoplift from the Slut trading
post. Lucy had gone after her, and then everything escalated
quickly between the Sluts and the Skaters. Lucy couldn't have

been prouder of her wound. It was proof that she wasn't afraid to fight, and that she had done her part for the gang. She had Naked Week to thank for her newfound confidence.

As soon as the Sluts got some distance from the market and turned the next corner, conversation in the group loosened up. Now that the eyes of the school weren't on them, the girls started cracking jokes about Skaters and feeling free to let their guard down and laugh. Lucy wasn't sure she should though. Even if she was officially one of them now, she was still the new one, which, to her, meant she had to play it cooler than the rest.

Raunch grabbed Lucy's bleeding arm and pushed her protective, prescription basketball glasses up onto her forehead to get a good look.

"Look who turned into a little badass!" she said to Lucy.

"No big deal," Lucy said, straining not to smile.

"No big deal, shit," Raunch said, laughing. "You laid that Skater out. She hit the ground like, *PWAP!*"

Raunch threw herself against the lockers and flailed her arms for effect. She banged her elbow, then grabbed it like she'd really hurt it.

"Ow, shit."

Lucy covered her smile with her hand. She was still trying to act like kicking a Skater's ass wasn't a big deal, but it kind of was. She'd chased that Skater girl and cold cocked her. It was nothing the old Lucy would have done.

Lucy wasn't the only one who had changed. In the quad, when everyone was waiting for the food drop that didn't happen, she'd witnessed Ritchie with the Skaters, in his new black mohawk, nod to Leonard by the Geeks, who looked like a genie in parachute pants and a vest, with no shirt, and a purple mini-ponytail. She'd seen Leonard then wave across the quad to Colin and Mort, who looked like blue-haired, undead versions of themselves. They'd given subtle waves back. But none of them even looked Lucy's way. Not even Will. Without knowing she was in the Sluts, they had no reason to look for her there, because she knew the idea of Lucy being a Slut was unimaginable to them. She wondered what they'd say when they found out.

"You made us look good out there," Raunch said.

"Thanks."

"So, hey . . . You think if this Gates guy pulls this move off, maybe you can get Will to get you some stuff? You're tight with him, right?"

Lucy stopped walking, and Raunch raised her eyebrows like she'd said the most innocent thing in the world.

"Hold on," Lucy said. "Is that why you're being nice to me?"

Raunch fell against Lucy like a pleading toddler. "Girl, you got no idea how bad I want some footie pajamas. The real soft ones."

Lucy smiled; she liked that Raunch didn't even bother to deny her motive.

"Footie pajamas," Lucy said. "Like what little kids wear?"

"They are soooo comfy, you don't even know. In fact, get yourself a pair. On me. Also, hook me up with a massage chair."

"A massage chair? Are you crazy?" Lucy laughed.

"You don't get anywhere thinking small, Lucy," Raunch said. "You think this guy can really pull it off? Do you think the parents are gonna deliver?"

"Honestly?" Lucy said. "Sam's parents didn't come this far to keep us safe. They came to keep him safe. I think they're gonna try. I'm pretty sure my mom and dad would."

"Yeah," Raunch said, wide-eyed and smiling. "Mine too. This is gonna rule."

"You are evil," Lucy said.

Raunch cackled, "No, Sam is. We're just finally getting something good out of it, thanks to Gates. I heard that before the quarantine, he took over an airport and threw a three-day party."

"I don't think so."

"I heard he punched, like, eight cops," Raunch said.

"I heard it was one. At a Kmart."

Raunch looked Lucy up and down. "You think he's bullshit, huh?"

"I'm just not convinced he's the school's savior like everybody else is, that's all," Lucy said.

"Well, I heard those St. Pat's kids were snobs, but after

today, I think I like rich kids. Especially ones that like to spread it around. I wonder if Gates has got a yacht. . . . "

It went on like that between Lucy and Raunch for the rest of the walk back to the cafeteria. Lucy had stopped arguing with her when she realized Raunch wasn't ever interested in resolving any points she brought up, she just liked to talk. Lucy had found her first real friend in the Sluts.

Lucy wondered if Will had gotten close with anyone in the Saints. In spite of the way he'd talked to her in the Stairs, she still worried about him. She couldn't help it. It was hard seeing him standing with a bunch of strangers. They didn't know him like she did, and she wasn't sure they'd be a good influence. But he had people looking out for him, and that was something. And as hard as she knew it was to ask for his epilepsy medication in front of everyone, she was proud that he was brave enough to do it. For a split second out there she had wanted to run to him and wrap him in her arms. In that moment she missed him like crazy. But that was pointless. They lived in different worlds now. He'd made his decisions and she'd made hers.

As Lucy walked into the cafeteria, Raunch was doing an impression of Sam with his face taped like a mummy. This was the third time she'd done it on the walk back from the market, but it got Lucy each time.

"Stop . . . stop . . . ," Lucy said between laughs.

Raunch said in her best Sam voice, exaggerated and fierce, "How dare you! How ... dare ... you ... " then she mimed being struck by the hammer. "Bwuh—"

Raunch fell into Lucy so she had to catch her trim little frame. They walked into the cafeteria and Sluts began to unload bags of food and supplies at the doorway to the pantry hall, while others started stripping down out of their food drop armor and hanging up their larger weapons.

Every Slut carried a knife. Lucy kept hers sheathed in a water-warped paperback that she tied around her thigh with cooking twine. It was a normal metal cafeteria knife, but the rounded tip had been ground into a nasty point, and the cutting edge had been hammered until it was paper thin. The metal was cloudy and scuffed from countless trips through a dishwasher, but an *S* painted on the base of the blade, in a curving, hair-thin line of red nail polish, gave it character. She hadn't pulled it on anyone yet, and she hoped she wouldn't have to, but most likely she would.

"C'mon," Raunch said, eyeing Lucy's bloody forearm. "Sophia'll fix you up."

Raunch and Lucy walked over to a long table where a bunch of Sluts were comparing injuries.

"Some Skater clotheslined me with a board," a flat-chested girl said. "I'm gonna need a boob replacement."

"You wish," another said, and the whole crew laughed.

"Check this out," one girl said and held up her middle finger with a strained grin. It was bent sideways at a sharp angle, a nasty-looking break but nothing a splint wouldn't fix. "A Skater stepped on it."

"Gimme your elbow, honey," Sophia said to Lucy from the other side of the table. She was the gang's Band-Aid girl.

Sophia was a perfect specimen. Everything on the girl seemed to push out; her cheekbones were round, her lips were pink pillows, her eyes gorgeous ovals with an elegant swoop. Her hair was a long shimmering auburn with bounce that defied gravity. She looked like the slow-motion girls in shampoo commercials.

"Am I going to need stitches?" Lucy said.

Sophia narrowed her eyes at the gash and twisted her lips in thought.

"Nah," Sophia said.

Sophia wiped the blood off Lucy's arm with some dampened toilet paper, and picked up a box of salt. Sophia tipped the box's metal spout over Lucy's arm and poured a long pile of salt across the cut. It stung a little, but Lucy was focused on her nurse. She had actually been looking for an excuse to talk to Sophia for a while now, but had never found a natural opportunity.

Sophia embodied sexual confidence, and that fascinated Lucy. The name "the Sluts" was misleading. Violent had chosen that name for her gang, for her own reasons. The girls in the Sluts weren't slutty, so to speak. It wasn't as if they slept with anyone and everyone who came along. They dated aggressively, and it was usually the boys who were the ones asking to make things exclusive.

"I like that Gates," Sophia said. "He's sexy."

"If you like pink eye," somebody said.

"Whatever, I'll just borrow Raunch's goggles," Sophia replied.

"Sophia, please go on a date with Gates and wear my goggles," Raunch said, laughing. "That would be so hilarious if you just never mentioned them, and acted like you looked all sexy and everything."

When Sophia laughed, she laughed with her whole body, twisting around and closing her eyes like she was savoring it. "You guys, I'm saying, I like a man that can take charge. That's hot. If he gets out of hand, whatever, I'll stab him."

The other Sluts laughed.

"Why do I think you're not kidding?" Lucy said.

"You'd be right," Raunch said. "Did you see those two Skater boys she was messing up in the market today? Soph, what are their names?"

"Rod and Tyson," Sophia said, concentrating on folding toilet paper into a neat rectangle for Lucy's cut. "Total assholes."

Raunch pointed at Sophia. "They're both her ex-boyfriends."

Lucy did a double take. "Wait, I saw them. You practically tried to kill them. You dated them?"

"How do you think I found out they were assholes?" Sophia placed the TP bandage on Lucy's cut, and began covering it with masking tape. "What about you?" Sophia said to Lucy. "When's the last time you got laid?"

"Um . . ."

It was the secret that had kept her from joining in conversations like this when she heard them. She still didn't want to say.

"Don't tell me you haven't gotten your rocks off since David," Raunch said, and with that comment, the girls nearby simmered their conversation and edged toward Lucy.

The other girls didn't know about David's death, she hadn't told them, so she couldn't blame them for bringing him up, but it still hurt her heart to hear his name.

"How big was he?" Lips said.

The girls leaned in. Sophia narrowed her eyes at Lucy and made the same face she'd made when she was deciding what was best for her wounds.

"Pretty big?" Lucy finally said.

"Was he good at giving head?" Sophia said.

"He was . . ."

"Tell us! You have to! Come on!" others chimed in.

Lucy couldn't think of what lie to say. All these girls asking her about the sex she never had with her dead boyfriend was making her mind spin.

"I bet he was rough," Lips said. "He was so nice all the time, the nice ones are always mean in bed."

"Did his missing eye make him fall over?" Raunch said. "Did you have to always do it on your side?"

Raunch scored more laughs with that one. Lucy stood up. She couldn't take any more of this, and she wasn't going to cry in front of them.

"What's wrong with you?" Lips said. "Just tell us."

Lucy saw Violent walking into the bathroom on the other side of the cafeteria. She walked away from the table of Sluts without a word.

"Hey, what the hell?" Raunch called after her.

Lucy ignored them and rushed to the bathroom. Inside, Violent was washing her hands. Lucy still trusted Violent the most of anyone in the gang. She was only able to get short and infrequent moments alone with Violent, so she always tried to make them count. The Sluts' leader had a way of putting things in perspective that Lucy was coming to depend on.

"Um . . ."

Violent rolled her eyes. "Just spit it out."

"How do you know when you're ready to have sex?"

"I figured you were a V."

Lucy couldn't help but feel disappointed that she was that easy to read.

"What, is it written on my forehead?" Lucy said.

"It's not a big deal, chill. You're ready . . . when you meet someone you want to do it with. That's pretty much it."

"Yeah, but what if I don't meet anyone like that? Will I get kicked out of the gang or something? 'Cause . . . I really like it here."

That made Violent laugh. "I haven't come across that yet." Violent stepped away from the sink and wiped her hands on a towel. "You're telling me there's no hot boys who turn you on?"

"Well, sure there are, I'm a human being."

Violent's amused grin hung in place. There was affection in her eyes, Lucy could swear it.

"Just do what you want," Violent said. "I don't get any benefit from you having sex. It doesn't affect the gang. Those girls out there are just messing around. Stay a virgin if you want to, who cares?"

"Right," Lucy said. "Who cares."

"We good?"

Lucy nodded. Violent walked past, and just before exiting, she gave Lucy a gentle pat on the shoulder. Lucy took a deep breath. She felt like a real weight had been lifted off of her. She was lucky to have Violent in her life. She turned for the door and headed back into the cafeteria. They'd be eating soon.

When Lucy stepped into the dining room she was met with a blaring chant, voiced by every Slut in the room, and the volume of it nearly knocked Lucy over.

"VIR-GIN! VIR-GIN! VIR-GIN! VIR-GIN!"

"I think we found you a nickname!" Lips shouted over all of it. They continued their joyous chant. "VIR-GIN! VIR-GIN! VIR-GIN! VIR-GIN!"

Lucy saw Violent laughing. She was doubled over, getting red in the face. She stood up, holding her chest like she couldn't breathe. She'd never seen Violent laugh so hard.

"I had to!" Violent yelled to Lucy through the laughing fit. "I'm sorry, I had to, I had no choice!" Violent's laughter took her over again, and she had to steady herself on a nearby table.

Lucy was set to break down, to fall apart from the sheer embarrassment of it, but the sight of Violent laughing made Lucy laugh too. She scanned the faces of her gang members and saw that the ones who weren't chanting were having a great time. There was no malice to anyone's laughter, and in a weird way, the mocking made her feel closer to them.

"You bitches," Lucy said with a smile.

19

IT WAS A JOYOUS FOOD DROP. THERE WAS

still fighting, vicious fighting over certain items, but there were far too many silly grins across people's faces to call it anything but joyous. The parents had come through. Junk food, candy, frozen pizza, and more. Half the kids were chowing as they ran. There were tugging matches over fresh jeans, boys getting knocked unconscious over porn DVDs, pig piles on top of two video game consoles in the mix. It was as if a giant piñata had burst over their heads and now they were going berserk with adolescent sugar lust.

"Will," a voice blared from above. "Was that the kid's name? The one that wanted the pills?"

Will looked up. The man with the motorcycle helmet stood at the edge of the roof, behind the razor wire, his black helmet and scuba tanks gleaming in the sun. The Saints said that the toxicity put off by infected teens only attacked the lungs, and that was why these adults were able to only wear oxygen tanks. It was a step down from the military haz-mat suits McKinley was used to seeing.

Will approached the wall. The man in the motorcycle helmet spotted him and held up a plain paper sandwich bag, then tossed it over the razor wire. It spiraled down like a leaf toward the quad floor. Will broke into a run for it, but there was someone already underneath it.

Bobby, the Freaks' leader, caught it. It landed perfectly in his hands, and he looked up at Will with a sharp-toothed smile and a flip of his blue mane.

"Uh-oh," Bobby said. "Looks like somebody's outta—"

Bobby never finished his sentence. Pruitt cracked him in the back of the neck with the butt of his rifle. Bobby jolted and dropped. Pruitt picked up the bag and tossed it to Will as he came running up. Bobby was at Will's feet, unconscious but still twitching, his blank eyes staring up at the open sky.

Will looked to Pruitt. "Thanks."

Pruitt gave him an apathetic nod and moved on.

Will tore open the paper bag. There they were. Two orange pharmacy bottles of Carbatrol. And another of Lyrica. He twisted the white plastic safety cap off the Carbatrol with such muscle he was surprised he didn't snap the plastic. He popped one of the blue and black capsules in his mouth, and dry-swallowed.

He felt cured the moment it was in his body. Carbatrol was

the medication he was on before the quarantine, the third medication he had tried and the only one that suppressed his seizures consistently. There was no way the pill had dissolved at all in his stomach, but the effect on his psyche was immediate. He felt unstoppable. Will ran into the fray. He was ready to have some fun.

Ahead, he saw Gates and a Skater both going for the same box of rum. Will expected a bloody struggle between the two of them, but when the Skater saw it was Gates, he backed away from the box with his hands in the air, smiling. Gates gave him a thank-you nod, and scooped up the box.

Will ran, past the new delicacies all over the ground, past the fights and the celebrations, and kept on going, in a circle, all around the quad. It felt so good to run. He felt whole again, on equal ground with everyone else. His body wasn't going to hold him back anymore. He wanted to take himself to the limit, go full blast until his legs gave out.

Will ran until all the goodies had been squirreled away by the sidelines, he never once tried to pick anything up. It was his victory lap for finally making one right decision and teaming up with the Saints. He met up with his new gang by the southwest corner of the quad. Gates stood before them, looking up at the sky, his head tilted to the side like a desk globe.

"We gave you what you asked for. Let the prisoner go," the man on the roof said.

"Prisoner? Don't you mean, your baby boy?" Gates said.

"Stop these games," the man above snapped. "We've held up our end."

"And I'll hold up mine. I won't kill him. This week."

"Where is he?"

"He's comfortable."

"We want to see him."

"No," Gates said plainly. It was a conversation stopper. The man clenched his fists and stared down.

"No one has to die," the man finally said. "We only want to take care of you. We want the same thing."

"Perfect," Gates said, his voice vicious and smooth in the same breath. "Then this should work out fine. You get us the same next week, and I'll let you see him."

Kids laughed through mouthfuls of Pop-Tarts and sugared cereal. The laughter spread and grew. They poured soda in each other's gullets while they gave the parents the finger. They threw crumpled beer cans up at the roofline. They were wild animals, depraved bastards, ungrateful brats, and they were loving every second of it.

"Let's hear it for the Saints!" a Geek screamed.

Saints! Saints! Saints! The cheers kept coming.

The peal of the crowd made goose bumps rise up all over Will's body. They roared for Gates. Like he was a pop star or a famous actor. Will looked to Gates, expecting him to take hold of the moment and make a speech. But Gates was unmoved. He wasn't smiling, he didn't seem proud, or caught up in the rush of the moment whatsoever. The cocky satisfaction with which he'd made his demands must have been all show for the crowd because now he looked depressed.

"It worked, man!" Will said to Gates, trying to get a little happiness out of him.

"Yup," Gates said. His demeanor didn't change.

"The market is going to get crazy. Hey, we should take requests for stuff you should ask for. That'll keep everybody on our side, then we won't have to worry so much about other gangs trying to take Sam," Will said, his mind lit up with possibility. "We'll be the most popular kids in school."

"You handle it," Gates said.

"What do you mean? You're not coming?"

"Don't feel like it," Gates said. He put his hands in his pockets and slogged out of the quad without another word.

20

THE SLUTS' TRADING POST WAS A MADHOUSE.
They had a line out the door, thanks to Violent's quick thinking during the drop. The Sluts only went for clothes rather
than spreading themselves thin picking up anything and
everything they saw. But just collecting clothes was no small
task. It was apparent how seriously the parents had taken
Gates's threats by how literally they'd interpreted his ransom
list. The parents had actually raided closets, nearly every one
in Pale Ridge by the look of it. Old, moth-eaten clothes lay
intermingled with new clothes that still had security tags
and the prices on them. While other gangs wasted manpower
lugging big ticket items like charcoal grills, the Sluts moved
swiftly and left the quad early, each one carrying garment
piles up to their noses.

Their classroom in the market looked like a Macy's after an
earthquake, but if anybody wanted a new wardrobe, they'd

have to come to the Sluts. Sure, there were tons of new good-ies in McKinley, but what good was having a bunch of toys at home when you were still walking around looking like crap? A new, clean outfit, on the other hand, not only made you feel good, it made people see you like they'd never seen you before.

Waist-high piles of underwear stood next to equally high piles of jackets, next to piles of pants, of dresses and skirts and socks and so on throughout the center of the classroom. Two Sluts were assigned to each pile to monitor shoplifting, while bartering tables ran the perimeter of the room, where a customer would take their clothes for payment. Violent and two other girls worked a tight door, allowing no more than twenty kids in at a time. The resulting line that gathered in the hall outside drummed up substantial word-of-mouth advertising, and by the time Lucy asked someone what time it was, she realized three hours had passed and business wasn't slowing down.

Sophia set a bottle of water down on the table in front of Lucy. Sophia had been working the floor, making sure that every girl dealing with customers had what she needed to do her best work, like a snack or a pen and paper. She even doled out the occasional massage.

"How are you doing?" Sophia said, when Lucy's most recent customer, a Freak with a binder ring in his nose, walked away with a pair of black leather pants and matching jacket draped over his shoulder. He'd paid with a five hundred count bulk box of condoms, and Lucy stashed it behind her chair, where a ridiculous pile of goods was heaped up. Lucy opened the bottle of water and took a long, patient drink.

"I'm good," she finally said, sucking in air and putting the bottle down, half empty.

"You look exhausted," Sophia said. "I'm going to bring Lips in to help you."

Lucy cringed at the mention of Lips. They hadn't spoken much since Lips had given her respect for knocking her ass on the floor the last day of Naked Week. She'd dyed Lucy's hair red, but even then, they didn't have much to say to one another. As much as Naked Week was just a test, the animosity she felt between herself and Lips was real. Now, even though they were both officially gang mates, that old feeling was hard to shake when she was around Lips.

"Don't bother," Lucy said to Sophia. "I've got this table covered fine."

"Not your call," Sophia said. "Violent's orders. She wants to up the number of customers she lets in at a time. It's two Sluts per table now to handle the overflow."

Sophia waved Lips over. Lips shoved her way past kids perusing clothes and pulled up a chair to sit next to Lucy behind the table.

"Make some room, Virgin," Lips said, frowning at Lucy.

"You've got enough," Lucy said. "Ugly."

"Ooookay," Sophia said, her eyes going wide and clapping her hands. "You two have a blast. If you fight, try to keep it away from the customers."

"Whatever," both Lucy and Lips said at the same time.

As Sophia walked off, Lips jammed her seat in beside Lucy, forcing her to scoot over. Lucy let out a long breath to keep herself calm. Getting into it with Lips wasn't worth it. She didn't need an enemy in her new gang. She told herself she could rise above it.

For an hour, they each dealt with customers, haggling. While Lucy left Lips alone, Lips felt the need to throw in her two cents about nearly every trade Lucy made, saying that she was letting customers get away with murder and that nobody in their right mind would make the deals Lucy was making. After what seemed like the hundred and fiftieth time, Lucy couldn't take it anymore.

"Shut up," Lucy said to Lips.

"Excuse me?"

"I don't care what you think is 'market value', okay? Do me a favor and don't talk to me."

Lips frowned, almost like her feelings were hurt. It wasn't what Lucy expected, mostly because she didn't know Lips had feelings.

"Just trying to help," Lips said. "Jesus. We've never had this kind of merch before, I figured maybe you needed help trying to figure it out."

"Well, I don't," Lucy said, and turned away from Lips and shouted to the line of waiting customers, "Next!"

A Geek approached Lucy with a pile of clothes. But it wasn't just any Geek, it was Zachary, King Geek in his golden plastic dress-up crown that tilted off the top of his grape-and-green-apple swirled dye job. He wore knee-high suede boots that looked like something Robin Hood might sport. His shirt was a ladies' nightgown tucked into his skinny jeans.

Zachary plopped down his merchandise in front of Lucy as Lips waved up her next customer.

"Chop, chop," Zachary said. "I don't have all day."

That was fine by Lucy; she wanted to keep this interaction as short as possible. Lucy started sorting through his pile of clothes. Midway through the pile, she plucked up a bra.

"That's for a costume," Zachary said, deadpan.

"I'm sure," Lucy said.

"Hey," he said, narrowing his eyes at her. "How do I know you?"

"You don't. So, don't try and butter me up now, Geek. Too late for that," Lucy said, keeping her eyes down on her sorting.

Back when she was helping David escape the school and they had Zachary prisoner, Zachary had told Lucy that if David died she wouldn't be able to go on without him. Zachary had said that Lucy would "fall apart."

But here she was.

She could get through this without him recognizing her. The last thing she needed was for Zachary to make a big scene out of who she used to be, especially with Lips all ears. Lucy got to the last item in the pile, the best of the bunch, maybe the most exotic thing she'd seen all day. A real, fox fur coat. Her mother had always wanted one like this.

"Oh my god, you're so slow," Zachary said, lifting a garbage bag onto the table and opening it for Lucy to see. It was mostly full with cereal variety packs, paper towel rolls, and batteries as a top layer. Underneath was a new pillow, a pair of work gloves, and a coil of bungee cords, none of it that impressive. "Here, just take this. That should cover it."

Lucy glanced over at Lips, knowing that she had an opinion. But to her credit, Lips kept her thin lips sealed.

"I got it," he said and pointed at her. "I know who you are."

"Congratulations," Lucy said, dry as sand.

Zachary covered his grin. "Look at you. A Loner in Slut clothing. I don't know about the red, honey. It's a little . . . desperate."

"Thanks for the tip." Lucy pushed the garbage bag to Zachary. "Now, I got one for you. You've got to spend more if you want more. This isn't going to come close to covering it. I'll take seven more bags just like it," Lucy said.

Zachary snapped his head back like she'd just pinched his nose.

"You're too funny, but let me tell you how it's going to be, big britches. That—" Zachary said, pushing the garbage bag back at Lucy "—is what I'm going to pay for this."

He laid his hand on the fur coat, his fingers disappearing in the softness. Lucy wrapped her hand around the reddish brown collar.

"Just this coat is worth thousands of dollars," Lucy said.

"Uh-huh," Zachary said. He nodded with a condescending tilt of his head that made his toy crown almost horizontal. "Out there, it is, but reality check—we're in here. And you've got no grounds to ask more than what I'm giving you. A coat is a coat. And if you keep pushing me, I might get offended. I might even ban my gang from trading here ever again. And how do you think Violent would feel about that, Ms. New Slut?"

Zachary tugged on the coat. Lucy let the collar slide through her fingers. This was her grudge with Zachary and she didn't want it to turn into a full-fledged gang rivalry. Lucy glanced at Lips again, whose eyebrows began to crinkle in frustration. Lucy remembered Violent's words from her initiation day: *We don't wait for permission, we don't take any shit.*

Lucy was quick with her knife, pulling it from its sheath at her thigh and sticking it into the table with a perfect *CHOCK*. The blade sunk in the faux-wood less than an inch from Zachary's fingers. He yanked his hand away with a yelp.

"Hands off the merch until you pay," Lucy said. "The price is set."

Zachary clutched his hand as if it had been stabbed. He studied Lucy with a curious sort of shock.

"Well, you've changed," he said.

"Pay up or move the hell out of the way," Lips said, standing for impact. "We've got other customers, Geek."

Zachary sneered, "Put my stuff on hold, I'll be back."

He snatched up his garbage bag and stormed off.

"Hurry up and maybe it'll still be here," Lucy said, grinning.

When Zachary turned away, Lucy and Lips met eyes.

"Sorry," Lips said. "Didn't mean to butt in."

"'S okay," Lucy said. "Thanks."

Lips nodded, then turned to the Skater girl that she was dealing with and pointed to the stack of T-shirts on the table in front of her. "Same goes for you. You browsing or buying?"

"Forget this, man," the Skater girl said. "I'll just put in a request with the Saints for the next drop. If you make out with Will a little he'll put you right at the top of the list."

The Skater walked away without the T-shirts. Lucy turned to Lips.

"What's she talking about?"

Lips shrugged. Lucy stood in a rush.

"I, uh . . . ," Lucy said. "Will you, uh . . . "

"Need me to cover you?"

"Yeah, that," Lucy said.

Lucy hurried through the classroom, weaving around piles

until she got to the door. Violent was doing a head count of shoppers and glanced at Lucy.

"Where's the Saints' table?" Lucy said.

"To the right."

Lucy stepped into the hall and up onto a folding chair that Violent had outside the trading post. She looked over the river of passing kids to the other side of the hall where three Saint boys sat behind a long folding table. Will was the one in the middle. They each had spiral notebooks on the table in front of them. Neither of the three seemed concerned with the line of kids waiting for a chance to talk to them. Their focus was on the girls sitting in their laps.

"Oh my god," Lucy muttered.

A Geek girl was sucking on Will's neck while a Pretty One chewed on his earlobe. She had her body wrapped around him like a python. Lucy felt sick. Will's eyes were wider than an owl's. He was laughing hysterically, but Lucy couldn't see anything funny. She felt like a fool for ever feeling sorry for him, for even thinking about him. Clearly, he wasn't thinking about her.

21

GATES SAT IN THE DARKENED BACK END OF
the school bus. It was his room now. Orange extension cords
snaked along the floor, which was littered with candy. He'd
removed all the bench seats except for a few, which he'd left
loose, like the two arranged end to end that he sat on now.
They worked as both his couch and his bed. The four TVs he
had arranged in front of him shined a modulating light on
his face. Three were hooked up to separate DVD players, and
one to a PlayStation. He was watching a porn, a supernatural
soap opera, a movie about bicycle racers, and playing a first-
person shooter video game, all at once.

He was bored.

Getting the parents on the roof to bend to his will was supposed to make him feel better. When Will had told him the
name of the motorcycle man's kid, he'd known he had to do
what he did right then. He'd figured it could ingratiate him

to the rest of the population by punishing their ex-tyrant, while also turning the tables on the evil pricks that had them locked up. But more important than anything, he'd figured it would be really fun.

He'd been riding that high for a week. These kids must have thought he had five-hundred-pound balls after what he'd done on the quad. It more than made up for not being able to free everybody when they'd first shown up at McKinley. Every day since he'd kidnapped Sam, he'd anxiously anticipated the parents next move, loving the constant tension of not knowing. But when they caved, and they delivered everything he asked for, it just . . . kinda sucked the fun right out of it.

His eye stung. It felt like there was a grain of sand under the lid, but no matter how many times he splashed water in it, the feeling persisted. He opened an individually packaged Rice Krispies square, and tried to see how big a bite he could take. His bite was so big, it started to hurt his jaw to try and chew through it. The chewy muck didn't taste that great. Like Styrofoam and a sweet version of glue. Glue wasn't sweet at all, he'd tried it. He'd always thought wood glue would taste sweet, because the color of it looked dessertish, but it turned out to taste awful.

With a burst of machine-gun fire, he died in the video game. He hadn't been paying attention. That had always been his problem in school. He couldn't pay attention to what the teacher was saying to him, even when he was talking right in his face, it was just too boring. His mind would start wandering in the middle of the teacher's sentence. He'd start thinking of how many dance club foam machines it would take to fill the whole school with bubbles. He'd fantasize about the girls he was chasing. He'd try to think of ways to embarrass the teachers. They all thought he was dumb anyway, just because he couldn't bear to listen to their boring bullshit. He found it really hard to focus during tests and he always tested terribly. He failed course after course, but his parents paid buckets to keep him enrolled. It made him feel like a fraud, like everyone thought he didn't deserve to be there, but they had to tolerate him anyway. He resented his parents for keeping him there. He'd never wanted to go to boarding school in the first place.

He did learn one thing at St. Patrick's though—breaking the rules is fun. It started with little stuff. He poured gin down the horn of his trumpet and kept it balanced against the wall as his secret liquor stash. He grew his hair past the acceptable length. He stopped wearing ties, and he'd untuck his shirt, both clear violations of the dress code. The school almost ran out of ties with all the ones they tightened around his neck when they caught him without one. He snuck into the girls' dorm at night. He started pulling pranks on other students, and on the teachers, but eventually, all that stuff got boring too.

So, he decided to throw a party in the old abandoned

boathouse, downriver from the dock where the crew team would put their shell into the water for morning practice. It was a bit of a hike, but it was far enough away from the main campus that they'd be able to make some noise and no one would know. Pruitt and Fowler had helped him set it up. The party was world-ending, it was so good. It was a brain-melter. He'd changed kids lives that night. It was that fun. Unfortunately, a groundskeeper heard the party, and they got shut down before the grand finale. He had been planning to clear everyone out of the boathouse at the end of the night and then set the rickety old thing on fire. It would have blown minds.

The boathouse party got him in a truckload of trouble. But the school had no proof it was him that organized the party. A hundred-odd kids had been brave enough to sneak out of their dorms, unnoticed, and leave campus to come to the party. They couldn't all be expelled. The St. Patrick's judicial council tried hard to get Gates to confess, they were looking for some way to trip him up and get him to reveal something, but he played dumb. Inside, he was celebrating. He took their accusation as a compliment. Basically, they were telling him, "Who else could have pulled off something so gigantically kick-ass? It had to be you, Gates."

He didn't get into as much trouble as he would have if they could have proved it. But his parents back home flipped. They were going to send him to military school but his little brother, Colton, talked them out of it. Somehow, Colton was able to convince their parents to enroll Colton at St. Patrick's so that he could look after Gates.

Once his little brother showed up at school, everything changed. Colton was the only one who could lift him out of the dark moods he got sometimes. Colton looked out for him, talked him out of his crazier ideas, and took the blame for more of Gates's fuckups than Gates liked to admit. He'd loved Colton, but he couldn't think about him without also feeling the crushing weight of how much he missed him. He'd only lost Colton a couple months ago, and he knew that was why he was so down. He hadn't been able to fully process it yet.

Gates fished around inside his beat-up camping backpack until he found his old phone, wrapped in a sock. They'd spent so much time hiding, away from electricity, that he'd hardly ever had the chance to charge it. It had lived at the bottom of his bag, a useless keepsake. He found the old charger wrapped in another sock. He plugged his phone into one of the extension cords and laid it on the floor. After a moment the phone chimed and a charging symbol appeared on the screen, but it needed more juice before it could turn all the way on.

"Gates?" a voice said from the front of the bus. He looked up to see Will poking his head into the bus. Will climbed up the short staircase with excitement. Gates wished he would go the hell away.

He liked Will in general. He'd saved Gates's life on the first day he'd met him and had only brought good things to their group so far. Plus, he hadn't dyed his hair some goofy color like the rest of the McKinley kids, so that had to stand for something. But Gates didn't want to talk to anyone at the moment. He hoped he didn't end up saying something horrible to the kid. He knew how easily aggravated he could get when he was down in the dumps like this. He had to keep a lid on his mood and hope whatever Will had to say was brief.

Will walked as he talked. "We missed you in the market, man! Everybody was shouting at us. It was like when you see the stock exchange in movies. A bunch of different girls made out with me to get their requests moved up the list. Can you believe that? We're like, heroes. I mean, it's all 'cause of you. It should've been you out there taking requests, really."

"Oh, yeah?" Gates said with no enthusiasm. "Did they taste different?"

"Huh?"

"The girls you kissed."

"Oh," Will said, and thought about it. "Sort of? One was kind of spicy now that I think about it. Why? Does that mean something?"

"Just occurred to me, I guess. Is that what you came to tell me?"

"No, I came because . . . it's a happy day in the school today, everybody's loving it, and I don't know, it just doesn't seem right that the guy responsible for it all is sitting alone in his room."

Gates let out a quiet sigh. "I'm in the middle of a bunch of things."

"You sure? You gotta see how much stuff people gave us at the market, it's ridiculous. Just come sift through it all."

"Maybe later."

"Right . . . ," Will said. It seemed like he was about to leave, but he paused. "Oh! Also, you know that observation room that looks out to the white room? They just got the control board hooked back up and you can control the sprayer thingee on the ceiling. We should get the Skaters to come pick up trash and we'll nail 'em with it."

"Eh . . . nah. Is that all?"

Will slumped, looking a little letdown. He went to leave, then stopped and turned back, looking uncomfortable.

"Listen, uh, I've never been one for telling people I appreciate them or whatever, but it's something . . . I want to start doing. Ugh, I hate how dumb that sounds. But you get it, we could be dead tomorrow and all. So, uh . . . anyway, I know I've only been a Saint for a week, and that isn't long, but, one week back was the lowest point in my life. If you hadn't made me that offer, I don't know if I would have survived. And like I was saying . . . today's like the best day ever. I didn't think people would ever treat me with that kind of respect again. You gave me a chance to erase the past from people's memories, man, and I'm going to treat it like a total fresh start. Anyway, I just wanted to say thanks."

Gates's phone chimed again. He glanced down to its bright screen and saw Colton. He'd forgotten his old wallpaper photo on his phone was a picture of the two of them in their St. Patrick's uniforms, before the infection. Gates had his arm around his brother. Colton wore his stupid black Ray-Ban sunglasses that he never wanted to take off. He thought his eyes were too close together, and he'd wanted to hide them. Colton's hair was cropped close, and parted precisely on the side. He always kept it short and neat, even for the year they'd spent on the run together.

Gates's mind flashed with the last memory he had of Colton alive. His brother was trying to turn himself over to the military. They'd been arguing about it for weeks. Colton believed the military was telling the truth, that there was a facility where the government would take care of them. He didn't want to run anymore, and he thought Gates was being paranoid. Colton snuck away when he was out scavenging in town with him and Pruitt. Gates ran after him, but he only got to him right as Colton was walking up to the soldier to turn himself in. Colton had his arms up in the air. The soldier raised his pistol and fired a round into Colton's head. The wind caught the cloud of red mist that puffed out of the back of his brother's head and carried the blood away. Colton's dead body flopped to the ground, the back of his head dug out like a ditch.

Gates cringed and tried to make the image go away with how hard he held his eyes shut.

"Hey, are you okay?" Will said.

Gates opened his eyes and clicked the display to sleep without looking at the phone. He turned to Will.

"Did you say I can spray people?" Gates said. Will grinned.

By the time he and Will had made it out of the bus, through the infirmary where they'd found the gurneys, and up the staircase to the observation room, Gates was already regretting leaving the bus. The control panel in the small room didn't even light up or anything. The observation room was small and long, and was really just a long desk underneath a long window that looked down to the white room. A couple file cabinets that had been emptied out were stacked at the end of the room. There was a black control board in the center of the desk, with loose wires coming out the back, and a microphone jutting out of it like an antenna.

"Here, use the joysticks," Will said.

Gates sat down in front of the control panel, and Will showed him how to trigger the water from the multi-hosed water sprayer on the ceiling of the white room, beyond the window. As soon as Gates got the hang of it, some people did come walking into the white room and he was able to nail two of them with the water jet. He scared the other one by making all eight of the contraption's mechanical arms come to life all at once. Will thought it was all hilarious and was laughing so hard that he collapsed onto the control board. Will accidentally ended up pressing a bunch of buttons.

Inside the white room, there was a large, square metal door in the wall that Gates and the others had never managed to get opened. But now, it crept up like an automated garage door. Beyond the door, inside a small room with bare concrete walls, was some sort of clear cube on wheels. Gates felt his first spark of real excitement since the parents had caved to his demands.

Gates whacked Will on the arm to get his attention and pointed at the clear cube. "Hey, guy who knows everything about this place, what the piss is that?"

Will stared in awe.

"No way," Will said. "I heard about this thing. The soldiers used it when the graduation machine was broken. I wonder if it needs keys."

Gates grinned. "I know how to hot-wire shit."

Gates had never driven a clear box before. Just the pure novelty of being inside a transparent cube as it rolled through the halls of McKinley was beginning to lift his spirits. He barely even noticed the sting of his eye.

People were starting to gather in the halls. He and Will had become quite the spectacle. Shocked and psyched faces came popping out of classrooms to ogle the rolling box. Kids started running after them, wanting to hitch a ride. He and

Will drank beers as they did a wide loop through the school. Will was driving at the moment and sitting in the only seat inside the cube. It was about the size of a golf cart on wide all-terrain tires. The walls and ceiling were made of half-foot thick slabs of clear plastic. He could see the clear epoxy they had used to seal it together, and the excess had squeezed out of the borders between the slabs and hardened. The only door was in the back, also clear, but the door frame, lock, and knob were all metal. Empty beer bottles rolled around on the diamond cut metal sheeting floor. The electric engine produced a continuous buzzing sound. Gates crouched beside Will, fiddling with the rubber glove that extended into the cube from the outside, so people could evidently test themselves. Gates had turned it inside out, and he was using it to reach out the front of the cube and high-five people they passed.

Will hadn't lied, the school loved him. Everyone seemed to know his name. When they saw him, they got really excited. They'd call out to him. Sometimes they shouted requests for the next drop. But most of the time they just shouted his name, or started applauding as he passed.

While Will drove, Gates took camera phone photos of the five Skater girls who rode on the top of the cube, their butts pressed into the clear plastic over their heads. The Skater girls were hitching a ride to Geek territory. When Gates started showing Will the pics he'd taken, the cube drifted too close to the wall and hit a few locker handles, jostling the whole thing. The girls squealed above and banged on the plastic.

"Watch the road!" one of the girls shouted.

"Sor-ry!" Will said, and both Will and Gates started laughing.

"You know what, this is good times, man," Gates said.

"I know. I didn't even get to see this thing last year. Never thought I'd be inside it!"

"Lemme try driving."

"Sure."

Will pulled over, and they switched places. Gates jammed his foot on the tiny gas pedal, while Will eased back to look up at the girls.

"This is what life's about," Will said.

"Oh, yeah?" Gates said, keeping his eyes on the hall.

"I think so. Life should always be riding inside a future car with cute girls on top."

"Ha-ha! Hard to argue with that."

Gates started weaving the cube from side to side down the hallway. The Skater girls shouted at him and began to hop off.

"Aw, come on, I was just weaving a little!" Gates shouted, as the last of the Skater girls lowered herself off the edge and dropped to the floor.

"Bye, girls," Will said, wistfully.

"Easy come, easy go."

"Totally."

They passed through a hallway intersection.

"My old gang used to live in a stairwell down that direction," Will said. "David would have loved taking a joy ride in the cube."

"Did he like to have a good time? Sounds like my kind of dude."

"Well . . . not really. He more liked to worry all the time."

Gates glanced at Will and saw that his mood had gone somber.

"Sounds like my brother, Colton."

Will sat up. "Really?"

Gates nodded. "He was always worrying about me, trying to keep me out of trouble."

Will nodded like he knew what that was like, then cleared his throat. "Uh . . . Fowler told me what happened to Colton. I'm so sorry, man. That's awful."

Gates tugged on the steering wheel, suddenly annoyed at how slow the cube was.

"There must be another gear or something," Gates said.

"Do you miss him?"

They were crawling along. Gates needed more speed. He felt all around the base of the steering wheel and around the boxy dashboard that must have once held virus-testing equipment. His fingers found a little plastic pull handle in a recessed nook on the underside of the dash. He pulled it.

There was a dull *thunk*, and the cube sped forward.

"Ho ho! E-brake! We've been riding with the brakes on the whole time!" Gates said.

"Oh shit," Will said. He gave the clear wall an excited double slap. "How fast does it go?"

The wobbly cube accelerated. The hallway began to race by.

"This thing can move!" Will said.

"We've got to see what she can do!" Gates said.

Will started laughing. Lockers and doorways whipped past. A group of Geeks had to dive to get out of the way when they saw a giant ice cube zipping toward them.

"Whoa! You almost hit them," Will said.

"She's still got more in her! She's still going."

The hallway ended at the open double doors to the basement, and they were fast approaching. The motor buzzed at a higher pitch.

"You gotta hit the brakes, hit the brakes," Will said.

"We gotta wait. We'll jump at the last possible moment!"

"What? Why?"

"It'll be intense!"

"We'll die. You'll break the cube!"

"Once-in-a-lifetime chance, dude!"

"Ah!" Will screamed. "All right! Go! Shit, this is crazy!"

Will was laughing as he kicked open the thick back door to the cube. Ten feet from the top of the stairs, Will jumped. Gates turned halfway around, getting ready to jump, but still holding the steering wheel steady with one hand. He watched the slanting ceiling of the stairwell rush toward him, and for a moment he didn't want to jump. A small part of him wanted to stay put, and hope the crash destroyed him. As the front tires were rolling over the top step, he jumped instead.

The sound of his torso slapping down to the floor was nothing compared to the cacophony of the cube crashing down the stairs. Will went running past Gates, to the top of the stairs. He pulled himself to his feet and rushed over to Will's side. At the bottom of the stairs, by the closed doors of the basement, the thick plastic walls of the tube had broken apart from each other, and now were piled with the black plastic trash bags at the basement doors. The motorized base was bent and missing a wheel.

Gates turned to Will, who still stared down at the wreckage of the cube. This was a moment Gates was familiar with. Usually at this point, when he'd taken things this far, whoever he was hanging out with would politely excuse themselves and then avoid ever hanging out alone with him again, or would start yelling and screaming at him about how stupid a thing to do that was.

Will looked up at him and grinned. "We got to get something faster," he said.

Oh shit, Gates thought to himself. He might just have a new best friend.

22

THERE WERE FOURTEEN CHOCOLATE HO-HOS
on a paper plate on the floor. That was what the Saints had
been giving Sam to eat. Junk. As worthless to him as eating
stacks of Post-it notes. If his father had taught him anything,
it was that his body was holy. This pile of shit cakes was an
insult. Fourteen cream-filled slaps in the face, one for every
day since the Saints claimed his father had delivered on
Gates's threat. But Sam refused to fall for that crock of shit.
They were trying to mess with his head.

All the stuff he'd seen those Saint kids carry past his clear
cell door, they must have somehow brought it in from the outside, before they'd gotten locked in here. It was all a show for
Sam's benefit. They wanted him to crumble and do whatever
they said. They needed him to be a blubbering baby in front of
his dad so that he would break down and stop starving them
out, which was really the truth of what was happening. But

his father would never give in. In all his life, Sam had never once seen his dad back down from a fight. So, neither would Sam. They'd stand against this together.

Sam sat on his cot, his hands behind his back, the only part of him still bound with packing tape. He was out of breath and sweating from his morning calisthenics. His body was getting weaker. It scared him a little, if he was being honest. He could feel his mind getting cloudier, and his eyeballs plumping out of their sockets. Starvation would do that to a person, but he'd been there before. He'd drink from the small sink to his right, by his toilet, awkwardly turning the faucet on with his cheek. Water was the only meal he'd had. He wasn't going to bend to the Saints' will in any way, he wasn't going to put those processed, sugar clumps they called food in his body.

He could wait this out. He could do it. He just had to last until his dad stormed the school with the other parents, and came for him. Only, it was taking longer than he'd expected.

Sam looked up. Someone stood beyond the door, in the shadows, watching him. Sam stared the kid down, even though he couldn't see his face. It was probably Will. He'd come and watch Sam for sometimes twenty minutes. Sam knew what that was about. Fear. The kid was in over his head and he knew it. Will was looking for some way to undo the knot he'd tied his dick into, but there was no way out for that kid. Sam was going to find Will when he got out. He was going to cut Will's throat out.

The door to Sam's cell opened.

It wasn't Will. It was Gates that stepped in. He kicked the plate of Ho-Hos forward a foot on the floor.

"You really should eat more," Gates said.

"Bring me a steak," Sam said, his voice cracking from so little use.

"No problem. All we have to do is ask your pops."

Sam laughed. Here's where it came, the part where they'd force him to make a plea to his dad, to pull at his heartstrings, to cry and scream and get his dad to cry and scream too, all so the parents would finally give in.

"In your fucking dreams, rich boy," Sam said.

"Whoa," Gates said, frowning. "Fine by me. I don't care."

Sam didn't quite understand the response, and it threw him off.

"You got a real temper, huh?" Gates said.

"You can't break me down," Sam said, getting more fed up by the second. "I'm never going to be your puppet. You can break every bone in my body, I am never going say what you want me to say."

Gates twisted his head with a confused look and smushed his eyebrows down like a caveman with a cell phone.

"I don't want you to say anything," Gates said. "They just want to see you. If that means I keep getting what I want, fine by me."

"Give up the act," Sam said, shaking his head. "I know he

hasn't given you what you want. That's why you need me to talk to him."

Gates started laughing.

"What the hell are you talking about, man?" Gates said. "Haven't you seen us walking by with all our new shit? Your dad gave us everything we wanted."

"I know that's all fake," Sam said, sweat pouring down his forehead, dripping from his eyelashes.

"Fake, huh?" Gates was laughing solidly now. "Wow. I thought you were slow when you couldn't figure out your gang sacked you, but this is bonkers—"

Sam thrust himself off the cot and charged Gates. He laid his shoulder squarely into Gates ribs, knocking the Saint off his feet. Gates landed on the toilet, but by then, Sam had already stomped his foot into the plate of Ho-Hos and sprung out of his cell. He scrambled left into the hallway and saw the doorway out of the processing facility, with no one guarding it.

He pushed off down the hall. He heard shouting behind him, hammering footsteps too. All he had to do was get to the red button to the right of the door. The white room was beyond it. He remembered it all from the day the Saints first arrived.

Something swung out from the doorway of an open containment cell. It cracked across his chest and knocked the wind out of him. His body crashed hard against the floor, and before he could catch his breath, Sam was surrounded by Saints.

Will stepped in, blocking Sam's view of the door. He wore a heavy down vest and held an aluminum bat over his shoulder. He looked down at Sam with a fierceness that made Sam second-guess everything he'd thought when he was in his cell. Gates threw his arm around Will and shook him with delight.

"Atta boy, Willie! What a hit!" Gates said, then turned to the other Saints. "Let's get the little prince out to the quad before his daddy has a breakdown. I can't wait to get my hands on the new stuff!"

The Saints hoisted Sam up. Nothing made sense. His father had really given in to their demands right away? He must have had no faith that Sam could escape himself.

A Saint peeled a long strip of duct tape and pressed it over Sam's eyes. The first image he saw when his eyes were closed was his father's glimmering key chain falling through the night sky. The Fighting Irish. It was a symbol of endurance to his family. His dad's alma mater, all four years on a full football scholarship. It was a message for Sam to stay strong and kick ass. But instead, Sam had gone and fallen apart. He could see it all clearly now. It had been game over from the minute he let himself get captured. He'd given his dad no other choice but to treat him like a baby.

Someone shoved Sam forward.

"Move it."

He did what they said.

23

LUCY STOCKED THE ALREADY PACKED shelves in the kitchen hall with energy drinks, sleeves of microwaveable popcorn, squeeze bottles of chocolate syrup, and whatever other goodies were in the bulk boxes on the floor. Such an excess of food should have been comforting to her. But it was beginning to gross her out. Lucy didn't like what the food drops had become. Initially, she didn't think she could trust the parents, but over time she saw that the parents were trying to help them, and protect them. Once she allowed herself to wonder if her mom and dad were up there with Sam's parents, then she couldn't get right with the way everybody, and Will especially, was treating them.

As Lucy tried to make room on the bottom shelf for a row of energy bars, she heard the scuff of feet behind her. She glanced back to see a Slut holding a flower in a clay pot. The girl held it close to her heart, and guarded it closely with her arms. The flower mesmerized Lucy. It was a ball of tiny petals, a pom of white on top of wide green leaves. She hadn't seen something so precious and lovely in all her time in McKinley. Where did she get it? Lucy had never seen any flowers in any of the food drops.

Lucy forgot about the energy bars. She stood and watched the girl pad toward the entrance to the kitchen. Lucy had seen her before, but they had never talked. Her name was Maxine. She was serious. Never chuckled, never joked, never seemed to even let her neck muscles relax. Sophia said that starting up a conversation with her was like trying to superglue water. Maxine didn't fight, she was barely ever around, but she could do as she pleased. There was good reason. Maxine was pregnant.

Getting pregnant was every McKinley girl's worst nightmare, because babies would die with their first breath. Their mothers were toxic to them. Lucy had known a girl named Rorie in the Pretty Ones who'd gotten knocked up. Hilary had sent her to a secret location in the ruins, where there was a Nerd you could meet there, and for the right price, he'd fix that kind of "problem." When Rorie returned to the gym, she looked like half the girl she used to be.

A single white petal fell off the flower. It fluttered to the floor behind Maxine, who failed to notice. She was walking at a brisk pace, enough so that her cherry ponytail flapped up and down to the rhythm of her scissoring steps.

Lucy hurried over to the fallen petal. She plucked it up with her thumb and forefinger. It was a curl of white, so soft that she was almost afraid to hold it. She didn't want to damage its tender silk. She smelled it. Its fragrance filled Lucy's nostrils. So alive, so fresh.

Maxine heeled it into the kitchen. Lucy entered after her, petal in fingers. The girl stepped to one of the deep, metal double sinks and held the clay pot so that a thin stream of water hit the dry soil. She jerked her whole body when she saw Lucy approaching. Her eyes flared.

"What do you want?!" Maxine said.

"Oh. I just . . . " Lucy held up the petal. "You dropped this."

Maxine looked pained at the sight of the petal, then her focus switched to Lucy's eyes. She didn't trust Lucy, that much was clear.

"Thank you," she grumbled. "You can put it on the counter."

"No problem. Great."

Lucy placed it on the cold metal countertop with care. Maxine continued to scrutinize her.

"I love your flower," Lucy said.

Maxine relaxed an inch. "You think it's beautiful?"

"Just the petal made me happy. Where did you get it? I'm dying to know."

Maxine straightened up and stood a little prouder. "It was on Mrs. Gemser's desk."

"Mrs. Gemser? That sounds so familiar . . . Wait, was she a history teacher?"

"Yup," Maxine said.

"I remember that from my class schedule," Lucy said. "I would have had her . . . fourth period! Yeah. If, you know, all this didn't happen."

"I had her in summer school. She was nice. You would have liked her."

They both nodded, each casting their eyes at a different spot on the floor.

"So . . . you're saying, this flower—"

"It's a hydrangea." Her tone was sharp, suddenly unforgiving.

"Sorry, this hydrangea. You've kept it alive all this time?"

"You think that's stupid?"

"No," Lucy insisted. "No way. I think it's so cool. How did you do it?"

"I came up with ways . . . ," Maxine said. She stepped forward and put it on the scratched steel counter, next to the petal. "Do you want a closer look?"

Even with the invitation, Lucy made sure to move slowly, so Maxine could see everything she was doing. Lucy crouched, getting to almost eye level with the flower.

"Hello," Lucy said softly.

"Her name's Minnie," Maxine said.

"Oh . . . I love that. Minnie."

Lucy reached for the flower, she just had to touch it. Maxine grabbed the pot and pulled the flower away.

"That's enough," Maxine said. She held the flower close to her chest, and walked out of the kitchen, as Raunch and Sophia entered.

"What was that about?" Raunch said.

"I was just trying to be friendly," Lucy said.

"You're barking up the wrong tree with that one."

"Maybe that's because nobody talks to her."

"Well, what's there to say?" Raunch said with an awkward shrug.

Lucy didn't answer. It was awful, but true. There was only so much to talk about with Maxine before you started thinking about the elephant in the room, that one way or the other, she had a terrifying ordeal ahead of her. It was what had kept Lucy, Sophia, and Raunch standing in awkward silence for the last thirty seconds.

"Hey, why don't you come out with us tonight," Sophia said.

"Really?" Lucy said.

An invitation to hang with Sophia was seriously flattering.

"We're going to this," Raunch said.

Raunch unfurled a single-page, black and white flyer that prominently featured a photocopied hand giving a thumbs-up and cut-up magazine lettering like a ransom note. It read: YOU'RE INVITED TO WILL AND GATES'S PIZZA PARTY.

Her mind flashed back to seeing Will in the market making out with one girl after another. Gross. Maybe it shouldn't have bothered her as much as it did. Maybe she didn't have the right to be offended that Will was getting so much female attention, but she was, and she certainly didn't want to revisit those feelings tonight.

"Oh . . . ," Lucy said. "I don't think so."

"What do you mean you don't think so?" Sophia said.

"They've been hyping it up like crazy," Raunch said. "It's gonna put every Geek show to shame. I'm freaking out, I can't wait."

"I'm sure it's going to be great," Lucy said. "But I can't . . . Will and I, we didn't leave on the best of terms."

"Were you dating or something?" Raunch said.

"No . . . I just don't think I'm ready to talk to him yet," Lucy said.

"Sounds like you were dating."

"No, we were . . . Ugh. He's hooking up with girls all over the market. I can't just go to his mega-party without a date, or I'll look like a loser."

"So we'll find you a date," Sophia said.

"If you could have any boy in school, who would it be?" Raunch said.

Lucy grinned. There was one boy. She'd seen him in the market a couple times recently. He was a Nerd. He had perfect teeth, and a really infectious laugh that always made Lucy smile.

"I don't know his name," Lucy said. "But he's friends with that Nerd, Peter, you sometimes hook up with."

"Which one?" Raunch said, getting excited. "What's he look like?"

"The one with the big hair, slicked back."

"Ooo, I know who you're talking about." Raunch clapped. "I'm on it."

Sophia smiled a wicked smile. "Tonight might be your night, Virgin."

Lucy opened the cafeteria door a crack, and peered out at the crowd of boys waiting outside the cafeteria for their Slut dates. It was a smattering of Freaks, a bunch of Skaters, two Geeks, and a Varsity who had a bad habit of letting his mouth hang open. Raunch was there too. She came walking up to the door, and slipped into the cafeteria.

"So, Peter said his friend's got the hots for a certain Slut we know," Raunch said.

"Me?" Lucy said. Her stomach fluttered.

"No, Maxine," Raunch said, then shook her head. "Yes, you, dummy."

"Sounds like love at first sight to me," Sophia said.

"His name is Bart," Raunch said.

"Bart?" Lucy said. She gave Raunch a skeptical look. "Really?"

"Oh, Virgin's getting picky now?" Sophia said.

"I still have self-respect," Lucy said, which made Sophia laugh.

"Whatever, I heard he's huge," Raunch said. "Lips said one of her friends saw it. She said it looked like a big snake, like it could eat hamsters."

"Well, when you put it that way . . . ," Lucy said. What Raunch was describing sounded like a horror movie.

"Hey, if you're not biting, I will," Raunch said. "Big bites."

Raunch laughed and elbowed Lucy. Suddenly, Lucy was nervous. The boy she thought was cute dug her. Did that mean she was going to hook up tonight?

"Quick, get wet. Here we go," Raunch said, as she pushed the doors all the way open and they walked into the hallway.

"Why are you so gross?" Lucy said, laughing. Raunch flexed her pelvis with three quick pumps and gave Lucy an exaggerated growl. Lucy laughed harder, and it made her butterflies feel a little better.

Lucy spotted Bart. He was smiling softly. At her. He had slicked his black hair back in a pompadour. A homemade skinny tie hung from his collar. He'd put on a tie for their date. She liked that.

"Make him work," Sophia whispered in Lucy's ear, then pushed off to meet her date. Lucy made sure not to trip as she walked up to him.

"Ding-dong, I'm Bart. What's your name?" he said and held out his hand for a shake.

Lucy looked down the lineup, praying that no Sluts had heard him and were about to scream out *Virgin!* None of them did, although Raunch pointed to his crotch and gave her a thumbs-up.

"Lucy," she whispered.

"Bartholomew," he whispered back.

"Oh, I like that better."

"I knew you would. Girls always like it better. I like Bart. It's kinda tough."

"It sounds like Barf."

"Hey-yo," he said and smiled with his perfect teeth.

"Hey-yo? Ding-dong? Who are you?"

He arched one eyebrow. "Don't blame me 'cause I talk cool."

All things considered, Lucy felt like this was actually the most normal interaction she'd had in months. She felt like a regular girl, flirting with a boy.

Bart nodded. "You want to wear my skate and I'll push you?"

Bart had a single roller skate hanging from his belt loop on his hip. He untied the roller skate with one pull of the lace. He handed Lucy the cream-colored, leather skate. On it, he'd drawn a miniature scene in blue ballpoint pen of an epic raging battle in the quad. A cartoon version of Bart soared over all of it wearing a single roller skate, while carrying a buxom girl in one arm and a blasting machine gun in the other. The girl held flowers and a heart-shaped box of chocolates. Lucy liked that he was a guy who even bought girls nice things in his drawings.

"You'll have fun, don't worry," he said.

Lucy gave Bart a look, then twisted off her boot and pushed it into Bart's hands.

"Carry this," she said.

He smiled as he tied her boot to his belt loop. Lucy dropped the skate to the floor and fitted her foot in. It was loose on her foot. Without asking, Bart knelt down and laced it up tight for her. It was kinda hot.

He stood and took her fingers in his. It was to help Lucy keep her balance, but to her, it felt like a gentleman helping her into a carriage. It made her smile.

"Bartholomew. Push."

She lifted her skate-less foot, turned away from him right after saying it, like there would be no discussion of the matter. But away from his view, she was trying not to laugh.

"Unbelievable," he said, but he still pushed.

They went slowly down the hall, away from the cafeteria, and Lucy was wobbly. Her one foot still slipped around inside the oversized skate. She stuck her arms out like wings. Whenever she'd start to tilt too far to one side, his hands were there to stabilize her. He walked beside her, pushing her when she needed it. They wove their way down the halls. She loved the sound of his laugh. The more he laughed, the more she found herself laughing with him.

"You're cool," Bart said in her ear, as he pushed her into the quad.

Lucy didn't answer. She was transfixed by the spectacle in

front of her. In the center of the quad's dirt lawn was the biggest bonfire Lucy had ever seen. It was bright and churning and tall. Like a giant Christmas tree set ablaze. All around the bonfire was what had to be the full roster of every gang partying their faces off together.

24

BOOZE WAS EVERYWHERE. IN THE TURBULENT
glow of the bonfire, Lucy saw countless orange faces with ink
black shadows, glugging it, pouring it, swaying from it. Falling, vomiting, and cheering. This was the real stuff. Not some
homemade swill that tasted like gasoline and Pez. Beer in
cans and bottles, wine, wine coolers, liquor, goofy alcoholic
lemonades, the works.

The whole thing was a wonder, and Lucy, for one, was
speechless. Bart returned to her, holding up a bottle of vanilla
vodka. The skate dangled from his hip.

"I got this for you," he said, and placed it in her hand.

The cool glass felt great in her hot palm. Lucy lifted it and
took a big sip. It tasted wonderful. Pure vanilla sugar. A swarm
of kids with lit sparklers ran past. She saw a lot of groping
in her peripheral vision. The burn of the alcohol rolled down
her throat, and then bloomed in her belly.

"Come on . . . ," he said. "Let's find Peter and your friend."

Lucy nodded with a smile, then took Bart's hand. They pushed through the crowd, past a slip 'n' slide made out of a greased-down roll of black trash bags. Slippery, shirtless people slid across it and crashed into a kiddie pool. There was a line of twenty or so microwaves, each on its own desk along the north wall, and they were all plugged into extension cords running into classroom windows. Kids would grab individual-sized, thawed-out, frozen pizzas from coolers nearby and cook them up, before moving on to hang with their gangs.

Lucy and Bart walked past a slurry of music made by the cell phones of stumbling, slow-dancing couples. Over the course of a few strides, they went from hearing Top 40 to country to R&B to metal. Beyond the couples, there were jam circles. Kids played new guitars and bongos and other instruments, while others lay on the ground, wrapped in blankets, and listened. It seemed like every sixth person was hooking up with the seventh. There was a circle of dudes standing around telling jokes. Lucy watched a girl eat chocolate espresso beans by the handful and then do a drum solo on her boyfriend's back. A group of laughing Freaks chucked batteries at each other, and in the fire's light it looked like they were throwing fireflies. She heard the faraway sound of a girl puking, and then the comforting words of her girlfriends. Footballs flew through the air. Frisbees too.

Lucy hated to admit it, but this party had lived up to the

hype. There was a kind of joy and camaraderie in the air that dwarfed anything she'd seen at Geek shows. Even if she was wary of Gates's tactics with the parents, what was happening here was good for everybody. Lucy looked up to the dark sky. She didn't see any parents, but it was so dark. At least one of them had to be posted guard up there. They always were.

"Let's go to the fire," Lucy said, and pulled Bart toward the massive flames.

The fire was eating the tower of wooden pallets and lumber. It was pure destruction, but it was beautiful. Lucy walked two steps closer than everyone else. The heat pressed into her. Whipping, snaking, furious tongues of fire filled her field of vision.

"Can I get a sip?" Bart said.

He took the bottle from her and tipped it back. Orange light twinkled off the vodka that clung to the crevasses of his lips. A gust of wind blew clouds of sparks off the fire. The sparks spun past Bart. He handed the bottle to Lucy and smiled.

Diagonally across the fire from her, Lucy noticed a big crew of Sluts. Raunch was among them, hooking up with her boy. Lucy pictured herself cutting loose like that, just losing herself to the pleasure of the moment. It didn't seem so far-fetched.

"On a scale of one to ten," Lucy said. "How lucky do you feel tonight?"

Bart's eyes widened, clearly surprised by how forward she was being.

"Pretty lucky," he said.

She laughed.

Movement in the crowd distracted her. The Saints were approaching. Kids from other gangs shook their hands and slapped them on the backs. They'd come a long way since their shaky start in the school. Now, they walked through the quad like they were a real part of McKinley. Like they'd always been there. They look excited, giddy even.

"Move back!" they shouted.

A really young-looking Saint girl, maybe thirteen years old, walked up and ushered the Sluts back. The Sluts complied since everyone else did, but they were surly about it. The Saints moved in two lines, pushing back at the crowd until the middle of the quad was cleared into one long strip, from one end to the other. The crowd had been split into two halves.

Gates came bursting out of the crowd, riding a wild hog. The animal was giant and muscular and ugly, and it didn't like having Gates on its back. He held tight to a leash that was choking its neck and he smiled like he was on an amusement park ride.

"I love this guy," Bart said.

Gates only made it about ten feet into the clearing before he fell off the snarling beast. The hog ran away, back into the crowd, squealing, and snorting. The crowd parted wherever the hog ran.

Gates got up, still grinning. From where Lucy stood, Gates was framed by the column of fire behind him. He wore a blue pinstripe suit with a crisp white shirt, although they were both stained with dirt now. He pushed back his long white hair.

"Welcome to the party, everybody. You guys like my new pet?" Gates hollered.

The cheering was immediate, and it hurt Lucy's ears.

"That's nothin'. Are you ready for the big surprise?" Gates said.

The party cheered again, but they were drowned out by a loud, nasty, echoing gargle that came from deep in the school.

"We got a special delivery last night. Top secret. And, it's a good one," Gates said.

The Saints laughed and nodded to each other.

The awful noise rattled like an angry chest cold, like a monster at the bottom of a well. It got louder. Closer. The crowd started to worry, and Lucy was right with them. The wretched, booming growl closed in on them. People backed up further, without urging from the Saints, making the gap in the middle of the quad wider.

Then Lucy saw it. A blur came ripping out of one of the hallways, and rocketed across the cleared dirt road, blowing a froth of dust into the air behind it. For a fragment of a second the speeding comet was right in front of Lucy, and she could see it clearly.

It was Will on a motorcycle.

The hallway was the barrel of a rifle, and Will was the bullet. He crushed his fingers around the Harley's handle grips. He'd crossed the quad in a flash, and sped right into the opposite hallway. People scattered ahead. Terrified faces bolted past him, bodies leapt out of the way, kids flattened themselves to the lockers like they were standing on the slim ledge of a high building. The hallway ahead shook in his vision. The bike was alive, vibrating underneath him like a giant buzz saw.

The hall ended at a T-junction with another hallway, and the hard wall rocketed toward him. Will fumbled with the brake, but couldn't get his fingers around it. He strained, hooked his fingers around the brake lever and the clutch, and squeezed, but he turned the bar a little as he did it, and the bike began to wobble underneath him. He suddenly wished his motor-cycle-riding experience was more than playing with his cous-in's dirt bike one weekend. He painted squiggles of rubber across the linoleum floor. The tires shrieked like a hurt ani-mal. Will shifted his weight to right it, but the motorcycle was too heavy.

The bike bucked, angry with him, and threw Will off. He crashed to the floor and the bike crashed on its side right behind him. Will and the bike skidded down the hall like air hockey pucks. His hoodie and T-shirt ripped away and the slide should have torn his skin up too, but Will had wrapped his entire upper body in duct tape, down to one inch strips around each of his fingers and fingertips.

The heavy bike wasn't slowing down. It caught up with Will and pushed him forward. The back wheel spun in his face. At least they'd remember him when he was dead.

Will felt the drag of the floor as his body slowed down. The bike cruised to a stop, and pushed him gently into the wall. On the wall opposite Will was a photocopied party poster with his face on it.

Will started laughing, it was just too funny. Not only was this whole idea bat shit crazy, but he started to imagine what the look would have been on David's face if he had been at this party. He would have had a heart attack.

"Buddy, that was amazing!" Gates said as he ran up. "Are you okay?"

"Think so," Will said.

Will gave each limb a turn, twisting it or bending the joints. Nothing felt broken, torn, or sprained. Gates grabbed his arm and helped him up.

"You are a maniac!" Gates said and slapped him on top of the shoulders. "People are going nuts out there."

"It was insane," Will said, still laughing.

Will pulled off his tattered sweatshirt and shirt. Blood seeped out from tears in his duct tape skin. Together, he and

Gates lifted the bike upright. It was scratched and scuffed, and the gas tank was dented, but the engine still started.

"I wanna ride the handlebars!" Gates shouted over the chugging motor.

Will mounted the bike, and Gates hoisted himself onto the handlebars.

"I can't see," Will shouted.

"I'll be your eyes," Gates said, glancing back at Will with a mischievous arch of his red-eyed eyebrow.

Will grinned. He eased into the acceleration. They cruised back down the hall. Gates held onto the steering bar and planted his feet on the front tire guard to keep his balance. The people they rode past in the hall were awestruck.

"FASTER!" Gates yelled.

Will cranked his wrist forward and poured on the throttle. Gates barely stayed on the bike as Will sped into the quad. When the crowd saw them, they lost their minds.

Will slowed the bike to a parade pace, he was going to milk every second of it. Gates was on front shaking his fists high for everyone. They cheered. Will revved the engine and they screamed louder.

Will's smile dropped when he saw Lucy.

She was at the front of the crowd. She wore heavy eyeliner that swooped up in the corners of her eyes like a cat. Her hair was flame red. Her old blue dress was now black and cut to ribbons like she was in a swimsuit calendar. It was full of holes. More holes than dress. The neckline was a plunging V that nearly reached her belly button. The two sides were held together by paper clip chains. Will stared at her dress in disbelief. The word SLUT was hand embroidered on the dress's bust, in haphazard, sloppily stitched red thread.

He brought the bike to a short stop right in front of Lucy and put his feet on the ground.

"Aw, come on, lets keep going," Gates said.

Will ignored Gates. The sight of Lucy in her new threads had rocked his world. He had to play it cool.

"You, uh . . . I . . . What the fuck? You're a Slut," he said.

"Yup," she said. Her eyes were cool and calm.

Gates whipped his head around to look at Lucy. His face cramped with irritation and his bad eye flickered.

"Who's this?" Gates said.

"When were you going to tell me?"

She stayed cool. "Didn't really see how it was any of your business considering the last thing you said to me. It was so . . . nice. It was such a really 'good friend' thing to say. What was it again?"

Will braced himself.

"Oh, yeah!" Lucy said, then she leveled her eyes at Will. "Fuck off."

Will leaned the bike on its kickstand and stepped off it, causing Gates to have to jump off the handlebars. Gates dug his finger into his eye with a fierce rub. Perturbed, he looked around at the crowd that had quieted and was watching intently.

Will stepped to Lucy. She didn't look happy with him, but even unhappy, she looked fantastic. He hadn't seen her since the Stairs. Somehow, he had forgotten how perfectly her face fit together. He'd also forgotten the inescapable pull he felt toward her, the ache in his chest that used to oppress him when he was this close to her. All the duct tape and popularity in the school couldn't protect him from that feeling.

"Look, about that night," Will said, keeping his voice quiet. "I'm sorry. I didn't mean what I said."

"Funny, that doesn't make it feel any less shitty."

"I was just trying to do the right thing for both of us—"

"Are you guys done?" Gates said. "Come on, Will, let's go. Don't let this chick ruin our party."

The Harley engine grumbled behind him.

"You go ahead without me. I'll catch up, man," Will said.

"What, just me?" Gates said.

"You can't party without your boyfriend?" Lucy said.

Ooohs erupted all around. Gates took a step toward her, and the Sluts broke through the crowd to flank Lucy. Knives out. Will kept his eyes locked on Lucy. It was clear that this wasn't what she wanted either.

"Whoa, easy," Will said. "No need for trouble, now. Let's chill out, put the weapons away."

Will gave Gates a stern look to make sure he was on board

with this plan. It was the first time he'd ever stood up to Gates so directly. The anger in Gates's face scared Will more than the fifteen-odd blades pointed at him. But in a blink, it vanished. Gates went full smile. He stepped back. He threw his arms up in the air dramatically.

"Anybody looking for fun, follow me!" Gates shouted.

Gates mounted the bike and gunned it, roaring away. The crowd closed the gap behind him with cheers, and partying resumed again.

Will turned to face Lucy. Neither of them spoke as the party swirled around them. Will felt at peace standing next to her.

"Should we talk?" Will said.

The tension eased from Lucy's face. She seemed like she was about to nod, but some Nerd with a pompadour stepped up beside her.

"We're gonna hit the slip 'n' slide," the Nerd said to Lucy.

Will looked him up and down. "That sounds good. Why don't you get lost?"

"What'd you say?" the Nerd said.

"Bartholomew," Lucy said quick, stepping between them. "Give me a minute, okay?"

The Nerd glared at Will, then walked away, shaking his head.

"Bartholemew, huh? Your friend has a stupid name."

She didn't react.

"Is this part of your new Slut personality? No laughing?"

Lucy twisted her face into a sneer. "No. We were all laughing our asses off a few minutes ago. When you showed up on a motorcycle."

"Oof," Will said with a nod.

"Pretty respectable party though," Lucy said.

Will shrugged. "I had to come up with some way to get you to show up and talk to me again."

"Yeah, right," she said and rolled her eyes.

"I knew the best Lucy bait was pizza."

Lucy laughed. Finally a sign that things between them weren't actually as bad as they looked, and that they didn't have to keep acting like they were enemies.

"So, really," Will said. "Why did you go Slut?"

"Are you really asking, or is this a set up for a joke?"

"I'll get back to you on the joke, but I gotta be honest, I'm still getting used to the red. I did not see that coming. Like ever."

"You got a problem with it?"

"I guess not. So, what do you do, just sit around all day cutting the crotch out of your jeans?" Will said, cracking up.

"Oh, I see," Lucy said. "You still think you're funny!" She pointed at his duct-taped torso. "Good thing you've never grown any body hair or it might hurt to take that tape off."

"Damn! Slut Lucy doesn't mess around."

"No, she doesn't."

Lucy held his stare. This was new. She didn't look away, or do something cute to break the awkward moment. This new

Slut Lucy was right at home with the tension.

"I miss you," Will said.

Lucy faltered. Will's emotion seemed to make her nervous. Bart walked over from the spot where he'd been standing, ten feet away.

"Lucy, we should get going if you're done talking to . . . this dude," Bart said.

"Beat it, Jebediah," Will said.

"It's Bart," Bart said.

"Bartholomew," Lucy said.

"Right, whatever. Don't you have a barn to raise or something?"

"Will, stop," Lucy said.

"Why? It's my party, and this big lump is messing up our vibe."

"Yeah, well we're on a date," Lucy said. "I'll see you later, Will."

She walked off with Bart. Bart put his arm around her, and she looked happy to let him. Will watched her red hair disappear in the crowd. It made no sense. The whole school loved him. Why couldn't she?

Will kicked the dirt. He'd started the night feeling invincible, but a few minutes with Lucy, and it was like she had taken a giant ice cream scoop to his middle, and left a gaping hole behind.

25

HILARY HAD COME TO SEE P-NUT.

They'd been secretly flirting for almost a year. Anytime he was near, and Sam wasn't around, P-Nut would wink at her, and blow her kisses, or steal a few moments with her at the market to tell her exactly how he would make love to her. At first, she was offended that he thought he was worthy of her. But he never gave up. And eventually, the fact that he was the only boy to ever approach her like that, when he knew full well Sam would wage war on the Skaters for it, started to turn her on.

Now that she was looking for a new boy, P-Nut was first on her list. She stood in the Skater's headquarters, the old administrative offices, with a crew of Pretty Ones. P-Nut balanced on the top rung of an aluminum folding ladder above her.

"Hand me that hammer, will ya, perfect?" P-Nut said.

He had the ball of one foot on the rung, his other leg

extended out to the side, keeping his balance. He wasn't wearing a shirt. P-Nut never wore a shirt. Hilary picked the hammer up from the floor and handed it up to him. He could have grasped it by the head, but he reached further, just to touch her hand.

"Thanks," he said.

In his other hand, he held a noose that was tied around the neck of a full-size, fully dressed, department store male mannequin. P-Nut hammered the end of the noose into the ceiling, defying gravity by staying on the ladder, and giving a Hilary an anatomy lesson of all the muscles of his torso in the process. The mannequin twisted and turned by the neck, his perfect face frozen in a white-toothed smile. Its hands were reaching out, with open palms, as if it meant no harm. P-Nut gave the nail one last solid whack, then hopped down to the floor.

"What's that for?" Hilary asked.

"To practice hitting people while you skate past them. Usually we use a duffel bag full of water bottles as a target, but that Gates dude got this for us."

Gates. Everybody loved to talk about him like he was God's gift to McKinley, but Hilary prided herself on her taste. She knew the difference between a boy that was built to last, and one that was a fad. Gates didn't smell like a winner to her. He'd burn out, or screw up, or do something wrong, and he'd end up going down hard.

"A mannequin?" she said up to P-Nut. "That's all you asked for?"

"One of the things." He took Hilary's hand by the fingertips like she imagined French boys did. "And now I got you here. What more could a boy want?"

"Are you serious?" she said, rolling her eyes.

"Hilary. I live for you," he said with a straight face. She giggled. She couldn't help it. No one really talked like that. "You got no idea how honored I am to have Hilary Bowden in the house."

"Stop it," she said, wanting him to go on.

"You want the tour?"

"Dying for it."

P-Nut put his hand on her lower back and led her forward. Very low on her lower back actually, closer to upper ass. He did it with complete confidence. She decided to let him. This had to go right, because too much had already gone wrong. She'd gone to George Diaz, a Varsity she thought she could build into something. He had the potential to lead Varsity as long as Hilary was pulling the strings. She told him how easy it would be to overthrow Terry, but he was hearing none of it, and said it would only make them look weaker in front of the whole school if they threw out another leader. George still wanted to fool around with her, of course, but she told him she has a rule against hooking up with bald guys. That shut

George up. His hair was already thinning, and he was only seventeen.

As Hilary walked past a row of administrative offices, P-Nut indicated the last one.

"Here's our skate shop," he said. "If you ever feel the need to ride, I will personally make your deck."

"Very generous of you."

Inside the room, Skaters were building skateboard decks on tables. The decks of their boards were broken pieces of wood from drop palets, desks, and other furniture. They ground them down to acceptable shapes with an array of customized tools. Others were hacking at the top surface of more finished boards with sharpened cafeteria knives, to give the surfaces more grip. In the corner, a worried Skater with all of his head shaved but a black sideways mohawk that went from ear to ear instead of front to back, stood watch as a Skater girl with a smiley face shaved into her head screwed one of his trucks into his new deck. He clutched his other truck by the wheels and held it to his chest.

Hilary and P-Nut neared the end of the hallway.

"Don't know if you ever got a chance to see the college resource library when it was . . . normal, but we kinda tricked it out," P-Nut said.

He opened the door to a room that was centered around the giant half-pipe. They'd bashed through the ceiling into the room above. Two Skaters dropped in from the room above and crisscrossed across the half-pipe's smooth linoleum tile surface. Hilary watched one soar into the air, past the old ceiling and the guts of the missing floor, up into the classroom above, where the Skaters had hung a blackboard vertically from the ceiling. When he reached the pinnacle of his jump, the Skater slapped a sticker on the hanging blackboard, not quite as high as the highest sticker, and dropped back down into the pipe. Skaters watching on both floors cheered his effort. The blackboard swung wildly from the brown and white extension cords that tethered it to the ceiling. The second Skater fell near the bottom, hit his head, and lay on his stomach, not moving. Other kids rushed to help.

Hilary ignored the kid's emergency and turned to P-Nut with an impressed smile. "Highest sticker is the best?" she said.

"You got it."

"And whose is that?"

"He'd like to invite you into his office."

P-Nut extended his hand. She took it.

As they walked hand in hand, she could see all the Skater girls in the room smoldering. A swarm of jealous reactions followed her across the whole room. It felt so good. She missed that feeling. She hadn't really felt it since Sam had been on top. She used to get it from the other girls in the school, just for the fact that she was a Pretty One. She used to get it from the other Pretty Ones, jealous that she had Sam. She felt at home. It did cross her mind that P-Nut might have slept with every girl in his gang, but that's pretty much what she expected.

P-Nut led her into a dark room. He closed the door. A lighter sparked. A little flame in the darkness. It was quickly blocked by the vague dark mass of P-Nut's body. He moved and there was now a second flame. A candle. He was lighting candles. It seemed almost as hokey as his line about how he "lived for her," but she wasn't complaining.

"Well, you get right to the point, don't you?"

"Ha, you're funny," he said, moving on to another candle. "I'm only trying to show you I care."

There were ten short, thin, brown candles lit around the room now and he was still going. It was an office with antique bookshelves, a plush reading chair, and an ornately carved wooden desk. All of it was lit by golden candlelight that revealed the deep red stain of the mahogany furniture. The air smelled calming and familiar, but she couldn't place it. She could have gotten used to a room like this.

"I don't remember any of this stuff coming in the drop," Hilary said.

"I guess Principal Warfield was a big antique freak. All this is from his office. I've kept them safe."

She liked that he had taste. It was the last thing she would have expected.

"And the candles?" she said.

The candles were finely made, smooth from trunk to tip. And Hilary would know. They were worthy to be sold at the Pretty Ones' market table. Well, they would have been, if Gates's free-for-all hadn't flooded the school with real beauty and bathing products that put their homemade ones to shame.

"Nah, I made them," P-Nut said.

"You are a fantastic liar."

"I did make them," he said. "You really think I'm just some idiot, don't you?"

"Kinda," she said. "You know how to make candles?"

"Of course I do. You think this vibe creates itself?"

"Okay, then what'd you make 'em out of?"

"Crayons I bought from the Geeks a long time ago. Melted all together."

"And the wicks?"

"Shoelaces," P-Nut said. "I unwove them and waxed the individual threads."

Why did that turn her on so much?

"I only break them out for special occasions. For special people."

"I'm that special?" she said, smiling on the inside only. It had been too long since she'd had even a decent compliment.

He walked closer to her.

"I want to talk about our future."

"Ew, stalker," she said and backed up, hoping he didn't see through her bluff.

"Don't talk tough. Be yourself with me. That's how it's gotta be if we're gonna do big things."

"What kind of big things?"

"A Skater-Pretty One partnership."

Jackpot. There was really no sweeter pleasure than something falling perfectly in her lap.

"I'm listening," she said.

He didn't say anything. He continued to stalk her around the room. She'd retreat, he'd advance. She couldn't wipe the smile off her face. She forgot how good it felt to flirt with someone she was actually attracted to. She slinked to the other side of the desk. He climbed up over the top of it and hopped down, landing with his face only three hot inches away from hers. This was her ticket. The Skaters had it all. Her girls loved the Skater guys, and P-Nut was hot. The only thing that scared her was she couldn't see a chink in his armor. She hadn't found that tender part of him yet, that part that she could twist and gain control. She had to trust that she'd find that part of him eventually. She always did.

He took hold of her head with both hands and pulled her into his lips. However many hundreds of girls P-Nut had kissed to get this good at it, she forgave him. P-Nut was soft but assertive. They were in sync. He moaned low as his lips told hers where to go. His hands slid all over her body. She could feel the heat of his palms through her dress.

It took all of her willpower to push him away.

"Slow down, Cashew. We haven't talked terms yet."

"Let's have some fun first," he said, and pulled at her.

"The Pretty Ones need to be taken care of," she said, struggling to gain her footing.

"New clothes," he said. "Daily laundry. Food. Your own rooms you can decorate like you want. And they'd only work a couple nights a week."

He placed his hands firmly on her hips. She pushed away.

"What did you just say?"

"People have more than they need now. They got stuff to spend. And I got just the thing for them to spend it on. I'm gonna open a gentlemen's club. I'll build go-go cages. I'll have a bar—"

Hilary laughed, she didn't know how else to respond. It was ridiculous.

"You can't seriously think that my Pretty Ones would strip for you."

"No," he said, like what she'd just said was the craziest thing in the world. It helped Hilary catch her breath. "Calm down. I got my girls for that. I'm looking for a higher class of girl, for those guys who are willing to pay the price. And I promise . . . It'll be a steep price, to spend a night with royalty."

It was a knife in the heart. She couldn't even find the words. She was so stupid. She shouldn't have let her guard down, shouldn't have let herself get excited about him wanting her. He hurt her feelings. No one hurts her feelings.

"Just think. You and me, Hil, we could make bank. 'Cause seriously, how long is this Sam hostage thing gonna last? All the good stuff is gonna dry up, but if we act now, we could collect it all."

She knew what some people thought, that the Pretty Ones were just concubines, that they were just in the business of pleasing Varsity to stay alive. Well, it was true, and it was something Hilary had been well aware of the whole time, but she had always been able to spin it to her girls as real, authentic companionship. And she'd seen actual relationships blossom from that "understanding." The more relationships there were, the more it kept the Pretty Ones believing that they had a choice. But this wouldn't fly, she couldn't say, *Hey, if we join up with the Skaters, you could all be whores! Whaddaya think?*

"Who do you think you're talking to?" Hilary said in P-Nut's face.

P-Nut shrugged like he was talking about what he'd like to have for lunch. "Well . . . ," he said. "Let's be real about your situation here. I'm guessing the only reason why you came here today is because you haven't been able to find a replacement for Sam. I'm offering you a way to stay the prettiest, with the finest things. You can stay on top, and you'll barely have to lift a finger. Isn't that what you want?"

P-Nut was ice-cold. She would have respected him for how ruthlessly he'd played it all if it didn't hurt so much. He wanted them to work in a whorehouse. Opening their legs for anyone with a backpack full of food cans, or a stack of fresh towels. It was unthinkable. She felt like she'd been molested from just hearing the offer.

She had to verbally murder him right here, collect whatever pride she had left off the floor. He looked at her with the same smile, like she wasn't understanding yet that he hadn't said anything wrong. The candlelight twinkled off his teeth. Sexy piece of shit. Hilary wiped her hands down her face, pressing her fingers down hard to keep from screaming.

She felt her tooth click out of place.

It was loose in her mouth. The glue had snapped. P-Nut stared at her. She couldn't open her mouth. She wanted so badly to shriek in his face, to tell him everything that was wrong with him and right with her. How he didn't deserve to speak her name, let alone put his hands on her.

She pushed past him, striking his ribs with a sharp elbow as she went. She tore the door open. She ran down the hall. She found her girls that had accompanied her were flirting with a crowd of Skaters. She waved at them angrily. They didn't see. She wanted to cry. She couldn't open her mouth to shout an order. She waved like an idiot. She walked up to one of them and slapped her across the face, as hard as she wanted to slap P-Nut. It must have stung. The girl, Michelle, was scared, red-cheeked, confused. She didn't know what she had done. The Skaters looked confused too. The tooth was under Hilary's tongue now, its sharp roots poked the thin skin of the bottom of her mouth.

Hilary turned and stomped for the door. Her girls followed. As soon as she was out the door, she sped up. She walked faster than all her girls, so that none of them could see her crying.

26

GATES LAY FACEDOWN ON A WHITE SAND beach. The hot grains of sand pressed into his eyes, his lips, his nose. He rolled onto his back. There were two oiled-up girls in bikinis and linen beach shirts with him, one lying on either side. He didn't know who they were and he didn't care.

The beach was long and crescent-shaped and empty. He and his female companions were the only ones around. The ocean had no waves, no movement, its surface was still, like a lake. He stared up and watched thousands of white dots appear across the deep blue sky, and then slowly grow larger. As they grew, he could see them better. Volleyballs. Volleyballs were raining from the sky. The first of them struck the soft sand and bounced back up high, like the sand was hard as asphalt. More balls hit the beach and bounced high, spraying sand in the air as they launched back up. White balls battered the beach all around where Gates lay, with his arms still behind his head, and his ankles crossed. None of them struck him or his two lady companions. Other things rained down. A falling cloud of shuttlecocks and Latin-to-English dictionaries pummeled the ground behind his head. Red neckties with little skulls on them came fluttering down. Hundreds of purple Super Balls struck the beach along with boxes of Boston baked beans that rattled when they landed.

The oily girls began to caress his shirtless body. One kissed circles on the skin of his neck, while the other whispered filthy promises in his ear. More objects rained down and struck the beach, kicking up more sand. The sand spray kicked up into the air, but it didn't fall back down, it hung in the air all around him. He reached out above his head, and swept his hand through the suspended sand, feeling it fall away at his touch.

"Where were you right then?" one of the girls said.

Gates turned to her. They weren't on the beach anymore, and they weren't lying down.

"What?" Gates said.

It was no longer daytime; it was night, the sky was black, and he was in Pruitt's backyard, where tangled Christmas lights had been draped all through the branches of a barren winter tree in the center of the yard. The girls from the beach stared at him, annoyed, and fully dressed, and holding plastic champagne flutes.

"Where were you right then?" one of them said again.

"On a beach," Gates said.

"Why are you acting so weird?"

When he looked back at them, their heads looked like fleshy marshmallows with black dots for eyes and no noses or mouths.

"Damn, girls. What happened to your faces?" he said.

"You like it?" one of them said. The area near her mouth seemed to pulse as she spoke, but he heard her quite clearly.

He wasn't sure if he liked it. Their heads were structureless blobs, but on the other hand, their skin was beautiful. It was luscious and healthy. He could see the hint of bluish veins under the veil of their delicate skin, and it made him want to touch their soft, puffy heads.

"What do you kiss with?" he said.

"We don't kiss. Straight to business," the other one said.

He nodded. "You girls are cool."

"Gates! You hear about the new hat?" Fowler said.

Fowler was walking across the yard toward him, holding a plain cardboard box in his hands.

"What new hat?" Gates said. The blobby-headed girls were gone, but he'd already forgotten them.

"A French fashion designer came up with the perfect hat," Fowler said.

"What do you mean perfect?"

"The design of it is so perfect that it makes anyone who

wears it look the best they could possibly ever look. It doesn't even matter what other clothes you're wearing, you put it on and poof, immediately you're better-looking than you've ever been."

"It's a magic hat?"

"No bro, it's scientific," Fowler said. "Just looking at the hat releases all this stuff in your brain."

"But how?"

"There's PDFs on their website; you can read all the research."

"That rules so hard," Gates said. "How much is the hat?"

"Free."

"You have it in the box?" Gates said, pointing to the box in Fowler's hand.

Fowler grinned. "You're never going to be the same, bro."

He pulled the top off the box, and inside was a green felt hat, with a pinched ridge running down the top, a baseball cap bill in the back, and three drops of white paint spilled on its front.

"Are you sure that's perfect?" Gates said.

"Just put it on, dude."

Gates took it out of the box and pulled it onto his head.

Instantly, he jolted with pleasure. It felt like his whole body was a tongue, the world was made of ice cream. He began to grow taller than everyone else. Girls came running out of the bushes, tearing their shirts off at the sight of him.

"Oh my God, Gates. There's no one better," he heard Lark say.

People were literally breaking out in tears when they saw how good he looked. He said his own name, "Gates." The crowd of girls encircling him simultaneously achieved orgasm. He said it again. "Gates." They fell to their knees, bodies quivering.

His fists grew to the size of boulders. He raised them up into the air and the girls all ran back to the bushes. He smashed his hulking fists into the ground, and made hot-tub-sized dents in the earth.

"Gates!" he screamed, and he launched into the air. Gates soared over all of Denton, spinning and twirling his way between buildings and over the trees, trying to swat all the birds out of the sky. He willed himself to go up, and he soared higher and higher, until the air got cold and thin. It pressed on his chest. He felt one with the wind, in complete control, but as soon as he thought that, he began to drift down toward the ground.

He tried to will himself higher again, but his powers of flight had abandoned him. He looked down at Denton, and saw that his slow descent was lowering him down to Capitol Boulevard, where most of the car dealerships were. His feet touched the ground in a cracked and overgrown parking lot, behind the local mini golf course. There were no cars, but five townie kids stood smoking weed by the light post. Their clothes were dirty, and two of them were shivering. They listened to a baseball game on a portable radio.

The weed smelled good. He wanted some.

"Hey, can I get a puff of that?" Gates asked.

One of the kids, who had droopy eyes and a dusting of facial hair over his plump face, passed the roach to Gates. He took a long drag, and it tasted like an orange Creamsicle.

"Where'd you get that hat?" one of the shivering kids asked him.

They were all eyeing it. The vibe had changed in an instant. He knew with absolute certainty that these townies all wanted his hat.

"You can't have it!" Gates yelled.

"Get that hat!" the droopy-eyed one yelled.

Gates ran. He tried to fly but he couldn't. He sprinted across the cracked asphalt, and over the tufts of grass and weeds that sprouted out from the cracks.

He looked back and saw that all the townies had vanished and only one person pursued him—his little brother Colton, with a bullet hole through his forehead.

Gates fell from the shock, and Colton was on him in a flash. Colton grabbed him and rolled him onto his back. Colton was never that strong before. Broken chunks of asphalt prodded Gates in his back. His brother straddled Gates's chest and pushed all the air out of him. His lungs were stuck empty.

Colton wore his black sunglasses, and Gates couldn't see his eyes, but his face was scrunched up in contempt. The wet rim of the bullet hole in his forehead glinted in the moonlight. Colton opened his dead, gray mouth and cold saliva came pouring out of it, like lemonade from a glass pitcher. It splashed over Gates's face and made him cough. The saliva began to shoot out of Colton's mouth like a fire hose, pounding down into Gates's head. Through the spraying saliva he could see how furious, how anguished Colton was. The saliva fire hose became a saliva water cannon as it began to blast down into his face so hard that he felt his upper lip and his eyelids begin to tear away.

Gates woke up on the floor of the bus. It was only a dream.

"Oh fuck, oh fuck, oh fuck," he said, touching his face to make sure it was still there.

The back of the bus was dark. The light of the main room shined through the shattered windshield, but couldn't make it all the way to the back of the bus. He pulled himself to his feet and kicked his way through food wrappers and empty soda bottles, and dirty underwear on the floor. He didn't bother changing into fresh clothes for the day or gathering his toiletries for the shower. He wanted to get out of the bus and away from that nightmare immediately.

He left the bus for the brightly lit front room of the processing facility. He had to squint at first to handle the light. Most

Saints weren't up yet; it was 6:17 a.m. There were a few shuffling through the room, trying to yawn the sleep away.

In one corner of the room there were two gaming chairs, the kind that rock back and forth, positioned in front of a flat-screen TV, and Will sat in one of them, playing a racing game.

Nice, Will was already up. Gates felt the tension of his nightmare washing away. He and Will always had fun together.

Gates ambled over, and plopped himself down in the free chair. He and Will high-fived, without either of them having to take their eyes off the screen to do it. They'd gamed so much together in the last few nights since the party that they might as well have slept in those chairs. He looked Will up and down. He wasn't sure but he thought Will was wearing the same clothes as the night before.

"Have you been up all night?" Gates said.

"Yup," Will said, his eyes locked on the screen.

"Is there a video game championship coming up that I don't know about?"

"Ha. No. I just kept playing."

"Wait. Should we have a video game championship?"

"We could," Will said.

"I actually can't believe we haven't done it already. Fuck, it could be so awesome. We could go all night. What games do you think?"

"I don't know."

"One fighting game, one-shooter for death matches, and

something that has split-screen multiplayer. Right? That's not bad. That covers a lot of bases."

"Sure," Will said.

"You're not excited about it? Look at you, you're mister gamer."

"No, I am, it sounds like a good time."

"You all right?" Gates said.

Will didn't answer, but Gates knew.

"It's about that Slut girl from the party?"

Will shrugged.

"Oh, come on. She's one girl. Who cares?"

"I like her."

There was something about the way Will said those words that made Gates pause. It wasn't their usual good time bullshitting kind of talk, Will meant what he said, and Gates could feel how deep his emotion ran when he said it.

He wanted to cheer Will up, Will had been his partner in crime, a fellow fun-hunter, and he didn't like seeing him so torn up like this. He knew Will thought this girl was really important, and in truth she probably wasn't. As far as Will had told him, this girl had done nothing but turn him down and lead him on, and Will kept going back for more like a loyal puppy dog.

"Best thing for you is to clean your palate with a new girl."

"Yeah," Will said with a sigh.

"Serious."

"Yeah, I know. You keep telling me."

"It's not just for you either. It's for this girl . . . what's her name? Luther?"

Will laughed a little.

"You know it's Lucy."

"Right, Louis. It's for Louis too."

That got another laugh out of him. Will's sullen shell was cracking.

"Nothing gets a girl interested in you faster than her seeing you with other girls," Gates said.

"Hmm," Will said. Gates could see the idea had needled into his brain.

"Besides, you KNOW Louis is in the Sluts, she's probably getting her ditch dug out by some guy, all day and night."

Will laughed, and cringed at the same time. "Damn! You're a dick," Will said, but he kept laughing.

Gates punched him in the arm. "Ah! You dirty motherfucker, you were thinking it. I know you were."

"I definitely wasn't."

"She's all unnnghhhh unnghhhh," Gates said, miming like he was a girl in ecstasy. "What? You want me to do five guys? Okay."

"Oh, come on!" Will said, smiling. He kicked Gates's plastic gamer chair over and Gates fell on the floor.

"Please make a line out the door, everyone," Gates said, "I

can only be humped by three guys at a time."

Will threw an open bag of Reese's Pieces at Gates and they hit him in the shoulder. Yellow, orange, and brown candies sprayed all over the floor. Gates laughed and scooped a handful out of the package. He chomped them and let the sugary peanut butter filling spread through his mouth.

"For real though. For real," Gates said. "Are you okay if I go completely real now? I might have to get real."

"Okay, okay, yes. Get real," Will said, amused.

"I'm just confused. Why do you have to be a humongous pussy?"

"That's it, I'm joining the Freaks."

"No, hold on. I'm fucking with you. What I want to say for real, is you should be fuckin' happy. We're on top. Everyone's coming to us, asking us for stuff. We're the cool kids."

"That's true," Will said, brightening another degree as he pondered the idea.

"I've got dates lined up for the next two weeks," Gates said, "and I told all of them they had to bring a hot friend."

"You did?"

"No lie. Now I could be throwing these girls Fowler's way, or Pruitt, if that's what you're telling me I should do."

"No one said that."

"Oh, why?" Gates said, torturing Will. "Are you interested in hanging out with new girls?"

Will took a deep breath, and when he let it out he smiled. "Yeah. I guess I am."

"That's the dude I've been looking for!" Gates said, and threw his fists in the air.

"You have one set up for tonight?"

"Yeah, with a Nerd chick. I heard her friend has a third nipple."

"Really? Full size?"

"You can only hope."

"Cool," Will said.

"This is gonna cheer you up. I'm going to make sure of it. We are going to party so hard for so long that you won't even be able to remember this Judy girl's name."

"All right, all right. You've convinced me."

"Perfecto."

"I gotta piss," Will said, and he got up.

"Great, thanks for letting me know."

Will chuckled as he headed off for one of the bathrooms in the mess hall. Gates put his chair right side up and sat in it. Its curved plastic frame let him rock back and forth. He picked up the controller off the floor and unpaused Will's racing game. He crashed the car almost immediately.

Gates heard the crunch of someone stepping on a plastic bottle behind him. He turned back.

Colton stood in the middle of the floor.

His skin was gray. He wore his black shades, and full St.

Patrick's attire, a blazer, tie and sweater, slacks, and penny loafers. His brown hair was combed neatly to the side. Black blood dripped from the hole in his forehead.

Colton walked toward him. Gates scrambled out of his chair and into the corner. How was this happening? His dead brother made fists of his hands as he strode toward him.

"Get back!" Gates said.

"Gates?"

Will was standing at the entrance to the mess hall, staring at him, perplexed. Colton was gone. One second he was there and the next he wasn't. Gates didn't know if he'd just seen a ghost, or he was losing his shit, but just like earlier when he had seen Will in the gaming chair, just Will's presence calmed him. He needed to stick with Will. He'd be safe with Will. He didn't know how he knew that, but he could feel that it was true in his bones.

"Hey, man," Gates said.

"Are you . . . messing around? You look all scared."

"Yeah. You know me. Can't keep it serious," Gates said, assuming a relaxed pose. He hoped he wouldn't have to talk about it anymore.

Will stretched and yawned. "So when does the partying start?"

"Right. Fucking. Now," Gates said.

27

LUCY WATCHED A NAKED GIRL DO PUSH-UPS
over broken glass. Her name was Frida. She'd been a Freak
since the gangs formed, but now she was fed up. She'd hooked
up with Bobby last year, but it wasn't that great and she'd
tried to move past it. Bobby wouldn't let her. He hounded her
with requests for dates, gave her creepy gifts, and got more
mad each time she turned him down. Finally he told her she
couldn't be in the gang anymore if she wouldn't date him.
Frida decided enough was enough and she came knocking on
the cafeteria door.

Now that she was staring at a pile of broken glass, with Lips
yelling at her in her ear, Lucy wondered if Frida regretted her
choice. The girl was on her sixth day of Naked Week.

"Thirty . . . ," Frida grunted out, as she pushed up and locked
her arms in place.

"What are you stopping for, bitch?" Lips shouted. "I wanna

see forty! I've been listening to this thirty crap for days."

Sophia walked away from the group of Sluts next to Lips to join Lucy, Raunch, and some others that were watching from a distance.

"God, part of me just wants to tell her how to make it stop," Sophia said, shaking her head.

"I'm so glad you said that," Lucy said. "Me too."

"She'll pull through," Raunch said. "She'll figure it out soon, I can see it in her."

Sophia nodded. "I know. It's just so hard to watch."

"That's what we have Lips for," Lucy said, and the others laughed.

The girls settled back into watching Frida struggle through more push-ups as Lips jabbed at her ribs with her foot. Frida began to lower herself toward the glass again. Lucy could remember that moment vividly, making the decision to push beyond her limits when she didn't know how it was humanly possible.

"Come on," Sophia whispered to herself, but it was meant for Frida.

"Fight back," another girl muttered.

Lucy never would have thought something so vicious would have warmed her heart. When it had been her in Frida's place, she'd thought all the girls around her were monsters. She couldn't understand how someone would treat another person in this way, but now that she was on the other side,

Lucy knew how much love there was in this room. Each one of these girls had suffered through similar trials and they were stronger for it. They only wanted the best for Frida, and none of them, including Lucy, had any intention of letting her fail.

This was Lucy's family now. Her life. She belonged. It was everything she'd hoped for when she'd joined up. So, why had she been thinking about Will every day since the bonfire party?

It still bothered her that their conversation that night hadn't gone the way she'd expected. Being in the Sluts had felt thrilling before she saw him at the party. And the look on Will's face when he comprehended completely that Lucy was a badass Slut had been the cherry on top. She'd wanted to see him eat his own words, feel horrible for the things he'd yelled at her in the Stairs. And he did, and he'd apologized, and he'd told her he missed her. That should have made her happy, but instead, it had only upset her.

"Hey, Virgin!" one of the guards at the cafeteria entrance shouted. "Somebody here for you."

Lucy swallowed hard. She wasn't expecting anybody. She looked to the other girls, who shrugged. Lucy walked toward the cafeteria entrance. When Lucy laid her hand on the door handle, she took a deep breath and hoped that it wasn't Will. Lucy pushed open the door.

Bart stood alone under a bright hall light. He had a crooked smile and his pompadour looked a little bigger than she remembered from last time. He gave her a big, friendly wave. Lucy felt her body relax at the sight of him.

"Hi, Bart."

"Yo."

So goofy. So cute.

"Wanna go on a date?" he said.

"Yes, she does!" Raunch shouted from somewhere behind Lucy.

Lucy laughed and stepped out into the hall.

When Bart had told Lucy they were going to the Geek show, she didn't know what to say. The last time she'd been to one was on a date with David. Those few hours she'd had with him, before everything went wrong, were immortalized in her mind. She could only recall the sights and sounds of that night as part of a perfect bliss. And so, Lucy was afraid that tonight Bart could only fail. She wouldn't be able to help but compare, and everything he did would only pale in comparison to how David did it.

She liked Bart, and she didn't want that. Thankfully, he was one step ahead of her.

Lucy's legs dangled over the metal ledge of the lighting catwalk, where Bart sat next to her. It was one of three catwalks that ran the width of the auditorium, each one mounted with powerful lights aimed at the proscenium stage at the far end of the room. A partying crowd, populated with heads of different colors, swirled below. Gangs mixed freely, in a way Lucy had never seen before, at least not from this perspective. Kids mingled. Pairs and threesomes from different gangs drank together, played games together, laughed together. The bonfire party had greased the wheels and started a phenomenon of impromptu parties that were happening nearly every day now. She'd heard about them, but this was the first one she'd been to since the bonfire.

"I can't believe it," Lucy said.

"Yeah, it's pretty cool up here," Bart said. "That Geek, Lane, you met, could only hook us up for a little bit before the show starts, but I figured it's way better than the same old Geek show stuff."

That wasn't what Lucy was talking about, but she was happy to keep it light. "Definitely," she said.

"I love heights," he said. "When I was little I was pretty sure I could fly."

Lucy laughed. "Really?"

"Yeah, one day I flapped my arms so hard I dislocated my shoulder. My mom freaked out when I came back in the house with one arm hanging to, like, my knees."

Lucy covered her mouth in shock. "No way."

Bart grinned. "The next week I built a pair of wings out of tree branches and bed sheets. I jumped off the roof and broke my leg."

"Shut up," Lucy said, snorting a laugh.

Bart nodded, his grin getting bigger.

"What did your mom do?" Lucy said.

"She just left me in the yard for a week. Said it was the only way I'd learn my lesson."

"What?" Lucy said.

"Honk. Sucka. Nah, she took me to the ER. Again. The doctor laughed at her. She didn't talk to me for a month. I was a pretty big spaz when I was little."

"I would've never guessed that. You're like the most chill person I know."

"My dad helped me focus after that. He was an engineer. I mean, is," Bart corrected himself. It was something a lot of people did when they talked about their families. "He taught me about drafting, and we started making designs for real planes. It's what I'm going to do."

"Build planes?"

"I'm gonna build one faster than the X-43," he said. Like he meant it. Like it was a fact.

Lucy didn't know what the X-43 was, but just the fact that Bart was so sure of what he would do in life, or that he would even have a life outside, was impressive.

"Maybe you'll take me up in it?" Lucy said, leaning over and bumping him playfully.

He shook his head. "You'd die."

"Huh?"

"I mean, it'll be too fast. It'll have to be unmanned."

"Oh," Lucy said. "Now I know why you went Nerd."

Bart laughed. That laugh she loved. He touched her knee. The glow of a blue stage light clamped to the catwalk railing above them made his perfect teeth gleam.

"Want to make out?" he said.

"Uh . . . ," Lucy said, a little surprised. It made her wonder if all of this, the catwalk, his plan to build jets, was all an equation in Bart's head that equaled "make out." It probably was. What boy didn't have a plan when it came to that?

"Yeah, okay," she said.

They leaned toward each other at the same time and kissed. He was pretty good at it. They scooted closer to each other, and he put one warm hand on her thigh and one on the back of her neck. Every move he made was steady, the rumble of the crowd below pleasantly filled her ears while she gave in to the pleasure of their kiss. It had been too long since she'd felt the rush of lips on lips. Long enough for it to feel brand-new and exciting. It was what she'd wanted the other night at the bonfire, but he'd never made a move. Maybe that was part of his plan too.

"Time's up," someone said from the adjacent catwalk. It was the Geek that had shown them up there. "Sorry, but Zachary's starting his show now, and if anything goes wrong up here with the lights, he'll kill me. Can't risk it."

Bart pulled back from Lucy and shrugged. "Bummer," he said.

He was so cool about it, it made Lucy smile, even though part of her wanted to smash Zachary's spotlight while she had the chance.

"Should we grab a seat?" Bart said.

"Sure."

Lucy had to hand it to Zachary. If he was good for anything, it was putting on a show. Just the set alone, in front of her, was impressive. Thanks to a delivery of new lumber and paint, courtesy of Gates, the Geeks had constructed a stylized version of McKinley High on stage. A looming row of gigantic lockers, nearly three times the size of real lockers, dominated the stage. Actual, piled-up salvage from the basement, clumps of tangled chairs and desks, gave the rest of the stage depth and dimension. In combination with the nightmarish lighting, the McKinley world onstage looked like some surreal wasteland.

"Way to go on the seats," Bart said when he walked up, holding two bags of microwave popcorn.

"Ooo, popcorn," Lucy said. "I can't remember the last time I had that."

"Well, keep dreaming, because they're both for me."

"Ha-ha," she said as Bart handed her a bag. He sat down next to her, reached across, and held her hand.

As the houselights went down, she smiled.

A spotlight cut across the dark and settled on a locker

onstage in the center of the row. The locker door flew open and Zachary stumbled out, wearing massively exaggerated shoulder pads underneath a football jersey. He wore a cartoonish coif of blond hair that immediately drew boos from the Varsity guys in the crowd, but peals of laughter from everyone else. Sexed-up moans and groans echoed out from the open locker, and anonymous girls' hands clawed at Zachary's jersey.

"Back, Pretty Things! Back!" he shouted in a faux-meathead voice, and he kicked the locker door shut. Zachary turned to the crowd and tugged at his collar with wide eyes. "Yeesh, sex slaves . . . can't live with 'em. Can't live without 'em."

Lucy snorted a big laugh. She couldn't believe what Zachary had just said.

"Oh, sorry," Zachary said. "Lemme introduce myself. My name's Dork Baloney. I know you all think every Varsity guy is just some total, complete, roided-out asshole that is looking for somebody's head to crush and—"

Zachary stopped suddenly and pointed at Bart in the crowd.

"What are you looking at, Nerd?! Do you want me to rip your head off?!"

The crowd erupted in laughter. Bart slapped his knee, loving it. Lucy looked behind her to see if Varsity was storming the stage. They weren't. They were laughing with everybody else. Not so long ago, what Zachary was doing might have started a riot, and Lucy wasn't sure it still couldn't. These jokes felt dangerous. Maybe that was what made them so funny.

Onstage, Zachary was shaking his head.

"Sorry, I don't know what came over me. What I was trying to say is that us Varsity guys are more sensitive than you think we are. And me, in particular, I was thinking about how there's been new kids in McKinley for months now, and nobody's given our new friend a proper tour of the school."

"Oooh," the crowd said in anticipation. Lucy gave Bart an excited look.

"Is he really gonna go after everybody?" she whispered.

"It'd be pretty pimp if he did," Bart said with a low-key shrug.

"After all, it's only the polite thing to do," Zachary said. "Right?"

"Suck a dick, Baloney!" someone in the crowd heckled.

"Maybe I will!" Zachary said in his most ridiculous meathead voice. "Follow me to the cafeteria!"

The crowd was giddy with anticipation of the Sluts getting roasted. Lucy knew Violent was in the audience somewhere. She'd headed out earlier in the night with a bunch of the others, and Lucy craned her neck to try and find them. She spotted Violent in time to see her watch a Geek boy onstage portray her as a brute who kicked Dork Baloney's ass when he tried to kiss her. Only three rows back from Lucy, Violent was close enough to see by the glow of the lit-up stage. Slowly, her flatline mouth turned up into a smile. It was all the cue the Sluts needed to laugh and really start enjoying themselves, Lucy included.

Onstage, Dork Baloney traveled to the teachers' lounge where P-Nut, depicted by a Geek in a harness and wires, was doing bigger and bigger, high-flying tricks on a skateboard. It was such fun to watch. He fake-crashed and fell on the floor, and started yelling that he'd broken his back and was going to die. A nurse girl came running to his side from offstage. The crowd was in hysterics as P-Nut's character tried to get his Nerd nurse to sleep with him, instead of stop the bleeding. The actual P-Nut thought it was hilarious and he applauded louder than the rest of the audience.

Sometime during that scene, Bart had let go of Lucy's hand. He'd put his arm around her instead, and now they were nestled up next to each other. She was crying from laughing so hard. Bart kept whipping his finger at the stage.

"Awww!" he said. "They got you, P-Nut! They got you!"

It was the first time Lucy had seen Bart this animated; he was usually so subdued. But everyone was caught up in it now. The crowd had tipped. There was a fever in the air. Gang lines had kept everyone on guard and frustrated for so long under Sam's rule that now that there was permission to laugh, it was like a tidal wave.

And that was just in time for Leonard's big stage debut. Lucy couldn't have been prouder. Dork Baloney was visiting the Freaks, and Leonard was playing Bobby. Because the Freaks had notoriously dyed their hair with blue toilet cleaner pucks, Leonard wore a giant papier-mâché urinal like a mascot would. His face barely poked out of a face hole. The urinal even had blue liquid by the drain. To Lucy's surprise, Leonard had a shockingly strong stage voice. He hammed it up as Bobby. He was a natural. Everyone cheered his performance. Everyone, except for the real Bobby.

Bobby stood up in the crowd. "I'll kill you, Geeks! All of you! You know that!"

The audience booed Bobby. Zachary never broke character, neither did Leonard. They never acknowledged Bobby at all, and it only made the crowd love it more. When Zachary's character moved on to the gym and Leonard exited the stage, Bobby's big moment was over. The more he protested, the more the crowd turned against him, until his fellow Freaks had to pull him down into his seat.

A Geek girl walked out onstage swinging her purse in a circle and smacking her jaw open and shut like she was chewing gum. She wore a blonde wig and a white dress and when she started telling boys in the front row that a blow job would cost them a sandwich, Lucy couldn't control herself. She knew who it was.

"Hooker Hilary!" Lucy said, way too loud.

Bart cringed with a laugh. "Oh, boy. We got a live one."

Lucy cackled. She knew it might lead to trouble, leading the crowd on this one, but Hilary deserved it. Sam had gotten his comeuppance for what he'd done, but somehow, so far, Hilary had managed to get off, unscathed. A laugh at her expense was the least Lucy could do.

Hilary stood up in a huff, like Bobby did. She was in the front row with a bunch of Pretty Ones. She was livid.

"I refuse to sit through this trash!" she shrieked.

"Then get the hell out!" Lucy shouted at her, and others in the crowd echoed her.

Hilary glared at Lucy with pure hatred. Lucy was unbothered.

"What are you looking at?" Lucy said, leaning forward in her seat.

Hilary sneered at Lucy, then widened her gaze to all the kids shouting at her. She looked uncharictaristically rattled. Lucy wasn't sure she had seen her blush before. She started pushing through her row in a huff. A string of Pretty Ones trailed her. As they reached the aisle and hurried for the exit, people whistled at them and shouted catcalls. They looked miserable, but Lucy didn't feel an ounce of compassion for the other girls. This was the life they'd chosen. If they didn't like what it had amounted to, then too bad.

"You're a wild one," Bart said with a grin.

Lucy fixed Bart with a charged stare.

"What?" he said.

Nobody had ever said that to her before. And she liked it. She planted a heavy kiss on him.

"Yee-ha!" somebody shouted from a few rows back. She had

a pretty good idea who it was. Raunch. "Get it on, girl!"

Lucy laughed through her tongue dance with Bart. Her whole gang must have been watching her now, maybe others too. It was a rush. She pushed Bart down in his seat, then hopped over the armrest into his lap, facing him. She straddled him like he was a horse and looked over to her gang. She threw up a fist.

"WHOO!" Lucy shouted back. They threw up fists and cheered for her while the play continued on stage.

Lucy leaned down and kissed Bart more. He couldn't have been happier. They made out for the rest of the play. It felt crazy just putting on a show for everybody around, but she was tired of being the prude all the time. Besides, Will seemed to be having a PDA marathon all over the school, so why should she hold herself back?

When the play ended and the lights came on, people got up from their seats and started to mill about the auditorium. Lucy and Bart didn't move. They were in their own little world. She wanted to stay close to him. There, on his lap. He couldn't look away from her. The stage lights sparkled in his eyes. He smiled his perfect smile. She wanted him. It was decided in a moment. Naturally. Just like Violent had said it would be. Bart was the one. He'd be her first.

Someone whispered in her ear.

"Make him wait."

Lucy turned and looked over to see Violent. Already moving

on. She couldn't see Violent's face. It made her anxious. She didn't understand.

"What do you want to do now?" Bart said.

Lucy looked back at Bart. He had a mellow grin.

"Uh . . . "

28

WILL WOKE UP WITH ANOTHER CRUEL HEAD-
ache. He felt like someone had spent the night standing over
him and beating his face with a rake. It probably wasn't the
best idea to mix booze with his medication, but he wasn't
dead yet. It had been three weeks of this, something like that,
partying day in and day out. In the mornings, it felt like it had
been three years. Each night, once the alcohol hit his system,
he felt ready to do it all over again. By then, the morning misery was long forgotten. Being bros with Gates was a full-time
job.

With bleary eyes, Will lifted his head and charted his sur-
roundings. He was on his back, on the floor in front of Gates's
school bus. All around him was a terrible mess. It wasn't just
the wrecked bus stuck in the wall, or the rubble around it, it
was the week's worth of party waste that littered the floor.
Food was spilled everywhere. Twinkies with footprints in

them. Cold cuts that had been thrown on the wall and had stuck there. A huge puddle of milk that someone had poured over a pile of cigarette butts. Dirty dishes covered in a brown crust of microwaved burrito filling. A soda-soaked pair of boxer shorts. Crushed beer cans and plastic party cups were everywhere. A knocked-over television played a porno, and there were two gaming chairs in front of it, but no one there watching. A series of croquet wickets were duct-taped to the floor, with mallets and balls strewn around. Gates had designated one corner of the room the "smashing corner," and it was where they threw glass bottles when they were done with them. Breaking bottles had bored Gates pretty quickly and he'd encouraged the gang to start destroying other things. In addition to the piled-up broken glass, the smashing corner had an eviscerated beanbag chair, bent lacrosse sticks, a bashed-up bicycle with slashed tires, and a pinball machine that had been set on fire.

Will didn't know how he'd ended up on the floor. The last thing he could remember was blending up mudslides with Gates and some Freak girls. He had a vague flash of hooking up with one of the girls in the supply closet across the room, but then things got fuzzy. That was pretty standard these days.

"There you are."

Will sat up and saw Lark walking toward him from the hall of containment cells.

"I have to talk to you," she said. She looked too serious for Will to handle right now. His head was murdering him.

Poor Lark. She was cute and clever and she liked Will. A lot. It wasn't hard to tell.

"What's up?" Will said to her.

Lark sat down in front of him and took his hands.

"I'm here for you," she said.

"Okay . . . "

"And it's not even that bad. Really, it's for the best. It's high time you moved on."

Will felt a twinge of panic. "What are you trying to tell me?

Lark sighed, "I know how hung up on you are on that girl, Lucy. And I saw her last night at the Geek show. And I don't know, I just feel like you can do better. 'Cause, you know, sometimes it's easy to make too much, like way too much, about the past, when the future is literally wide open. Right in front of you—"

"Lark. What are you talking about? You said you saw Lucy."

"Yeah. At the Geek show. I think she's got a new boyfriend."

What was it with Lucy and making out with guys at Geek shows? Unbelievable. Even though it wasn't David this time, it still hurt. Last time this happened, Will ran away crying. He wasn't about to do that again. He had to go talk to her.

Will pulled on clean clothes in his room, and headed out into the hall of containment cells. He passed Sam's cell. Sam paced in his locked cell like a tiger at a zoo. He froze when he saw Will and charged the clear door. He spat on the thick plastic between them.

"I'm gonna kill you," Sam shouted. Will could only read his lips; no sound passed through the door.

Will ignored him and continued on toward the closed metal door to the white room. Sam continued to beat on his cell door. The air in this hall had never lost a pungent chemical smell, and it made Will feel more ill than he already did. Will hit the red door button on the wall, and the door to the white room slid open, disappearing into the wall.

The white room was a pool of two-foot-deep water. A folding table had been laid on its side and duct-taped against the other side of the doorway, and towels had been stuffed under it to keep the water from flowing out. Another table sealed up the doorway to McKinley on the other side of the white room. The water's surface reflected the bright ceiling and the white tiled walls. Water poured down in continuous streams from the eight hoses of the sprayer contraption on the ceiling. Saint boys and girls in their underwear cavorted in the water. Some floated around on inflatable mattresses. Gates and Pruitt stood in the middle of the room. Gates wore mirrored aviator sunglasses that shined with the same bright white of the rest of the room. He was shirtless and he'd cut his pinstripe suit slacks into board shorts. A tie was wrapped around his head like a headband, with the knot off to the side.

Pruitt was the only person who was fully clothed, with his trousers rolled up above his knees. He had his giant hands on his hips, and loomed over Gates.

"Why do we have to talk about this now, Pru?" Gates said. "Can't it wait till, like, a group powwow or something?"

"Dude, we haven't had a powwow in I don't know how long. When's the last time we even all ate together?"

"I don't know."

"Months. Since before we got Sam. No matter what was going on, we used to all at least gather around the campfire and say what's on our mind."

"What do we need a campfire for? The lights are on."

"You know what I mean," Pruitt said.

It was weird seeing Pruitt upset. He never talked this much. But it was a big enough event to keep Gates occupied, and that was what Will needed. He'd never get to the cafeteria if he got sucked into Gates's orbit. Will pulled off his shoes and socks and rolled up his jeans to his knees.

"Party pooper," Gates said to Pruitt.

Pruitt poked Gates with a fat finger. "I don't have a problem with having fun, I got a problem when there's no time for anything else."

Will stepped over the table dam and into the pool, hoping to walk out unnoticed, but Gates saw him right away.

"There's the guy! Get over here, Will! Isn't the water great?"

The water was freezing cold against Will's skin.

"Pretty great," Will said.

Gates walked toward Will.

Pruitt threw up his hands. "So, is that it? I'm just supposed to walk away now?"

Gates ignored Pruitt, keeping his eyes on Will. Will sloshed toward the school. He couldn't get cornered.

"I'm heading out," Will said. "Be back in a bit."

Will sped up a little, the drag of the knee-high water was slowing his stride.

"Where you going?" Gates said, sloshing through the water to meet Will in the middle of the room.

"I . . . just need some air."

Gates got in Will's way, and Will had to stop. Meanwhile, Pruitt tromped back into the processing facility.

"Hold up. I forgot to tell you. There's these three Pretty Ones I met. They want to party with us tonight." Gates slapped Will's chest. "They're jonesing for a little more Gates and Will."

Will laughed. "I'm gonna pass."

"You hear what I'm saying, right? They want to party. They're sure things. And they're hot."

"I'm not really in the mood tonight."

Gates looked annoyed for a moment, but he shook it off with a smile.

"Yeah," he said. "You're right. Girls can wait. Some other night. What should we do instead? Want to go break some windows?"

"Uh . . . not really."

"Yeah, that sucks," Gates said, then gasped. His eyes lit up. "Forget it—I got it! There's still a little gas left in the motorcycle, let's take it on one final joyride through the halls, let every gang hear it fuckin' rumble. Whattaya say?"

"I just—"

"Then, we torch it. You'd love that."

Will snapped. "I don't want to right now! All right? Will you let me go?"

Gates said nothing. Will thought Gates was staring at him, but all Will could see was the dual reflections of his own frustrated face in the lenses of Gates's shades. The pause went from awkwardly long, to crawl out of your skin long, but then Gates raised his hands in the air and stepped out of Will's way.

"Do whatever you want, I don't care," Gates said.

The room had gone quiet again. Will couldn't get a read on whether it was okay with Gates that he was leaving or not.

"All right. Later," Will said.

He kept his eyes forward, and walked the last few feet to the steel doors to McKinley, then stepped over the table dam. Will continued on, into McKinley's front foyer. The leakage from the white room had spread into a giant puddle that covered most of the foyer's burned and warped floor. He heard the party ramp back up behind him.

"Oh shit!" he heard Gates say from the white room. "We should ask for a shark!"

29

"I'M HERE TO SEE LUCY."

A Slut with long, red feather earrings sneered back at Will through the cracked-open door to the cafeteria. She looked at him like he was a homeless man trying to wander into her art gallery.

"She's not here."

"I don't believe you," Will said.

"Go away," the Slut said, and started to close the door. Will stopped the door with his foot and leaned against it. The Slut grimaced as she pushed harder.

"What do you want?" Will said to the Slut.

"What?"

"From the parents. What do you want me to get for you?" Will said.

The Slut didn't hesitate. "A teepee. Twelve footer," she said.

Will wrinkled his brow, "All right . . . weirdo. I'll make it happen."

"You better not be lying."

"I'm sure you'll kill me if I am. Just let me in."

The Slut stepped back from the door and opened it for him. Will walked into the cafeteria. He didn't get more than three steps before a bunch of Sluts had him pressed against the wall and were going through his pockets.

Out came his weapons. A Swiss Army Knife, with five blades, that Gates had gotten him. His new Maglite. The chain he kept wrapped around his forearm to make his punches heavier. The brand-new hatchet he kept stuffed in the back of his pants. They even found the razor blade he kept taped under his belt.

"I'm gonna need all of that back."

"Depends if you behave yourself or not," a big Slut said, and gave him a cheap slap in the crotch. Will winced. He would have fought back but he couldn't screw up his chance to see Lucy.

They shoved him forward. He couldn't believe how clean it was in the cafeteria. They walked him through a door on the other side of the dining room. Will knew the Sluts had claimed a full hallway of classrooms off the cafeteria, including a small student lounge, but he'd never been inside.

They led him into the triangle-shaped lounge. All of the

plastic covers over the fluorescent tube lights in the ceiling were transparent red. The light they gave off was so dim Will had to work to see people's faces. He felt as if they were all at the bottom of a glass of red wine. Sluts lounged in well-preserved, plushy love seats and cushioned chairs that populated the space. Any of them could have been Lucy in the deep red of the room.

Seven angry girls, all with pale skin and dark lips and thin eyebrows that slanted down toward the bridges of their noses, followed him as he walked. He passed pretty girls who seemed dead inside. Some of the girls had dates, guys interspersed in the group. Will peered at the dudes. Some ignored him, others casually tried to hide their faces, and then there were the ones that scowled at him until he continued walking past their girl, then they went back to not caring. A skinny girl with a red bob growled at him like she wanted to kill him. A Slut with black lipstick and a train track of gold safety pins pierced through her left eyebrow screwed up her face at Will and flipped him off. He didn't let any of it shake him. He was a man on a mission.

"Will?"

There she was, in the red, lying on her side on a sofa, her body twisted away from Will. He had to squint. She was wearing a shirt that was hardly a shirt. It draped too loosely on her, threatening to show too much. She wore a pair of sweat shorts that stubbornly refused to cover the bottom of her butt.

That kid, Bart, was lying next to her. He had his stupid arm around her, and she looked cozy as hell all nestled into his side, except for her face, which was stiff with shock. She sat up and straightened her shirt. Bart kept his hold on her.

"What are you doing here?" Lucy said.

"Can we go somewhere and talk?" Will said.

Lucy looked to Bart, concerned. "I'm kinda in the middle of something."

Will wanted to explode.

"Please, I really need to talk to you."

Lucy opened her mouth, but no sound came out. Will stayed patient.

"Will . . . what else is there to say?"

"I love you."

Lucy stared at Will. Bart started laughing.

Will ignored Bart and pushed on. "Listen, we had a string of really shitty luck and it ended badly, and that sucks. But I want to take care of you and I'll do whatever it takes to get you back in my life."

Through the heavy red light, he saw a hopeful little smile bloom on her face for just a second. And then she looked at the other Sluts around her and dropped it.

"Oh god," Bart said. "That was so lame."

"Fuck you, Nerd."

Bart laughed again, harder than before. It was the most annoying laugh Will had ever heard.

"Will, I think you should leave," Lucy said.

"Lucy, it's me," Will said, and he touched her arm.

As soon as he touched her, Sluts converged on him. In a few simple, strong moves, they ripped Will's hand free of Lucy and wrenched his arms behind his back. He strained and twisted against their grip.

"Get off me," he said through gritted teeth.

They pulled Will away from Lucy. She stood, but didn't stop them. She didn't care.

The Sluts lifted him off of his feet and carried him like they were going to use him for a battering ram. He would have screamed if they hadn't brought their knives to his throat so quickly.

They carried him out of the lounge, through the cafeteria, and sure enough, opened the door with his head. They threw him out into the hall. His weapons were tossed out after him. He landed on the floor, next to a pile of trash bags that leaked a puddle of red onto the floor.

30

"I GOTTA GO TO THE BATHROOM," GATES SAID
to Will, in a hallway near Freak territory.

That sounded great by Will. Will could use a break from the
guy, even a short one. He'd been hanging with Gates nonstop
since Lucy shut him down. He was exhausted, and Gates was
beginning to grate on his nerves.

"Go for it," Will said. "I think there's a bathroom up there to
the right."

Gates paused.

"Actually, you want to come?"

Will stared in disbelief. Gates wasn't kidding. It never ended.

"No, I'm good," Will said.

Gates frowned. "Are you sure?"

"I'm good. I already went."

"I don't remember you going."

"Well . . . I did," Will said.

Gates narrowed his eyes at him.

"What," Will said. "You don't believe me?"

Gates pursed his lips, and stared at Will until the awkwardness was painful. Will prayed for him to leave.

"Yeah, okay," he said. "Maybe I just didn't notice or—yeah, you know what? I'll go later. Let's keep looking for it."

Will sighed, and the two of them continued their search, poking their heads into classrooms that they had no business looking into. Will carried a six-pack of canned beer in one hand and an extension cord lasso in the other. Gates held a spear made from a whittled wooden flagpole.

"This is where that Freak girl said she saw it?" Gates asked.

Will nodded. "Yep. Second floor. Near room 213."

"Soo-ey," Gates yelled. "Soo-ey! Here, piggy piggy."

Will stood in silence, watching Gates as he snorted like a pig. He didn't know if he wanted to laugh or cry. Gates could be super fun, but Will just couldn't keep up anymore. Nobody could.

Will tossed his empty and cracked another beer. He'd already thrown up once that night, but he'd kept drinking. Gates was easier to take when Will was drunk, and so was the crushing pain of missing Lucy.

"When's the last time you saw the hog anyway?" Will said.

"I don't know," Gates said. "The party?"

"Which one?" Will said, but he didn't really care.

"The first one, buddy. The best one, our pizza party. Come on!"

"Oh, yeah," Will said. There was no hiding the boredom in his voice.

"What the hell's the matter with you?"

Will shrugged.

"Please tell me you're not still obsessing about Lucy, man. She's ruining your life. I told you to keep away from her, didn't I? How many times are you gonna let her treat you like dirt?"

"I don't want to talk about it," Will said.

"Well, I do. This is my life too. And she's ruining it 'cause if you're in a bad place, then that brings me down."

"I'm fine."

"I'm fine," Gates mimicked Will with a slack jaw and a dead voice.

"What are we gonna do when we find this thing?" Will said, trying to shift gears back to the hog.

"I just want it back," Gates said with a twinge of annoyance. "It belongs to me. It's my pet. Why should somebody else get it?"

"Because you let it go in the first place."

"Hey," Gates said and bashed his spear into the nearest locker for effect. "If you were gonna be like this, then why'd you come along?"

Will had the urge to tell Gates off, but Gates was acting so odd that he felt a twinge of fear as to what would happen if he did.

"Did you hear that?" Gates said, his annoyance morphing into excitement.

"Nope."

"Listen."

Will tuned into the silence, and then he did hear something. It was faint like the distant sound of someone scraping ice off a driveway, but deeper, darker, wetter.

Gates eyes went wide, and for a moment, Will felt a tickle of a thrill.

"Let's go," Gates said, hushed, and snuck forward.

They crept up on a darkened classroom. Will and Gates planted themselves on either side of the doorway and peered inside. Just from the stink, Will had a feeling this was a Freak dumping ground. One room to pile up all the nastiness and trash from two floors of turf until the Skaters got around to hauling it all to the dump. They'd gotten lax on their garbage business lately.

A loud snort blasted out of the darkness.

"Light it up," Gates whispered.

Will softly set down his beers and pulled his Maglite from the back pocket of his jeans. He clicked it on and pointed it into the room. The beam slipped across piles of filth, some as high as four or five feet. A miniature landscape of deflated garbage bags, wet clothes, and rotting food.

"There!" Gates said, still whispering. "Go back."

Will traced the beam back between two mounds of black garbage bags and he saw it. "Oh god," Will said, holding the beam in place over the massive hind region of the hog. It was on its side and its head lay flat on the floor.

Thick, coarse hair. Black. Stiff. It covered the hog's entire body. Long white whiskers angled off its rumpled, bucket-ended snout, which glistened in the beam of Will's flashlight.

"What's wrong with it?" Will said.

"It's sleeping, I guess."

"Why is it sweating? Do hogs sweat?"

"I don't know," Gates said.

"It looks sick, man."

The hog snorted again, and it sounded like a belch of air from a clogged sink. Both Will and Gates jumped at the sound, then Gates started cracking up. He covered his mouth. The hog's breath was fast. Will felt like they should help it, but he didn't know how to even start. He and Gates just stared at it like it was the engine of a broken-down car.

Will trailed his light across its muscled bulk. It had to be three hundred pounds. Its long thin tail waggled violently. He shined his spotlight on the tail. It was still, then flailed around with more spastic jerks. Its ass bulged.

"Oh, motherf—" Will said.

Around a dark hole in its rear end, a donut of flesh pushed out.

"The thing's gonna have the shits all over the place!" Gates said.

The hog farted, and the slimy head of a piglet popped out. It stayed there a moment, wearing its mother's body as a turtleneck. Then the rest of the piglet's slick sausagelike body slid out. It landed on the concrete floor. Its flesh was pinkish where it wasn't black, and the pink skin looked see-through, like raw chicken breast. Its snout was short and stubby, and it writhed on its side.

Gates had reached out and grabbed Will's arm for impact. Both of them stared with their mouths wide open and their jaws jutted out.

The piglet's little slimy eyes opened. The mama hog roared. It was a horrible sound somewhere between a lion's roar and a volcano with bronchitis. Will flinched. His flashlight beam seesawed. When he tilted the beam back onto the hog, he nearly fell over.

She was looking right at him.

Her long, heavy-boned head was craned just far enough over that she could stare at Will out of the corner of her right eye. She had eyelashes. Soft brown ones. And the white of her eye was prominent from this angle, a crescent of brilliant white. It made her eye look entirely human. A woman's eye in the head of a pig.

The sight of it made Will's stomach lurch, and he took off

running. He got all the way around the corner to the next hall before Gates caught up with him. He was dying laughing.

"Ho-lee shit . . . ," Gates said, "have you ever seen anything like that before?!"

Will shook his head. He was trying to forget about it. It all seemed so wrong. That thing didn't belong in here. Those little things didn't deserve to be born in this place. But they were here because of Gates and Will.

"We gotta go back," Gates said.

"What, why?"

"Those are my little piggies!" Gates laughed, and Will recoiled. "I betcha there's like eight of 'em coming. Dude, we could train 'em, like attack dogs. Attack hogs! How badass would that be? You mess with me, you mess with my hogs!"

"Just leave 'em be. You shouldn't mess with its babies. Everything's not here for your amusement, okay?" Will said.

Gates's face drooped like he'd been the birthday boy and Will had just popped all his balloons. Will didn't care though, he'd had enough Gates for today. All this partying and thrill-seeking, it wasn't working anymore. He felt like he needed to sleep for a week just to think straight again.

"Fine," Gates said. "Be a little bitch about it."

"Whatever dude, I'm heading back."

Will turned and strolled down the hall. He didn't hear anything from Gates behind him. *Let him stay here and stare at his piglets,* Will thought. And that sounded like what he was going to do, but then Gates piped up again, and Will died a little inside.

"Wait up, we'll go together."

31

LUCY WAS GOING TO SLEEP WITH BART.

Lucy and Violent walked up the stairs to the library. The
only noise was the jangle of Violent's necklace made of sharpened cafeteria cutlery. They'd done this walk before, under
crazier circumstances, on their way to the ruins, when David
was dying by the minute. It had all gone wrong in the library.

Lucy didn't anticipate Bart to be some rape-crazy maniac,
but Violent's intention had always been that Lucy feel over-
prepared for the moment. And Lucy was definitely that. She
had five condoms so Bart couldn't pull any lame excuses. She'd
been practicing her scary voice every morning with Sophia,
so things didn't have to get physical if he tried anything she
didn't like. And if he did, Lips taught her eight different ways
to hit a guy in the nuts. Raunch gave her a pouch of salt in her
pocket to throw in Bart's eyes if things got out of hand. And if
worse came to worse, she had her blade to cut him from neck

to nuts, to use one of Violent's more quotable phrases.

"I feel like you're my mom dropping me off at the mall for the first time," Lucy said. "You really didn't have to walk me."

"I didn't have to, I wanted to."

It made Lucy smile a little.

"Really?"

Violent nodded.

"Thanks," Lucy said, and they walked the last flight up in silence.

"I heard some shit went down with Will in the lounge," Violent said when they reached the third floor.

Lucy blushed. "That'll never happen again—"

"That's not what I'm saying. I heard he said he loved you?"

"Yeah, he said that. So?" Lucy said. She could feel her stomach cramp with anxiety. She got tense every time she thought about that day. Will had a bad habit of hitting her with huge emotional bombshells that put her on the defensive. She resented how vulnerable he could make her feel.

"Do you love him?" Violent said.

Lucy couldn't believe she was hearing these words out of Violent.

"Is this another test?" Lucy said. "I can never tell when you're messing with me."

"Not a test. I'm just saying from experience, love is scary shit. I ran from it, and I don't feel any better for it. I wouldn't want you to make the same mistake."

"I don't love him," Lucy said. She straightened as she did, and she faced the door ahead. "Now, are you done being a pain in my ass, or should we go find a couch somewhere and talk about our feelings all night?"

Lucy held on to her warrior face until Violent smiled.

"All right, pincushion . . . ," she said as she headed back down the hall. "Go get yourself stuck."

The fire door opened. Belinda stood in the doorway. She wore a gray sweater and khakis, her curly hair was black now and shoulder length. She'd put a little weight back on, but it suited her.

"Ahhhhhh!" Belinda squealed at the top of her lungs, with her arms spread out like she was trying to catch a beach ball. Lucy squealed too, by automatic girl reflex.

They hugged and Belinda pulled her inside. "I can't believe you're here," she said.

"Me neither. It's so good to see you, Bel!"

"Look at your red hair! You are such a badass now."

Lucy laughed. "No, I'm not. Come on."

"No, but, you are. Have you looked in a mirror? I'm not the only one that thinks so either. I ran into Mort and Ritchie at the market, and, like, we were, like, all talking about how none of us ever saw this coming. You better watch out, I think Ritchie might ask you out."

"What? No way. Ritchie?"

"Uh huh, he, like . . . couldn't stop talking about how you look," Belinda said, nodding.

"Weird."

"Totally."

They struggled through an awkward pause. Lucy had done so much living in the past few months that Belinda knew nothing about, and Lucy was sure the same was true of Belinda.

"I think about the Stairs sometimes," Belinda said, her voice tinged with emotion. "But there's nobody here that can relate, so I just keep it to myself."

"Me too." Lucy nodded. She understood. But she didn't want to think about what they couldn't get back. "So, where's your guy?"

"I'll introduce you."

Belinda led Lucy down a long book-lined aisle where books were replaced by bedding on each double-wide shelf. She wondered what kind of Nerds slept in which section.

"He's right there." Belinda pointed to a boy standing in a circle of other Nerds. "Isn't he so adorable?"

Lucy looked the boy over. He was a little chubby around the face. No hint of an ability to grow facial hair. While the other boys talked, he stared up and to the side, like he was lost in thought. His mouth kept flirting with a grin. His shirt was on inside out and his sneakers were so worn out, they looked like mummy feet. He stood with his hips forward and his stomach out, and let his arms hang straight down at his sides. His fingers fluttered like he was playing piano.

"Definitely adorable," Lucy said, for Belinda's benefit.

"Freddy-bear!" Belinda said.

Freddy came trotting over and planted a big clumsy kiss on Belinda's cheek.

"Hi! I'm Freddy Golden," he said with a friendly smile. He shoved his hand out, fingers splayed. Lucy shook his hand.

"Hi Freddy," Lucy said. "I'm Lucy."

"Cupcakes here talks about you all the time," Freddy said.

Freddy went behind Belinda, put his arms around her, and slid his hands into her front pockets. He rested his chin on her shoulder. Lucy liked him immediately.

"Aw. Well, I miss her a lot too," Lucy said to Belinda. "Cupcakes, huh?"

Belinda blushed. "He calls me that."

Freddy blew gently on Belinda's neck. He whispered something in her ear, and Belinda blushed and giggled.

"Do you want to do puzzles with us?" Freddy said to Lucy.

"No, she's got other plans, Freddy," Belinda said.

"Oh, right," Freddy said, then flared his nostrils with an immense smile. "Bart's waiting for you at the information desk."

"I'll walk you over there," Belinda said.

"Don't be gone too long, Cupcakes," Freddy said.

Even as Belinda tried to walk away, they still held hands, like lovers at a train station. He pulled her close again, gave her a final squeeze and nuzzled her neck, before letting Belinda and Lucy walk away. It was beyond sweet.

"I think he's great," Lucy said as she hooked her arm through Belinda's.

"I think we're soul mates," Belinda said.

Lucy placed her palm to her chest. She was genuinely touched by Belinda's happiness. She'd never seen her friend look more uninhibited or comfortable in her own skin. And soul mate. No one in the Sluts even said words like soul mate. "You're a lucky girl, Bel."

"What about you?" Belinda said.

"Hmm?"

"Bart! He is sooo cute," Belinda said.

"He is. I don't know if he's my soul mate though," Lucy said. She was surprised by how gruff her own tone sounded, but Belinda was kind and smiled anyway.

They stepped into the expanse of the library's main room. It was well-lit and quiet, like Lucy remembered it before everything went crazy last time. She couldn't help but carry the tension of the old ambush with her in every step she took. Thankfully, she felt like she could handle herself more with every Nerd she passed. In her red, scoop-neck shirt, with slashes in it that showed peeks of her black bra, and her skin-tight black jeans, she was dressed more confidently and provocatively than anyone around her. Every Nerd watched her closely, some with curiosity, some with fear. It made her grin.

"Lucy?" Belinda said.

"Yeah?"

"I just wanted to say, maybe he's not your soul mate, but I'm really glad you found someone that you care about with Bart. I know how hard it was for you to lose David. You more than anybody," Belinda said, then paused. "Except Will, I guess."

"Thanks," Lucy said, but she felt that same queasy feeling in her stomach again at the sound of Will's name. Why did people have to keep bringing up Will? She didn't want to think about him right now. And hearing it out loud, she was even uncomfortable with the idea that she had "found someone" in Bart. Her thing with Bart was casual, just for fun, and that's why she liked him. He was relaxed, and lightweight. She still thought of that moment where they stood by the bonfire that first night together. She had her girls around her, she was having fun, the heat of the fire was warming her body, and Bart was smiling at her. It was a moment where anything seemed possible, and everything seemed simple. Then Will tore across the quad in a motorcycle and complicated things. She'd been trying to get back to that bonfire moment with Bart ever since, but Will kept getting in the way.

Lucy saw Bart. He was sitting on top of the librarian's circular information desk, sketching on graph paper. She felt more relaxed at the sight of him.

"Ding-dong," Lucy said.

He looked up and smiled. "Check it out," he said and held up his drawing. It was a scribbly ballpoint pen drawing of Bart driving a speedboat, with a bikini girl water-skiing behind it.

"Fun. Is that me?" Lucy said, pointing to the bikini girl.

"Let's say yes," he said.

"Jerk," she said with a smile.

Belinda said good-bye, and Bart showed her more of his drawings. They were all of Bart, and he was always doing something impressive in them, like punching a hole through a wall, or turning into a werewolf. Her favorite was a drawing of a 747 jet with his smiling face where the cockpit should have been. He'd pulled some books for her as well, and he showed her some of his favorite jets of all time. He gave her a tour of the library, and it helped Lucy to see it as his home rather than a battleground. They joked around, flirted, and talked for a long time, until most of the Nerds were heading off to sleep.

"Wanna see something cool?" Bart said after a while.

Lucy nodded, and he led her to a quiet study room. He closed the door behind them, and locked it. There was a sheet pinned up over the window so they could have total privacy. Bart opened a laptop. He showed her bunches of videos that the Nerds had stolen off of people's phones when they'd brought them to be serviced or loaded up with music at the Nerds's trading post. Bart told her that most of the time they left people's content alone, but every once and a while they'd come across something too good to pass up. And they'd have to save a copy.

He showed her a video compilation of people falling, tripping, and injuring themselves. It was pretty funny. He showed her a private video diary entry made by Bobby where he cried the whole time and talked about being misunderstood. He showed her a camera phone picture of P-Nut and a Skater girl in bed, P-Nut was smiling big with his arm around the girl. Then, Bart showed Lucy another photo of P-Nut in the same bed with a different girl. Then, about thirty more, all in the same bed, with a different girl each time and P-Nut always smiling the exact same way.

It was all funny stuff, but the whole time Lucy felt like she was working to get back to the energy she'd had at the Geek show. She didn't feel as wild as that night or the night of the bonfire. Thankfully, she didn't have to grapple with that too long before they finally started making out. That got her out of her head.

Bart took off Lucy's shirt. He cupped her breast and held it like it was a rare and delicate artifact. He started to kiss her neck passionately. His warm lips and wet tongue were all over her now. She groaned. It felt so good, and it turned her on to feel how much he wanted her now. He craved her. He was heating up. This was a moment she'd been fantasizing about. It was about to happen.

Bart unbuttoned her jeans. He reached inside and slid his hand down between her legs. She clamped her thighs together; no one had ever touched her that close.

"It's okay," he said.

But it suddenly wasn't. She felt queasy. She couldn't relax. Something was off, and she didn't know what.

She pulled away to look him in the eyes.

"Does this mean anything to you?" she said.

"Yeah, it feels so good," he said in a low, smooth voice. His hand was still.

"No, I'm saying . . . do I mean anything to you?"

He blinked and furrowed his brow, like she had just asked him a riddle.

"I think you're cool, and . . . I've been having fun hanging out."

"But, do you have feelings for me?"

"Um . . . "

Lucy pulled his hand out of her pants.

"Bart, I don't think I can do this."

"Why not?"

"'Cause . . . I don't love you."

"Well, I don't love you either; what's the problem?"

"I think . . . I would need to love someone to sleep with them."

Bart looked confused. "I think you're in the wrong gang," he said.

"I'm gonna go."

Lucy stood and pulled her shirt back on.

"No, stay. We can get back on track. This was just a speed bump."

"I don't think so," she said. "It's not going to work out with us."

She walked to the door, opened it, and stepped into the main room library. Lucy headed for the exit.

"Wait, Lucy," Bart said from behind her.

She paused and looked back at him. He was standing in the doorway of the study room, his belt undone.

"Do you think Sophia would be into me?"

She didn't answer. She didn't want to see Bart ever again.

Lucy hurried across the library floor. The whole place was quiet. When she got to the exit, she had to shake the shoulder of the Nerd girl who was supposed to be keeping watch over the fire door. The girl had dumpy black hair and snot trails encrusted above her upper lip, and a T-shirt that was too small for her thick body. She'd been sound asleep. It was a miracle she hadn't fallen off her stool yet. The girl's eyes barely opened.

"I want out," Lucy said.

The girl unlocked the door and pulled it open like a zombie. She may not have ever really woken up as she let Lucy walk through and shut the door behind her. Things never went well for her in the library.

Lucy headed down the stairs. With every step down, she felt more confused. What the hell had happened up there? She felt oddly proud of herself for not going through with it, but she was still kind of turned on. Lucy thought back to that couple she and Will had seen the day of Kemper's graduation. The scene played so passionately in her mind. She'd imagined that the couple's connection was so deep, but maybe all they'd been were desperate strangers just trying to cope with life in McKinley. By the time she reached the second floor, Lucy felt naive, like her innocence was nothing she could shake, no matter how long she hung out with the Sluts. Violent had told her to be smart about her choices, but Violent had said it full of regret about her own past, almost as if she and the Sluts were a different breed and Lucy was someone they were simply corrupting.

Lucy stepped out of the stairwell into a first floor hall. She walked close to the lockers, moving at a good clip, until she turned a corner and saw a girl rummaging through an open locker. Lucy slowed. The girl pulled her head out of the locker. It was Hilary.

Lucy froze in place, still in shadow. Hilary went back in for more. Lucy had never seen her like this, down on her knees, clawing through a locker like a Dumpster diver. Rumors about what had gone down in Hilary's private meeting with P-Nut had been getting wilder and wilder since the Geek show, but it looked like the gossip must have finally taken its toll. When Lucy had been a Pretty One, Hilary would make her and the other girls walk as a group to different lockers throughout the school. It was usually after Hilary and Sam had a big blow-out, and Sam wanted her to be nice to him again. He'd give Hilary a locker number and a combination, and inside he would leave her presents. They all had to *ooh* and *ahh* to make Hilary feel good about what Sam had given her.

Lucy stared at Hilary, and the fog of doubt from her walk down the stairs burned away. Mocking her at the Geek show wasn't enough. Hilary had tried to starve Lucy out, she'd made the other Pretty Ones shun her, she'd kicked her out of the gang for disobeying and had encouraged Varsity guys like Brad to go after her, and he would have raped her if David hadn't done what he did. And even after Hilary had done all that, she'd stabbed out her boyfriend's eye. But, now things were different. Hilary didn't have Sam anymore to protect her, and she didn't have any Pretty Ones with her either. She was all skinny and alone, scavenging one of Sam's old stashes. For anybody else, that wasn't so bad. For Hilary, this was rock bottom.

Maybe this date was going to have a happy ending after all.

"Wow. This is just sad," Lucy said.

Hilary looked up and saw Lucy. She looked surprised at first, but not scared like Lucy had hoped for. In fact, she didn't look scared at all.

"I'm gonna enjoy this," Lucy said, cracking her knuckles.

Fifteen Pretty Ones ran into the hall from a classroom.

"Are you?" Hilary said.

Lucy realized too late that she'd made a horrible mistake. She tried to run, but they tackled Lucy to the ground. They sat on her chest and they slapped her face. They dug their nails into her skin, they slashed her with them, they drew red lines all over her body with their sharp claws, and they kicked her ribs and stomach. Lucy was bruised, bleeding from countless little cuts by the time they finished. Hilary stood over Lucy, keeping her distance as if she was disgusted by Lucy's existence.

"She's so ugly now," Hilary said. "Remember when she used to be pretty?"

The Pretty Ones laughed.

"I like her hair though," another Pretty One said.

"Ooh, that is a nice shade of red," Hilary said. "I want it."

They grabbed her head. One of them pulled out a knife. She tried to stop them, but there were too many. They yanked at her hair, and gathered it into a ponytail at the back of her head. With a sawing motion, the one with the knife cut Lucy's ponytail off. They shoved Lucy's head down and the back of her skull cracked into the floor. She could feel the ends of her new, shorter hair tickling the backside of her jaw.

Hilary took the ten-inch long clump of Lucy's red hair from the other Pretty One. She pulled a pink hair band off her wrist and looped it around the base of the ponytail, then dangled it over Lucy's face.

"Thanks, Slut. I think I'll turn it into a toilet brush," Hilary said. "Let's go, girls."

Hilary and her crew walked off down the hall. They left Lucy squirming on the floor. Just when she'd thought she couldn't get any lower, she realized that she was going to have to go back to the cafeteria, face her gang, and admit that she hadn't been attacked by burnouts or Freaks . . . she'd had her ass handed to her by a bunch of Pretty Ones.

Some Slut she was.

32

THE BLOWING WIND WAS COOL AGAINST THE
spit that ran down Sam's arms. The people who used to quake
before him, they spat on him now. They cheered when Gates
threw him around like a bag of books. They blamed him. They
thought everything that had happened after the quarantine
was his fault. Idiots. For the past few food drops, Gates had
brought Sam to the quad for show, but this was the first time
Gates hadn't bothered to blindfold him. This time, he got to
see all the faces of the people who hated him, he got to see
their glee at seeing him demoralized. He was a punching bag,
a prop, a trophy.

Saints held his arms, which were bound behind him with
duct tape. His mouth was gagged. Sam stared at the ground.
He didn't want to look up, he couldn't bear it. His father was
up there, witnessing every second of Sam's failure.

TOTAL DOMINATION.

That was his father's favorite phrase. He'd shout it at Sam during their father-son training sessions at five a.m. They'd start with an hour of strength and conditioning in the basement. Then it was immediately on to a liquid breakfast, his father's creation: veggies, protein powder, a mix of seven carefully chosen powdered sports supplements, water, a cup of Pedialyte, and a teaspoon of vinegar. Sam had never touched fast food until he'd started dating Hilary. He was his father's science project. His perfect athlete.

Dominate! Dominate! his dad would yell from the bleachers on game day. Sam could remember seeing how uncomfortable it made the other parents around his father. He could remember how it made him feel, hearing it when he was on the field, in the huddle, his father screaming when no one else was making any noise. Nobody else could understand his father's disgust with imperfection. But Sam had been raised under it. His dad didn't just need Sam to win, he needed him to do something new that no one had ever seen, every game. And almost every game, Sam couldn't do it.

When he would return home, there would be no love. His father would shun him after a loss. It was guaranteed he wouldn't acknowledge Sam's existence for at least a day. And every flaw spotted brought a punishment with it. He might take away Sam's bed for a week and make him sleep on the floor. He'd take away his computer, or put all the TVs in the house in storage until Sam got another win. He lived by his dad's rules, down to the detail, to get an occasional nod from his father, or a rare smile. The guy didn't love him, not as far as Sam could tell. He loved the win, and he loved when Sam didn't get in the way of that happening.

Sam could only imagine what his father thought when he looked down at the quad. It killed him that his father had never had the chance to see what he'd built with Varsity. Instead, all he got to see was his son as a hopeless victim.

Gates was in the center of the quad, stalking around the pile of food and supplies. The pile was about a third of the size as usual, and it was mostly comprised of something Sam hadn't seen in almost two years. Fresh vegetables. Squash, spinach, green beans, and lettuce.

"What the hell is this?" Gates shouted up to the sky.

Gates walked over to the pile and kicked over a crate. Deep green cucumbers spilled into the dirt.

"This isn't what we asked for!" Gates shouted up at Sam's father in the motorcycle helmet. "Where's the Tempur-Pedic mattresses I asked for? Huh? Where's the above-ground pool? I asked for two matching chain saws, where are they?!"

"We can't do this anymore," Sam's father's voice blared down from above. Sam knew that tone. His father was fed up, officially disgusted with Sam. He wasn't going to play along anymore. He'd decided Sam wasn't worth it.

Gates pointed at Sam. "Do I have to remind you what the score is again?"

Sam dared to look up. Other masked parents had appeared on the roofline. They moved toward Sam's father.

"Goddamnit, we've given you everything you wanted," Sam's father said. "This stops now. One of our men, a good man, died yesterday in Colorado Springs trying to get your precious above-ground pool. Killed by a pack of teens."

"Waaaah," Gates said, imitating a baby's cry.

"This has gone far enough, you little—"

His mom approached his father on the roof, sunlight glaring off her lilac helmet. She touched his arm, talking him down the way she always did when he got like this. Seeing her gentle way here, in McKinley, was too much for Sam to handle. Sam felt his eyes get hot, grow wet, and overflow. He was crying. Sam didn't cry, he hadn't cried since grade school. An easy breeze made the tear streams go icy on his cheeks.

"If you'd just give us another chance, we could all work together, and figure this out," Sam's mother said without amplification. Her voice was small and sounded far away.

"Oh, you want us to work now?" Gates said.

Gates pulled a yellow metal box cutter out of his pocket and held it up for Sam's mother to see. He extended the triangle of razor blade out of the box cutter's handle with a push of his thumb. Then he began to cross back toward Sam, box cutter in hand. Sam let out a fearful grunt that was muffled by the tape over his mouth. His legs shook uncontrollably. Sam knew

Gates was out of options, a message had to be sent, the only thing that would make an impression was to go to town on Sam like he'd never done before. Mutilation beyond recognition. It's what Sam would have done.

"No, Jason, don't!" Sam's mother shouted.

His father pushed his mother away, and she fell back. He flipped his motorcycle helmet visor up. He pulled a rifle up from the ground, and laid the long black barrel over the razor wire.

Instant screams erupted from the crowd, and people scattered. They ran for the exits.

The rifle cracked. Sam jumped. Dirt kicked up beside Gates's feet. Sam's father lifted the rifle for a reload. An empty casing ejected from the gun and spun down three floors to land in the quad.

"You stay away from my boy, you bastard!"

Never in his life had Sam heard his father express that sort of emotion about him. He stared up in shock as the Saints ran for cover, leaving Sam alone, unguarded. His father pulled the rifle butt up to his shoulder and leveled the sights at Gates.

"Run, boy!"

Sam didn't hesitate. He obeyed his father's command at once. It felt like old times. He took off, running as fast as he could with his hands bound behind him. Sam dodged. He weaved. His father kept firing. Nobody was trying to grab him, they were running for their lives. Sam worked his way through the chaotic crowd, and escaped into the hall. Every gunshot he heard told him how wrong he'd been.

His father loved him after all.

33

"CHECK THE CLOSET!" GATES SAID.

Will pulled open the closet door. Empty. They were in the middle of a mad search for Sam, in a first-floor classroom that smelled like rotten milk.

Pruitt ran into the room, clutching a rifle that he'd fashioned into a club. The barrel was wrapped in athletic tape for grip.

"No sign of him in this hall," Pruitt said. "I checked all the lockers."

Gates punched the blackboard nearby, and Will was surprised to see it crack.

"HE SHOT AT ME!"

"Gates, calm down," Will said, keeping his voice as measured as he could. "We'll find Sam, and everything'll be fine. There's only so many places he can hide."

Gates started pacing and muttering to himself.

"You know what Sam would do if he was in our place? He'd get on the PA," Will said. "He'd have P-Nut giving news updates until there was nowhere left to hide. Let's get every gang organized. I mean, we're all in this together, right?"

"Nobody else gets him," Gates said. "Sam belongs to me."

Pruitt crossed the room. "Listen to Will, he's making sense . . ."

Will felt huge relief that he and Pruitt were on the same side of this.

Pruitt continued. "It doesn't matter who captures Sam—"

"I want him!" Gates said, squaring off to Pruitt. "I want that motorcycle helmet fuck up there to see exactly what happens when he crosses me!"

"What are you gonna do?" Will said.

Will looked to Pruitt whose forehead was crinkling with concern.

"You can't kill him," Pruitt said.

"I can," Gates said. "Right in front of their eyes. They've had it coming for too long."

"Get a grip, Gates," Pruitt said, walking toward him, using his size to get his point across. "Those adults up there are not the same adults that made our life miserable before. It's only gotten this bad because you took it too far!"

Gates's eyes were crazy. "How can you possibly be on their side in this?"

"I'm not on their—"

"They're evil, Pruitt! Adults are the enemy. You know this! Why aren't you furious?!"

Pruitt wanted to answer, but Gates didn't give him a chance.

"You know what they did! They told my baby brother they would take him to safety. The military said they'd protect him—"

"That's not how it—"

"You were there, Pruitt! That soldier shot Colton in the head!"

Pruitt threw his rifle across the room in a rage and it clattered against the wall. It made Will jump. He didn't know what to say or how to help ease the situation. This was something he wasn't a part of. Pruitt pushed Gates, who stumbled back to the blackboard, confused.

"You're right!" Pruitt said. "I was there. Except what I remember doesn't match this story that you like to tell people."

Pruitt loomed over Gates so completely that Gates had nowhere to look but up into Pruitt's shaggy beard.

"And I can't stand to listen to you keep lying," Pruitt said. "I don't care if Will's here. Let him hear this. He needs to hear this."

"What are you talking about?" Gates said, shrinking.

"You, me, and Colton were out scavenging in that subdivision. What was it called?"

"Deerlake . . . "

"Deerlake, right!" Pruitt said. "Then, we saw one soldier. In a haz-mat suit. You remember that?"

Gates shook his head. "There was a mobile unit. It was picking up infected—"

"No, Gates! There was one soldier. He saw us and ran. We couldn't let him get away, he'd come back for more. So we went after him."

Will watched Gates closely. He blinked like his eyes were on fire. His cheeks trembled with his lips.

"No, that's not how I . . . ," Gates said. He shook his head continuously.

"You and Colton were always faster than me. The three of us split up, and searched all around that neighborhood. And when I caught up with you behind that big yellow house, someone came running around from the side yard and you shot, and he went down."

"That's not what happened," Gates muttered.

Gates was clutching his long hair. His eyes were flared wide, like he was seeing the whole scene play in front of him. He was breathing in soft pants. Will stared, speechless.

"You were a mess when you saw Colton on the ground. You couldn't talk, nothing. And I didn't blame you. That's why I told you to go back to camp. Somebody had to bury him, and you were too out of it," Pruitt said.

Gates was sobbing now, moaning and covering his face. His long white hair draped over his hands.

"When I got back to the others and heard you'd told them all that a soldier shot Colton when he'd tried to turn himself in, I went along with it," Pruitt said. "Because it was an accident and it only would have hurt morale if they knew. But somewhere along the way, you started believing your lie."

Pruitt put his big hand on Gates's shoulder and shook him. Gates still covered his face, shaking underneath.

"I know it's hard, but you've got to face it and move on. You shot your brother, Gates. You killed Colton."

Gates screamed. He pulled something out of his pocket and jabbed it into Pruitt's gut. Pruitt stumbled back with a groan. Gates charged the giant and tackled him to the ground. Will could feel the impact through his sneakers when Pruitt's heavy body hit the floor. Gates and Pruitt grappled. Pruitt couldn't move as fast as Gates, who slipped behind Pruitt and wrapped him in a headlock.

Will moved toward them. "Guys, stop it. We should be—"

Will stopped short when he saw what Gates had hit Pruitt with—the yellow box cutter he'd threatened to use on Sam in the quad. He dug the triangular blade into Pruitt's left temple and dragged it across his forehead, just under his hairline. Pruitt howled. Will jumped back in horror and fell over a nearby chair.

Gates dug his fingers into Pruitt's open wound, and the giant screamed louder. Gates's hooked fingers bulged under Pruitt's skin. He tightened his grip on Pruitt's scalp and pulled. The wound opened like a mouth. The underside of

Pruitt's scalp was a red, wet carpet of nerves without skin. The exposed cranium below was ivory white. Pruitt's scream went silent. He must have been in shock. When Will looked back, he saw Pruitt squirming on the floor, trying to hold his loose flap of scalp on.

Will stood up and bolted for the door, but Gates jumped into his path. He held the box cutter up, pointing it at Will. Pruitt's blood dripped from Gates's hand. Will put his hands up and backed away from the blade.

"Don't do this, Gates," Will said. "Whatever's going on we can— I don't know, man. It doesn't have to go like this."

Gates looked at the blood-smeared box cutter in his hand, then back to Will. Pruitt groaned low. Gates's face was red from strain, his cheeks were inflated and spit bubbles percolated at his lips. Will kept one eye on the open door twelve feet behind Gates, waiting, hoping, praying that someone would walk past.

Gates closed his eyes. When they popped back open the turmoil that had raged across Gates's face was gone.

"I love you, Will," Gates said.

Will remained perfectly still. Gates walked to him and placed his bloody hand on Will's shoulder. Gates backed him into the wall. The bloody box cutter was still gripped in his hand.

"You love me, right?" Gates said.

Gates's desperate eyes flicked over Will's face. His face was way too close to Will's. A thumb's width away. Every direction that Will tried to move his head to look away, Gates would move his face there.

"Come on," Gates said. "Say it back."

"Uh . . . " Will's throat had gone dry with fear.

"I need you to say it. It's not so hard," Gates said. "Friends say it all the time."

"They don't," Will said, but he didn't know why he was bothering to talk sense into Gates. The guy was sick. There was something wrong with him. Will might have had a glitch in his brain, but this dude's brain had a fatal error.

"You're stalling, Will. Just say it. Don't make it weird," Gates said.

Gates's pupils were bottomless. He blinked and scratched at his red eye.

"You'd do it for David," he said. "Do it for me."

"David's my brother."

"David's dead! And I've given you everything!"

The air around them was still and silent. Will started to sweat all over. He could feel Gates's breath on his face. His stomach flip-flopped.

"You're not mad at me, are you?" Gates said.

"No, hell no," Will said. As long as he had that box cutter, Will had to say whatever would calm Gates down.

"'Cause it seems like you're mad at me," Gates said.

"No," Will said.

"You swear," he said.

"Yeah, Gates, I swear."

"But you do love me though, right?"

"Eh . . . ," Will said. He'd never felt so uncomfortable in his life.

"Just say it!" Gates screamed.

Gates clocked him. A real punch, knuckles to eye socket. Will's legs went jelly. His ass hit the floor and his head smacked the wall. Gates was on his knees, hugging Will, almost immediately.

"No-no-no, I'm sorry," Gates said. "That was a mistake. We all make mistakes, right? I didn't mean it."

Tears streamed down Gates's face. Will was dizzy and discombobulated from the punch. Gates hugged him even harder. His wet cheek pressed into Will's, and their skin slid across each other's. Beyond Gates, Will could see Pruitt on the floor. He'd stopped moving, his face was turned away, and there was an oblong pool of blood extending out from his head.

"You have to forgive me," Gates moaned. "That wasn't me just then. Please. Will, please, I need you to forgive me. Please forgive me."

He was a sobbing, psychotic, mess.

"I forgive you," Will managed to say.

"You do?" Gates said and he pulled back from Will. Desperate hope lit up his face.

Will nodded, his eye swelling with pain by the second.

"And you love me?"

Will sagged. He didn't want to die. Not here. Not at the hands of this maniac. Will took a deep breath and ignored the alarm bells ringing in his head, the itch in his blood, the intuitive sense that this was a titanic mistake.

"I love you," Will said.

Gates's tears doubled, but they were happy. They dripped around his smiling lips and off his unbrushed teeth.

Gates continued to cry, and to hug Will, for a long time. Will had to keep on telling him that he wasn't mad at him, that he loved him and he forgave him. After what seemed like the hundredth exchange, Gates seemed convinced that Will did love him, and wasn't mad at him. Gates had finally worn himself out. Scalping a friend and having a breakdown were apparently exhausting.

"I'm tired," Gates said.

"You know what we should do, buddy?" Will said.

"What?"

"We should go home and get some shut-eye. We've been partying so hard."

"Yeah. That sounds good." Gates nodded. "We should make bunk beds."

Will forced a trembling smile. Gates stood up, and then Will did. Will glanced down at the box cutter. He wasn't out of the woods until he stepped out of that classroom door and into the hallway beyond.

"Let's go home," Gates said, and started off toward the hall.

Will followed steadily, with no sudden moves. He could feel the box cutter blade carving across his forehead, and the ripping pain of Gates tugging his scalp off his skull.

As Will stepped into the hall after Gates, he was holding his breath. There was a mixture of gangs in the hall, maybe a hundred strong, trading information about Sam.

Will dashed into the crowd.

"Will . . . ," he heard Gates say behind him. "Where are you . . . "

"Gates found Sam!" Will said. "He needs help!"

The crowd started running past him. They swarmed Gates, and Will kept moving, pushing past body after body.

"No!" Gates howled after him, but Will didn't look back. "Don't leave! DON'T LEAVE ME!"

The tortured cry cut through the confused talk of the crowd and reverberated through the halls. It was a sound that rang in Will's ears long after he'd lost Gates. It chilled him to the bone.

34

"I NEED A BREATHER," SOPHIA SAID. "GONNA grab some water. You need anything?"

"Nah," Lucy said. "I'm good."

She sat down on one of the stools by the cafeteria doors, and wiped the sweat off her brow with her sleeve. She and Sophia had been sparring for a half hour, and Lucy had held her own. Sophia had said it was good for making their guard duty hours go a little faster, but Lucy was afraid the suggestion was about something else. Pity.

Not only was Lucy the girl who cried wolf when it came to sex, she was the one Slut the rest of the gang had to worry about in a fight, the weakest link in the chain, thanks to her recent run-in with the Pretty Ones.

Lucy pushed up her sweaty sleeves. She looked at her arms. They were marred by wide, crisscrossing, scabbed-over grooves made by the Pretty Ones' claws. She looked like she'd had a tussle with a weed wacker. Her face hadn't fared much better. Hopefully, she wouldn't look like Ritchie once they healed. And then there was the ultimate humiliation, they'd chopped off her hair. It was too short in the back, and it did not look cute.

Soft footsteps approached. Lucy looked up to see Maxine walking across the dining hall, toward her. One hand held that perfectly potted flower, the other held her little pregnant belly.

"Taking Minnie for a walk?" Lucy said.

"Looking for you," Maxine said.

"Me?"

Maxine nodded. As long as Lucy had known the girl, Maxine had never looked for anyone. She avoided them. Maxine settled to a stop in front of Lucy. She swayed ever so slightly side to side. A sweet smile spread across her face. Another first.

"My baby's going to live," Maxine said. She laughed and cried as she spoke. She was bubbling over with feeling. "She's going to live, Lucy!"

"What do you mean?"

"I'm graduating," Maxine said.

That special cocktail of emotion came over Lucy, the one she felt every time she heard someone say those words. She was happy, she was jealous, and she was sad at the thought of losing this person from her life. But the sadness was minimal this time. Everyone's prayers for Maxine had been answered. In an instant she'd gone from the girl you couldn't look in the eye because of the doom she carried in her belly, to an expecting mother, about to start a new life.

Lucy took Maxine's free hand and squeezed it. She would have hugged the girl, but she was afraid she might crush the flower.

"Congratulations!" Lucy said. She couldn't stop smiling. "You deserve it."

"I want you to have Minnie."

Lucy stared at Maxine, who held the flower out.

"Really?"

"I know you'll take the best care of her. You know how important she is," Maxine said with a nod. She pushed the flower into Lucy's hands.

"I don't know what to say," Lucy said.

"You have to say yes. You have to keep her alive."

"I will," Lucy said.

"I wrote down everything you need to know," Maxine said, and pulled a folded piece of paper out of her pocket. "These are the directions to her room."

"Her room?" Lucy said, taking the paper.

"It's on the third floor. She needs to be there at sunrise, every day. Promise."

"I . . . promise," Lucy said, unsure about what exactly she was promising.

Maxine smiled and then walked to the cafeteria doors. Lucy looked to the flower in her hands. She ran the back of her fingers across the petals. She allowed herself a single, gentle squeeze of one petal, and it was lovely. She could feel the water inside it. She could feel how it would break apart if she were just to press a little harder. For a moment, Lucy lost herself, completely whisked away into a memory of a different time, of a different place, when she was little, when a pleasure like this was as big as life got.

Maxine left the cafeteria. As the doors drifted shut, a blood-spattered hand shot in between them. A boy's hand. Lucy jumped. Somebody was trying to get in, and she wasn't doing her job. She placed the flower on the stool and reached down to the paperback strapped to her thigh. She pulled her knife, sheathed between the pages, and charged the door.

Will pushed through the doors from the hall.

"Lucy!"

Lucy lowered her knife. "Will, what are you—"

The flesh around his eye was stained by a fresh red and blue bruise.

"Oh my god," Lucy said. "Are you okay?"

Will's face was pale with terror.

"Gates killed Pruitt," Will said.

"Who?"

"He's a Saint. At least, I think he killed him. I just had to run . . . I had to get out of there—"

"Will, slow down," Lucy said. "You're freaking me out. I don't know what you're talking about."

"It's Gates . . . he's obsessed with me. He's crazy."

"What do you mean he's obsessed with you?" Lucy said. She was getting more anxious as Will went on.

"He's lost his mind. He's going to come after me. He's not going to stop. He killed his little brother . . . "

"Oh god. Okay, well, um . . . you can't stay here. I can't let you bring the Saints down on the Sluts."

He nodded. "I know," he said. "I like your hair."

Lucy touched the bob she'd fashioned from what was left of her hair, then got ahold of herself.

"Will—" she said in a sharp tone. "This is serious."

"Look, I know I shouldn't have come here. I just had to see you."

"You did?"

"In case it was the last time."

"Everything okay?" Sophia said as she walked out of the kitchen. Lucy looked back to her, then to Minnie the flower, sitting on the stool.

Lucy picked up the flower and took Will by the arm. "I gotta go," Lucy said to Sophia. "Cover for me."

Will crawled through a ventilation shaft behind Lucy. The last time he'd been in a shaft with her, things between them hadn't been so hot—it had been that dead silent crawl back from the Varsity pool. He was pissed at her then, but not now. He was grateful. She was putting herself in danger to keep him safe from a psychopath.

"I think this is it," she said.

She was ahead of him in the narrow metal tunnel. Lucy was paused in front of a vent cover. She hovered her phone light over a crumpled piece of paper. She looked to the vent, reached out, and gave it a push. It fell away.

Lucy stuck her head into the pitch-blackness on the other side.

"Oh, wow," he heard her say.

She pulled herself into the void, and she disappeared from view. Will pushed the potted flower ahead of him until he reached the opening. He looked down into a small room that was lit only by moonlight through a single narrow window that looked out on to the quad.

"Hand me Minnie," she said.

"It has a name?"

Lucy reached up. "She," she said. "She has a name."

Will handed the flower down to Lucy, then lowered himself out of the shaft. Will's feet touched down on a Xerox machine, and he jumped down to the floor from there. There was another copier in the room. It was pressed up against the only door. Like a lot of other doors in McKinley that weren't meant to be opened, the handle had been removed.

He walked over to flip on the light switch.

"Don't," Lucy said.

Will turned to her, confused. She held up the crumpled piece of paper, her phone light still on.

"It says to never turn on the lights at night. Don't want to attract any attention to this window, it says, on the off chance somebody's in the quad."

"What is this place?"

"A secret," Lucy said. "I think you'll be safe here."

Lucy moved to the window and placed the potted flower on the sill. She gave it special attention, more than Will thought a flower needed. She turned it until it faced out the window, as if she wanted it to have a view of the quad below. Will walked to the shelving unit that spanned the entire wall opposite the copiers. The shelves were stocked with pickle jars and plastic cups full of quad dirt. In some of the dirt was dried fruit left to rot slowly. There were a couple spray bottles and a hot plate with a pot on it. At the end of one shelf was a black light that looked like it came from a science lab.

"Is all of this for that one flower?" Will said.

Lucy turned and nodded. "Makes you wonder what else is in this school we don't know about."

She crossed the room to a mattress of blankets on the floor next to the opposite wall. Lucy sank down to the makeshift bed, sitting with her back to the wall. Will sat down beside her. The room was as quiet as a snowed-in house. The madness he'd left behind in that sour-scented classroom seemed so far away. For now, he was safe from that demented red eye, but it would find him eventually. That thought made him treasure every moment he had alone with Lucy.

Her posture was better than ever before, her back was parallel with the wall. Moonlight made her short, red hair a shimmering purple. It highlighted the cuts that latticed her arms and the long thin scabs that lined her face. He hadn't mentioned them before, in the cafeteria. He didn't want her to feel self-conscious, but he was pissed off that anyone would lay their hands on Lucy. It was all part of the new her, he guessed.

"Who did that to you?" Will said.

"This is bad, Will. It's really bad."

"I know. I'm sorry I pulled you into this."

"Yeah, but you always do this! You always do shit that means somebody has to bail you out! I'm not your babysitter."

"I said I'm sorry," he said, raising his voice.

"Can't you ever just do the right thing? Why do you make friends with these lowlifes like Gates and Smudge? Does it make you feel better or something?"

"Feels better than being rejected by you every five minutes!" Will yelled back.

Lucy's face flushed red, and their eyes locked. She grabbed his head and kissed him. Will's mind reeled. How was this happening? Her lips were soft and hot. They felt unbelievable. They separated, but only a few inches. They stared into each other's eyes. They were more intensely connected than Will had ever experienced with someone. She wasn't pulling away either. In the Saints he got to ask for whatever he wanted, and he usually got it, but it never really made him happy. Right now, he was truly happy. The thing he really wanted, the thing he wanted most in the world, was still Lucy, and she wanted him back.

He took her head in her hands and kissed her. That second kiss would have been enough for him, but it was only the spark. It led to more kissing, and groping. Lucy's raspy moans sent an electrical current crackling through his body. Soon, Will was tugging off her clothes and she was doing the same to him. He grabbed, he caressed, he tasted. He kissed around her bruises.

This was real. They were going to have sex. Will didn't want to screw it up. For all the hours of porn he'd seen, once it was really happening, he felt like a tap dancer on a frozen lake. He wanted her to love it. Each thing he did, he did with a terror that she'd push him away and look at him like he was a pervert, or a child. She'd realize that he wasn't good enough, that he'd never done this before, and she'd be disgusted. She'd demand that he stop.

She didn't do any of those things. She kissed back with equal passion. She sucked on the skin of his neck. She grasped him, and guided him inside. Heaven.

35

WILL STARED AT THE COPIER ROOM CEILING.
It was lit by sunlight now. He didn't know how long he'd been doing it, picking out weird faces and shapes in the patterned tiles, like he was staring at a cloudy sky. It was impossible to sleep with Lucy in his arms. Her head was tucked warmly below his chin. He didn't dare move and make her stir. He wanted her so happy she'd never want to leave. Her hip filled his hand. His heat mixed with hers until he couldn't discern the border between them.

She purred. He felt her eyelashes tickle his chest. She must have opened her eyes.

"You awake?" he said.

"Mmm-hmm."

She lifted her head and turned to face him. She smiled.

"Fancy meeting you here," she said.

One look, and she could dissolve him until he was nothing but a shadow in the shape of a boy.

"Wish we had something to eat," Lucy said.

"Well, darn it, I forgot to go to the store."

"That's dumb," she said through another smile.

"You're dumb."

He squeezed her and she squeaked, and he wanted to hear it again and again. Their clothes were strewn over their naked bodies like blankets.

"What time is it?" Lucy said.

Will groaned and pulled her closer. "Who cares?"

"Nobody knows where I am. I should've told Sophia. They might get worried."

"Really? What do the Sluts look like when they get worried?"

Without missing a beat, Lucy bore her clenched teeth at him with wild, furious eyes. She looked like a constipated piranha. Will cracked up. Lucy shook with laughter, trying to hold the face until she couldn't anymore. She covered her mouth and snorted a giggle. Will put his forehead to hers, she settled into him.

"I'm serious, what time is it?" Lucy said.

Will sighed and found his phone in his pants, which were laid over Lucy's calves. The screen was shattered, but it was still in one piece. He clicked it on. The upper corners of the display were discolored, pinkish, and the rest was littered with dead pixels.

"Eleven a.m.," Will said.

"What's that?"

Lucy was looking at Will's phone, the screen still illuminated. She sat up, holding his and her clothes to her front. She took the phone out of his hand to get a better look at his phone's wallpaper. It was a dim snapshot of the Loners gathered around the TV he'd stolen from the Freaks and hung in the Stairs lounge. Lucy sat in the middle, in her pale blue dress, looking back at the camera and sticking out her tongue.

"I don't remember this picture," she said, staring at the pic, the phone's blue light gleaming off her bare shoulder. She seemed mesmerized by her former self.

"It was a while ago."

"Do I . . . ," she said, still puzzling over the picture. "Do I seem different to you now?"

"You definitely look different."

"Yeah, but . . . am I different?"

"You mean aside from eating bricks for breakfast and punching babies in the face or whatever you Sluts do?"

"Hey, I'm serious!" she said, and gave him a hard slap on the chest. He laughed.

"No, not really. You're still the same."

"Oh," she said, clearly let down.

"But, I like that person. I'm having a great time with that person."

"I know. Right," she said.

He'd upset her, and he wasn't sure what he'd said wrong.

"I'm gonna go," she said. Lucy started gathering up her clothes.

Will sat up. "Come on, don't go. The Sluts can wait."

"It's not them," she said. "You've got to eat eventually. I'm going to go to the market and stock up for you."

She pulled on her clothes. Will looked at Lucy standing above him. Her short red hair tousled. Sleeveless white T-shirt, torn all to shreds with a drawing of a chain saw on the front. Tight, burned-up jeans that showed off taut muscles that Will was sure she didn't have before.

"By yourself? I should go with you."

Will stood and pulled on his pants.

"Will, stop," she said. "You know you can't leave."

Will was afraid of Gates, but he was more afraid of letting Lucy leave. Things were so perfect up here, in their third-floor hideaway. This little place of their own. Outside, anything could go wrong.

"I'll come up with a disguise—"

"Will, Gates is crazy, you told me yourself. You know you have to stay here. That's the whole point."

"It's not safe."

"I can handle myself," she said. She stepped up onto the copier to climb into the vent.

"Well, that's something," Will said.

"What?" she said from above him.

"The old Lucy never would have headed out alone like this."

Lucy smiled.

"I guess she wouldn't."

She knelt down until they were face-to-face and she kissed him. He'd done something right.

"I'll be back later," she said, still smiling. "Take care of Minnie."

Lucy hurried down the hall, on her way to the market. She was desperate for a bathroom after spending all night in the copier room, but still she couldn't help feeling light on her feet. Alone, she was finally able to really enjoy what had happened. The push and pull of the pleasure. How alive her body felt after it was over. The warmest, deepest night's sleep she'd gotten in a long time. She was maybe the happiest she'd ever been. Once she was in Will's arms, she knew that, after all her turmoil over who she'd lose her virginity to, and whether she would, she'd ended up in the right place, with the right person. Her first time had been perfect.

Lucy pushed open the door to the girls' bathroom. This particular bathroom had become a sort of public works project for all girls, initiated by the Sluts. They had installed new stall walls and stall doors that had long ago been destroyed, so that girls from any gang could pee in peace. Over only one sink, a mirror had been reassembled like a jigsaw puzzle out of odd, mismatching shards. Another mirror was in the works soon, sponsored by the Nerd girls. And girls from every gang chipped in when they could to supply toilet paper. It wasn't a perfect system, but today was Lucy's lucky day. A full roll was waiting for her in her stall. Lucy closed her stall door and began to unbuckle her jeans.

A conversation in the hall, just outside the bathroom, made her pause. Some girls were arguing. She heard the door open. One of the voices cut through the others; it was higher, sharper, more vicious. It was unmistakably Hilary.

"Watch the door, girls. Don't slouch, Tabitha. No one needs to see your gut," Hilary said.

Lucy very quietly stepped up onto the closed toilet seat, and crouched there.

"Nobody comes in here until I come out," Hilary said. "You included."

She heard the noise of the hall quiet. Hilary must have shut the door. Lucy could hear her footsteps. Lucy lowered her hand to the handle of her knife and wrapped her fingers around it. She waited for Hilary to throw open the stall door. It didn't happen.

Hilary walked away from the stalls. Through the space between the stall door and stall wall, Lucy had a narrow line of sight on her old gang leader. Hilary looked at her distorted reflection in the mirror mosaic. She placed her little white purse on the edge of the sink, leaned forward, and began to examine her teeth.

Lucy stepped down from the toilet, quiet as a cat. She crept to the gap and pushed her eye closer to get a wider view. Lucy nearly yelped when, in the mirror, she saw Hilary pull one of her teeth out.

"Oh my god," Lucy mouthed silently.

The tooth had a strip of duct tape along the back of it. Hilary panned her head back and forth, examining herself. Her lips were peeled back to reveal a gaping black space on her upper row of teeth, to the right of her front incisors. Just that one, empty, gummy arch between the otherwise perfect row of white Chiclets made Hilary look sickly and sad. She tongued the gap.

Hilary held up her tooth and peeled the duct tape off of it. She balled up the tape and chucked it on the floor. Hilary delicately placed the tooth on the corner of the porcelain sink. She removed a small roll of duct tape from her purse and began to fashion a fresh strip of adhesive.

Lucy couldn't stop staring at that tooth. Hilary's pride, her power, her vanity was resting on the edge of the sink.

Hilary dropped the roll of tape by mistake, and it rolled under the row of sinks.

"Ugh," Hilary said. She got down on her hands and knees to

pick it up. Lucy yanked open the door and ran for the tooth. She snatched it off the sink, and bounded back into the stall.

"Hey!" Hilary yelled.

Lucy kicked the toilet's flush handle, and looked back in time to see the terror seizing Hilary's face.

"NO!" Hilary wailed, and charged at Lucy.

Lucy dropped the tooth into the flushing toilet. The whirlpool of water carried the little pearl straight down the tube. Hilary shoved her hands into the toilet bowl, frantically feeling around for it. Lucy ran for the door.

A Pretty One threw open the bathroom door, and Lucy kicked her in the shin. The girl buckled. She punched another one in the nose, just like Sophia had once shown her. She elbowed past the next two Pretty Ones in her path. They didn't chase. They were probably too busy trying to figure out why their leader was clawing through toilet water like a dog trying to dig under a fence.

Lucy booked it down the hall, laughing with pure joy. Hilary had it coming.

She knew Hilary would try to make her pay for this at some point but she didn't care. At least for a while, at least for today, Hilary was ruined.

She neared the cafeteria. She'd have to gather some stuff to trade at the market. The ceiling lights by the front doors to the cafeteria were functional, but the fifty feet of hallway between her and the doors was blacked out. Lucy didn't bother to take out her phone for the weak light it would cast. She ran in the dark.

Lucy saw movement in the unlit hall. Shapes. Murky lumps lurking in the corners of her vision. She slowed her pace. Were her eyes playing tricks on her? The shapes grew distinct. They were boys and girls standing still in the darkness. Lucy slowed more. And when she did, the boys and girls began to walk toward her. They converged on her from all around. She whipped out her phone and clicked it on. They had white hair. Saints. What felt like ten pairs of hands grabbed her.

Someone plucked Lucy's phone out of her fingers. The boy who did it, he shined her phone's screen up to his own face. Her heart went cold. It was Gates, his face screwed up with tension, and his one red eye shut.

"Well, look who decided to come home," Gates said.

36

WILL SMILED LIKE A FOOL. HE COULDN'T stop. He had everything he wanted. The afternoon sun streamed in through the window of the copier room. It had nearly set behind the roofline, on the opposite side of the quad. He watched the last little curve of blazing light as it disappeared.

Will sprung to his feet. He took a spray bottle from one of the shelves nearby, and walked to the flower in the window. Will gave it six squirts from the spray bottle, just like the directions required, covering the flower in a fine mist. Lucy cared about this thing, and if it was important to her, he wanted to take care of it right. He leaned in and smelled its wet petals. He thought of how fantastic Lucy smelled. He thought of the wonders of her body. Her skin against his. He wished she was there with him right then. He wanted another thousand nights, just like the last one.

A faraway noise drifted in from the hallway on the other side of the door, beyond the copier. It was muffled, merely a murmur, but still, it was familiar. It was definitely someone talking, but he couldn't make out a single word. He'd crawl into the vent and see if he could hear it better. No matter what Lucy had said, he couldn't bear to stay put any longer. He felt too powerful to just lay around. Maybe this was what being a man felt like.

Will jumped up on the copier and pulled himself into the vent. The vent cover was dangling down by a string, a convenience made by whoever repurposed this room. He lit the shaft with his phone. He slid through, making sure to keep the bend and pop of the metal to a minimum. The voice was still speaking, still unintelligible, but a touch louder than in the copier room. It was an announcement over the PA system. It had to be, no normal voice would be loud enough to carry this far.

Will knew better than to head out into the stairwell when he reached the next vent. He knew better, but he still did it. Will popped the vent cover off. It dangled down by another string. He slid out and placed his feet on the third floor banister. His balance was precarious as he clicked the vent cover back in place, but eventually he got it, and jumped down onto the stairs. The stairwell was quiet. He maybe thought he was losing his mind, until P-Nut's voice resounded from a hissing PA speaker located only a few feet from the vent.

"I get it," P-Nut said. "You want me to stop playing it. I want to stop playing it. It's a little on the weird side. But I'll play it for a month if that's what old Gates wants. I think he's going to be one of my best customers when I open my new strip club, the P-Nut Gallery. You heard that right. Come forget your troubles with our lovely ladies, opening soon. But anyways . . . back to our regularly scheduled programming."

There was a click, and Gates's voice replaced P-Nut's, icing Will's blood in an instant.

"Will . . ." Gates's voice was heavy, full of emotion. "Lucy is with me now. If you want to see her again, then you have to come back, buddy. I'm not mad at you. I know you think I'm mad, but I'm not. It's not safe for you out there. I can't keep you safe when you're not with me. Please. I'm begging you. Come home, Will."

Will knocked hard on the door to the cafeteria. He wore a gray hoodie that was three sizes too big for him. The front was splattered with deep brown soil stains thanks to what looked like a year or so of use as a rag for potting and unpotting the flower. The hood covered Will's face though, as long as he kept staring at the floor. It had kept him from being identified so he could get here, and that's all he needed from it.

The doors swung inward. A Slut with six paper clip wire hoops piercing one nostril peered out at Will. He edged his foot forward to block the door from being slammed shut in his face. It never came to that. The Slut grabbed Will by the sweatshirt just below his neck and yanked him in. Before he knew it, more hands were on him, and they were moving him fast. They dragged him into the dining hall and threw him forward.

Will stumbled and he came to a stop behind Violent, who was screaming at someone.

"Lips, I told you to—"

"Boss!" one of the Sluts that threw Will said. Violent turned and looked down at Will.

"You," she said. Her lip curled and the corners of her mouth sunk.

"Yeah, me."

"This is your fault."

"Maybe."

"Not maybe! Yes. What is it with you, huh? Why are you such a shit magnet?"

Will tried to stop his temper from flaring, but her words had already kicked the furnace door open.

"Why are you such a towering bitch? You can act like this is my fault, but you're the one that's got her walking around school like she's bulletproof—"

Violent grabbed his hood, spun him round, and slammed him into a table. She was surprisingly strong. He felt something sharp pricking through the crotch of his jeans.

"Whoa, whoa!" he said, throwing his hands up. He looked down to the knife pressing into him. "Slow down."

"She's too good for you, you little bug!" Her pupils shook like the epicenters of micro-earthquakes.

It was a weird thing; despite the knife at his crotch, Will felt he could trust her.

"You love her, don't you?" he said.

"I've never loved anyone."

Will smiled. "Liar."

He thought he saw a smile begin to arc her mouth upward just before she bared her teeth and jabbed him in the Adam's apple with her fingers. Will couldn't breath. He hacked and coughed, and his throat ground against itself like it was full of pumice grit.

Violent withdrew her knife. Will coughed so hard he felt the blood swell in his head. He saw spark clouds all across his vision.

"I should hand you over to Gates right now!" Violent said.

Will sucked in a desperate breath, and then another, and the cough subsided. He looked at Violent with snot dripping from his nose and tears in his eyes.

"That's exactly what I was thinking."

37

SAM WAS SO CLOSE. ESCAPE WAS ONLY A FEW minutes away. He could feel his own body heat in the air around him. Sweat stung his eyes, and slicked his whole body. His right arm was pressed against the metal wall, and it was cool. Three horizontal slashes of light from the locker vent striped his face.

He spied the hall. A herd of Freaks had just passed by, whining, posing, snarling at imaginary enemies, dressed like they'd raided a party store at Halloween. He'd barely gotten the locker door closed before these Freaks came moping around the corner.

There was a time when the idea of hiding from those loser Freaks like a monumental pussy would have been something he and Anthony or Dixon or whoever would have had a good laugh about. It was Sam's reality now, and his friends had all turned on him. They despised him like the rest of the school.

When he was the Saints' prisoner, all Sam had wanted was revenge. But now, he was free and he didn't give a shit about any of them, what they thought, what they'd done to him, any of it. It was the greatest relief he'd ever felt in his life, and it was all because his father loved him. Sam had been losing for months, unequivocally losing, and his father still loved him. It was a feeling like nothing he'd ever known. For the first time, he was looking forward to life on the outside.

Sam pressed his ear hard against the locker vents. The Freaks were gone. There hadn't been any sound for the last two minutes. He opened the locker door and stepped out into the dusty, cooler air. He clutched a heavy wrench to his chest and limped on, down the hall. He'd sprained his knee running in the hall, after he'd escaped the quad, and the pain had only gotten worse since then. He must have torn a muscle too. Only two short hallways and he'd be in the quad. Sam scanned every locker handle as he went, always aware of where the next locker without a lock on it was, always ready. Jumping locker to locker was how he'd made it this far, undiscovered. He'd been hiding in the ruins since he got away from Gates, waiting for the frenzy over him to die down.

Sam heard something around the next corner. Footsteps. He moved to the nearest locker and gripped the shiny metal handle. Sam opened the locker. A boy with shoulder-length black and orange hair, blue lips, gray skin, and slit wrists crusted over with blood, fell out of the locker. A dead Geek. He left it. There was no time. He went two lockers down to the next one without a lock. He tore it open. It was empty. He jumped in and pulled the door shut.

Even if it was a ninety pound Nerd girl with a heart of gold who was about to walk around the corner, Sam didn't trust that she wouldn't try to stab him with something, or at least scream at the top of her lungs so that other, bigger people, could come and stomp him to death. He was too close to happiness to take any chances. He choked up on the wrench in his hand and stayed perfectly still until the footsteps faded away.

Around the next corner it was only one short hallway to the quad. Twenty feet. He could feel his body charging up. The pain in his knee faded. He knew this feeling, from game nights. It was time for Sam to run the ball all the way to the end zone. This was the last second, winning play, the ultimate one he and his dad would talk about for decades to come. He'd get to the quad, he'd call for his father under the cover of night. He'd be pulled out. They'd get out of Colorado. They could start over.

Sam stepped out with all his weight on his good leg. Something big crunched under his foot, the size of a two-liter bottle. It squirmed. Sam looked down to see an animal under his shoe, its head flat on the cold linoleum and its body bent up like a lady's high heel shoe, hind legs slipping messily. It looked like a piglet, maybe a couple weeks old.

"Yuh—" Sam said in a panic.

He lifted his leg up and stumbled away. The piglet made no noise, other than the chaotic scratching of its little hooves on the floor. It panted but didn't scream, it couldn't. Sam had crushed its spine under his foot, and it was in the last throes of panicky death. The little thing fought to hold on. Even in its small newly complete brain, it seemed to know that this was too soon.

"I'm—"

Sorry, he was going to say. But before he could, Sam heard a furious gallop behind him. He turned, but not fast enough. Something rammed his legs. He felt a pop in his knee. He was thrown back, away from the piglet. The wrench flew from his hand. He hit the floor and slid into a row of lockers, his head crunching into the thin metal baseboard.

Sam groaned at impact. He pushed up to face his attacker. He didn't know what he thought he'd see, but what he hadn't expected was another pig. A big one. A burly beast, all stomach and shoulders, with black shining hooves and jutting, bottom-row tusks on which its rubbery top lip rested like a drape. Gray-black teats swung from its belly with every nudge it gave to the dying piglet. It was the mother, that much was clear. Five other little piglets poked their snouts out from the dark of a neighboring classroom. They shuffled and pushed against each other to see what their mother was doing, but they never ventured into the hall.

Sam slowly pulled himself up to sitting. The pain in his knee was torturous. He watched as the crushed piglet's little hooves gave one last scrape against the floor. The mama pig had her nose buried under the piglet's belly, trying to lift it up, trying to make it move again.

He scanned the hall in search of the wrench. Too far. Sam pressed his palms to the floor and pushed through the pain to scramble to standing.

The mama pig gave one last blast of hot breath from her nostrils, a final pat on the piglet's head to say good-bye. Then, the mama pig swung her thick muscled neck to point her head at him. She locked one dark marble eye on Sam.

He limped to the next corner. It was almost a hop. He was unable to put any weight on his knee. At the end of the short hall, through the half-open double doors, Sam could see blue moonlight shining into the quad. His father was only seconds away. So were the clacks of pig hooves behind him. He didn't want to look, but he should have. Maybe then, he could have dodged the attack.

The pig hit him squarely in his bad knee again. She knew. His leg buckled. He collapsed like a beach chair, and fell face forward onto the floor. Hooves dug into the small of his back as the pig mounted him. Sam twisted under the pig. He would find her eyes. He'd dig his thumbs into the oversized greasy black olives and pop them out.

The pig slipped off Sam. He flipped onto his back with his hands tense, thumbs poised to stab. But the pig was faster. Her long jaws clamped down on the soft meat of Sam's throat. She tore it away. His neck was a hole. The tubes of his throat spilled out. Sam couldn't breathe. Blood in his lungs. The beast bit at the wound, clamping down again and tearing more of him away.

Sam didn't understand. His hands pawed at the animal's hefty chub, doing none of the damage he'd planned to impose. This was wrong. This wasn't the way it was supposed to go. His mind was flooded with regrets. All the while, the pig dug into him, shaking him like a pillow. His body became warmer, more numb. She threw him down. His cheek pressed against the cold linoleum. As his vision blurred, the whitish blue light of the quad became a richer blue, then black.

He wanted to go home.

She stood there above him, huffing through her shotgun-barrel nostrils. Sam's blood dripped from the coarse hairs on her chin, and it was painted all around her mouth.

The pig turned away from her kill and trotted back to the den where her babies were waiting for her. They would be hungry.

38

LUCY LAY ON A GURNEY IN THE COMMONS,
the same giant room where she'd fought the Skaters along-
side the Loners and Will had broken all their boards. It was
where she'd first drawn blood in a battle. That seemed like
ages ago.

There was no fighting to be done now, her wrists were duct-
taped to the metal pipes on the gurney's sides. She strained
against them, but she couldn't slip her hands out. It was
almost time for the exchange. She watched the hallway that
eventually led to the cafeteria, where the Sluts would be coming from. Saints lurked in the shadows just outside the pools
of orange light that polka-dotted the vast floor of the commons. Wide concrete columns dominated the space.

Gates was playing golf. He stood ten feet from her. There
was a tipped-over bucket at his feet, and a pool of golf balls
was spread over the floor around him. She watched him bend

down and place a golf ball on the toe of an old sneaker, which he'd been using as a tee. He gripped his club, a big titanium driver, and took a heavy swing. The ball shot off the shoe and ricocheted off the concrete columns, and the hard floor, ping-ponging around the room. *Tack-a-tack-tack!* Saints ducked to avoid getting hit by the speeding ball. Gates teed up another and let it fly. She flinched when the ball cracked off the concrete column next to her head.

She saw a squat, round-faced Saint getting pushed toward Gates by the other Saints. "Okay, okay," he said. The round-faced boy approached Gates with caution.

"Hey . . . um, Gates?"

Gated took another big swing and hit the shoe this time. The shoe twirled into the air. Gates threw his club to the floor. "Boring!"

"Uh," the round-faced boy said.

"What is it, Fowler?"

He turned and looked at Fowler and his red eye fluttered. There was a little glob of yellowish gunk on the bottom lid, some sort of puss, that would jump and stretch across his eye with every blink.

"We were wondering. Why is it so important we get Will back again?"

"I told you, he knows where Sam is."

Fowler didn't look convinced.

"Some of us think we should just be searching for Sam."

"Who's some of us?" Gates said, insulted. "How many times have I saved all of your lives? How many times have we been done for, and I've been the one to lead us all out of it?"

"A lot of times, man."

"That's right. And I'll lead us out of this one. You have to trust me. Haven't I earned that?"

The look on this boy Fowler's face said it all. He was frightened of his leader. Gates was losing his gang.

"Will doesn't know where Sam is. He's lying to you," Lucy said to Fowler and the others.

Gates turned to her, enraged. She shouldn't have said it. What had she been thinking? She was a sitting duck. He stomped toward her, his hands in tensed into claws.

"Hey, Eyedrops!"

Gates stopped in his tracks and jerked his eyes toward the hallway.

It was Violent. And all the Sluts. Sixty-three of them. They leaned against columns with smirks, or took a seat on the floor, picking their teeth with their blades. They glared at the forty-odd Saints with menace.

"I got something for you," Violent said.

Will stepped out from behind the red hair and the knives in an oversized gray sweatshirt. He was one white head of hair in a sea of red.

Lucy's heart leapt.

"Oh my God!" Gates shouted. He was covering his open mouth with his hand. His bugged-out eyes quivered as they looked at Will. It turned Lucy's stomach that Gates's response to seeing Will seemed to match the same kind of emotion and excitement that Lucy felt inside.

"I believe that redhead there belongs to me," Violent said.

"Send him over first," Gates said, still staring at Will in wonder.

Violent walked beside Will as he crossed the gap between the gangs. She held her knife in her hand; its entire handle had been dipped in red nail polish. Will looked scared, but he gave Lucy a little nod as he walked. As they got closer, Violent broke away from Will and came to stand next to Lucy's gurney.

"What's the plan?" Lucy whispered to Violent as Will continued his walk toward an emotional Gates. Will's oversized gray sweatshirt made him look like a kid in a grown-up's clothes.

"No plan," Violent whispered back as she cut Lucy loose. "Let's go."

"Wait, what do you mean? How is Will getting to get out of this?" Lucy said.

"Pretty sure this is as far as he's thought things through."

Colton walked toward Gates. He wore a big gray sweatshirt that was too big for him. Gates was still in shock. He hadn't expected his brother to walk out from the Sluts. He'd been expecting someone else, or something else, but he couldn't remember what it was. It didn't matter now. Colton had returned.

Every step Colton took toward him brought Gates closer to joyful tears. Colton looked healthy. His brown hair was combed neatly to the side, as always. He walked stiffly though, and he wasn't smiling. He still wore those same damn black sunglasses, and Gates wanted him to take them off now more than ever. He needed to look into Colton's eyes and know what he was feeling. He needed to connect with him.

Gates opened his arms wide, and wrapped Colton in a warm hug. Colton's arms stayed down. Gates never wanted to let go again. The tears began to squeeze out of his eyes. The pain of not having his little brother in his life was transforming by the millisecond into gratitude. He didn't care how this was happening, he didn't need an explanation, they were together again. All the irrational guilt he had felt, that it was some-how his fault that Colton had tried to turn himself in, that maybe he had said something wrong, or had taken Colton for granted, that all evaporated.

Colton had never died. He hadn't been shot by a soldier. That was just Gates's mind playing tricks on him. His brother was alive and well and everything was fine. Gates wasn't to blame for anything.

"Guys, get him his presents! What are you waiting for?" Gates said, while still squeezing his brother.

Behind him, the Saints jumped to his orders, dragging out old beaten boxes from the shadows, full of toys, and sports equipment, and DVDs.

Gates sensed movement to his left. He looked up from his hug and saw Lucy rushing up to him with Violent running after her. Lucy held a knife with a red handle, and before he realized what was happening, she plunged the blade into his side, just under his ribs. The pain made his legs buckle and his hands instinctively went to the wound. He fell on to his side on the floor, and looked at the red knife handle sticking out of his waist like a flagpole. Lucy pulled Colton away.

Saints ran past Gates, going after Lucy, which made the Sluts charge the Saints. A gang battle erupted through the commons.

Gates grasped the glossy red handle of the knife, and pulled the bloody blade out of his body, inch by excruciating inch. He was gagging from the pain by the time he got it all the way out, and let it clang down onto the floor. Thick blood came belching up out of the hole in his side.

Gates clutched his side, and grunted through the pain to stand up. He frantically scanned the sea of swinging weapons in search of Colton. He saw knives everywhere. He saw Sluts slicing at eyes and necks. He saw them kicking crotches. He saw a Slut eat a rifle butt to the face. He saw Tiffy swing a croquet mallet into a Slut's stomach. He saw Lark on the floor shrieking over her dislocated jaw. He saw all that, but he couldn't see Colton anywhere.

He had finally gotten his brother back. The only thing that mattered was Colton. And Lucy had taken him away again. He couldn't breathe.

"Don't take him from me!" Gates shrieked at the top of his lungs. He kept looking everywhere. "GIVE HIM BACK!"

"Shut up, rich boy," Violent said. She came running out of the fray, and tackled Gates to the ground. His stab wound exploded with pain. She attacked him with fists and fingernails. Gates clamped his hands around the bitch's neck, and saw her startled eyes blast wide open. He crushed down on her throat with all his strength.

Will and Lucy ran out of the commons, and down two halls. The further they ran, the more the battle sounds faded. Will pulled her into an empty classroom and shut the door. They clung to each other. She hugged him with all her strength. He was alive, and away from the grips of that psychopath. They separated.

"I have to go back," Lucy said.

"What?"

"I have to help my girls, they're only in this fight 'cause of me."

"No, you can't go back there."

"I have to."

"Gates is gonna be going ballistic. I don't want you around him."

"You're the one who shouldn't be around him. You need to go back to Minnie's room and hide."

"Come with me," Will said.

"I can't, Will, I told you—"

"I'll let you kiss me."

She laughed. She couldn't help it, she wasn't expecting that. Will smiled at her. For a moment, she smiled too, but her face went slack when she saw twin lines of blood pour out from Will's nostrils.

39

WILL AND LUCY DASHED DOWN THE HALLWAY,
toward the quad, holding hands.

"I have another year," Will said. "I'm supposed to have another year."

"We don't know anything until you scan your thumb. It could be anything. Maybe you got hit," Lucy said.

"I told you I didn't get hit."

"I don't know, Will. Maybe the air's too dry."

He wasn't buying it. And he knew she wasn't either, but she kept trying to keep him calm.

"It can't be the virus," she said. "That just doesn't make sense."

Unless Will's body was just done with puberty. He guessed it was a possibility. He hadn't grown any taller in months. No matter what the answer was, he still might have to leave school. He should have been thrilled to finally get to leave.

To have this all end. But, not now. Not when he'd just gotten Lucy back.

The two of them slowed. There was a corpse on the floor ahead of them, a boy. His legs were splayed, with one shoe off and one shoe on. The white floor around him was a mess of smeared blood. It wasn't until they were closer that they saw where all that blood had come from. The whole front of the boy's neck was gone. The flesh had been torn away, and Will could see the front of his spine nestled into the red mulch of shredded neck meat. Above the ragged wound was a face they knew all too well.

Sam's mouth was open. His eyes were too. They had gone gray. His face was twisted in agony. It was a painful death. Horrible. But Will guessed it was inevitable.

"Oh my god," Lucy said, staring down at Sam. "Who would do that?"

Will searched inside himself for the satisfaction at seeing Sam destroyed and he couldn't find it.

"We should keep moving," Lucy said, and pulled Will forward.

"Wait," Will said, staying put. He took off his oversized sweatshirt and flung it out like a bed sheet. He let it fall across Sam from his chest to the top of his head. He turned to Lucy and gave her a nod. "Okay."

They ran for the open door to the quad. Outside, it was raining hard. The air smelled clean. Will and Lucy rushed into the quad. It was one giant square of mud. Will scanned the razor wire perimeter, three floors up, and spotted an adult standing on top of the east wall.

"Thumb check!" Lucy yelled as loud as she could.

The adult lowered the boxy machinery of the disembodied thumb scanner. It dangled from a long pole extended over the razor wire. As they ran for the wall, the figure above became clearer. Rain splashed off his black motorcycle helmet. It was Sam's father. The thumb scanner spun as Sam's dad lowered it. When it was ten feet above them, Will could see that the scanner was sealed up in a ziplock freezer bag.

Will unzipped the blue-green seal, wiped his hand on his jeans, and stuck his hand into the bag. He planted his thumb on the scanner.

The rain poured.

"You're transitioning," the man shouted down without the benefit of his amp.

Will shook his head.

"No," he said, his voice barely a rasp. "It can't be right. This doesn't make sense."

If there was pain in Lucy's face, it was only for a second. A storm gust blew it away. Her hair whipped in her face, and she looked up to the sky.

"He has to be lifted out!" Lucy yelled.

"No," Sam's father said. He reeled the scanner back up.

"What do you mean?" she shouted. "He has to graduate! You have to let him out."

Sam's father pointed a gloved hand at Will.

"I know who you are, kid," the man said. "You want out? You bring me Sam, alive. That's the only way you're getting out."

"Will's going to die if he doesn't—"

Will put his hand out to stop Lucy short.

"No problem!" Will said.

Lucy looked at Will like he'd gone crazy.

"Just be here waiting when we show," Will shouted up. The man turned away from the quad. The conversation was over. For now.

"Will, what are you doing?" Lucy said under her breath.

Will shrugged.

"Worth a try."

Lucy and Will stared at Sam's body. They had propped his blue-ing body up to sitting, against the lockers. They'd stripped him of his blood-soaked shirt and dressed him in the over-sized sweatshirt Will had worn. They'd stuffed their own socks into the gaping wound in his neck so that the blood wouldn't seep into the sweatshirt fabric. It was the best they could manage in the time they had, but he still didn't look close to alive.

"This isn't going to work," Lucy said. "They'll see he's dead."

"No, they won't."

"You can clearly see he has no neck! Oh god, and they aren't going to let you out," Lucy said, going nearly as pale as Sam.

"Hold on," Will said and he knelt down beside Sam. Will took up both ends of the hood's drawstring and cinched it tight. The hood closed around Sam's face in a perfect oval, like an Eskimo. "There. What about that?"

Lucy tilted her head slightly and studied Sam. "Actually," she said, the tension in her face easing slightly. "That's not bad."

Will stood and overcompensated with a big smile. "See? I told you, it's going to work. I'm gonna get to leave."

Will's stomach dropped out of him when he said those words.

"Okay," Lucy said. He didn't want her to say "okay." He wanted her to say, "Don't go! Never leave me!"

"I don't want to leave you," he said.

"You have to."

"It's too soon."

"I know."

"I just got you back," he said.

"I know. But we don't have a choice."

"How are you so calm about this all the sudden?" Will said.

Lucy's face was unaffected, flat, still.

"I'm just trying to keep my shit together," she said. "The second you leave, I'm going to lose it."

Will forced himself to slow his breathing. He nodded. She was right. There was no point in crying about it now. Will went in for a kiss, and he made sure to make it count. It would have to tide him over for a year if this ridiculous plan worked.

And if they failed, this would be the last time he would kiss her without a death sentence hanging over his head. He kissed her slowly; he wanted to feel every moment of it. Her lips pushed back with a feather's weight. Lucy pulled away.

"What's wrong?" Will said.

Lucy looked away. "We shouldn't waste any more time."

He knew what she really meant. The more they lingered, clutching each other, touching and kissing, the harder they were making it to say good-bye. Lucy moved to Sam's body. Will sighed and followed. He bent down and slung one of Sam's limp arms over his shoulders. Lucy did the same, and they lifted his scarecrow corpse up. They looked like Sam's best friends, each with one of his arms over their shoulders, as they hurried him down the hall. Sam's dead feet dragged on the floor. They threw open the doors to the quad, to the wall of rain beyond.

They charged onto the quad. Sam's toes dragged through the mud. They carried Sam along as fast as they could. The rain was pounding now, making a haze of gray that was difficult to see through. Sam's head bobbled.

"He's unconscious!" Will screamed, twisting Sam's head up toward the roof ledge to reveal Sam's face. "He needs medical attention right away!"

They stood in the middle of the quad where the crane would meet them. They stared up and shielded their eyes from the falling raindrops.

"Come on, man!" Will shouted to Sam's father, who now held a pair of binoculars to his eyes, under his flipped visor. Will prayed that he was satisfied with what he saw. The man took his time with his decision.

"You promised, now do it!" Lucy shouted up to the sky.

Sam's father raised his arm to someone above they couldn't see. The graduation harness lowered into view, attached to the crane arm high above. The harness twisted on the crane cable.

"Just strap Sam in," his father said. "We'll do you after."

"It's both of us or nothing! That's the only way it happens!" Will shouted.

The harness finally dangled low enough for them to grab it. Will bear-hugged Sam's corpse, so Lucy was free to strap Will in, one limb at a time.

"You're ready," Lucy said.

Will wasn't sure if it was tears or rain on her face.

"It's okay," Will said because he thought he should. "I'm not going to abandon you, okay? I'll find a way to help from out there. I promise. You know that, right? I swear to—"

"I'm sorry, Will," she said.

"You're sorry? Why are you sorry?"

"I should've gone with you," she said, her voice more frantic by the second. "I should've gone with you to live in the elevator. We could've made it work. We would've had more time. You never would have teamed up with Gates. . . . I never would've—"

"Ssh," Will said. "Don't. It's okay . . . "

"We could've had more time," she said, her mouth down-turned in sadness. "Oh, Will."

Lucy went in for the kiss. Her lips got within an inch of his before he was tugged up into the air. The harness bit into his flesh. Sam's body was ridiculously heavy, and Will had to squeeze with all his might.

"Good-bye!" Lucy shouted up.

Will heard a guttural rumble from the hall. The revving of an engine. He knew who was coming.

"You have to go!" he shouted at her.

"What?" she called up.

Gates came roaring onto the quad on the motorcycle. Lucy broke into a run.

"Colton!" Gates screamed when he saw Will in the air. He poured on the throttle. Gates stood on the pedals, and reached up for Will as his bike zoomed by underneath. His fingers barely grazed Will's right foot.

Will kept ascending, giving thanks for every additional foot of space that grew between him and Gates. Then, he saw something horrible. Lucy had only managed to run fifteen feet in the mud. As Gates dropped himself back down into the saddle seat of the motorcycle, he carelessly clipped Lucy with the handlebars as he raced past her. She spun off her feet and flew into the mud.

"Lucy!" Will shouted.

Gates wobbled and crashed. Lucy wasn't moving.

Will crested the roofline of the school and rose up to eye level with the parents who had gathered behind Sam's father at the east wall. He stared into the black visor of the motorcycle helmet.

Will looked down to Lucy, who still lay motionless in the mud. He wriggled all around trying to look past Sam's body to see where Gates was. He lost his grip on Sam's slick, rain-soaked body, and Sam's heavy bulk began to slip through his arms. Will instinctively clamped down to hold on, and got his forearms underneath Sam's jaw.

Sam's weight pulled down hard against his forearms and Will heard a snap.

Sam's body fell out of the sweatshirt. It tumbled down and thumped into the mud below. But Will held Sam's disembodied head, still in the sweatshirt's hood. The rest of the empty sweatshirt flapped in the wet breeze.

Will heard the adults scream. Sam's father fell to his knees, completely silent. He gripped his helmet in agony as he stared at Will holding his son's dead head. Will dropped it. The woman in the lilac helmet screeched and screeched. Far behind them, he could see six more adults running toward the roof ledge.

The crane began to turn and swing Will away from the quad. He looked down into the quad. Lucy was in the same spot, but writhing around on the ground, beginning to stir.

He saw Gates. He reached his hands up toward Will. He might have been screaming but Will was getting so high, and so far away from the quad, that he couldn't hear it through the rain. Someone had to come help Lucy.

Will looked up to see the tip of the long, orange crane arm, high above him, and the arrows of rain zipping down toward him from dim gray clouds. Beyond the school, he saw a wall that went around the whole McKinley campus. It was made of big rig trailers, stacked three trailers high, the work of the crane Will assumed. The wall went all around the front hill and the parking lot and circled back behind the school to include the football field, until it disappeared into the gray haze of rain.

People walked on top of the truck trailer walls, patrolling with rifles. In the front lawn Will saw a forklift, a tractor, and more heavy machinery. He saw new prefab buildings along the wall. He saw a triple chain-link fence at the only break in the trailer wall, by the entrance to the parking lot.

There was other movement within the walls. Will saw horses. Pigs. Cows grazing. There were chickens too. He saw what looked like an unfinished barn and stubby grain silo. Will squinted and strained his eyes to understand what was happening on the football field. There was something off about it. The grass was too tall, it was swaying.

It was a field of wheat.

40

GATES PALMED SAM'S HEAD AND LIFTED IT
up to gaze into its eyes. He studied the slack, dead face with
an unhurried curiosity. Sam's open mouth was full of mud and
rain. The defiled head of the king. There was a spray of rain
bouncing off both of their heads. There was a bleeding stab
wound through Gates's cheek, to go with the one Lucy had
given him in his side. The motorcycle's engine still hacked
and popped and coughed. The bike was tipped on its side, on
the ground by Gates's feet.

Lucy was on the ground twenty feet away. It felt like the
quad was spinning. The motorcycle accident had disoriented
her. Her clothes clung to her, drenched.

Gates chucked Sam's head over his shoulder like a water-
melon rind at a picnic. It landed in the mud behind him with a
splatter. He stared up at the sky, to where Will had gone.

"He's gone forever," Gates said.

Gates's gaze lowered to Lucy. She didn't flinch, she didn't look away, but inside she was petrified by whatever mental, lunatic dialogue he'd had with Sam's head. What grisly thing had he resolved?

He took off his pants.

A wave of nausea melted Lucy. She swallowed and blinked. She clenched her jaw and forced herself to sit up and brace for the horror of what might happen next.

"You took him from me," Gates said.

Lucy got to one knee. Pain spread all through her body. She made herself stand. If the Sluts had taught her anything worthwhile, it was to never let your enemy know your fear. She didn't quiver, she didn't whimper, she didn't cry. She gave him nothing. All those feelings were for her alone.

He pulled off his blood-soaked T-shirt and dropped it. The wet fabric slapped down into the mud. The skin of his chest was a mess of red dripping holes, the bite marks of Slut knives.

The quad's spinning slowed. Lucy's vision sharpened. Whatever Gates had planned made Lucy want to vomit. But what truly shook her, what obliterated all the heat in her body, was the sight of Violent's many-bladed necklace around his neck. It shimmered in the pale light.

"It's your fault," he said, standing there in pale blue boxers and mud-covered sneakers.

No one was coming to save her. The Sluts had probably disowned her after she'd forced them into a gang brawl they didn't want and then ran away with a boy none of them liked. David was dead. Will was outside. The Loners were no more. She had no ideas, no tricks up her sleeve. He might kill her right here. This could be the way she died.

She took a step forward, and it didn't hurt too much. Then another. She walked toward him.

The surprise on his face was genuine. So was the confusion. "Are you serious?" he said.

She sped to a jog. Her hips hurt. Her lower back clicked.

He seemed almost delighted to see her heading for him, but the coldness in his eyes took all the heart out of his smile.

Her jog became a run. She kicked through the mud, all the way to where he stood, by the motorcycle, fists up, stance wide. She kicked for his balls, and she connected, but mostly with his inner thigh.

He slapped her with a heavy hand, and blood burst from torn scabs left by the Pretty Ones' claws, and streamed down her cheek.

She raked at his face with her fingernails. She made a grab for Violent's necklace next. If she had a knife she could take him. But she never got the chance. He punched her in the stomach first.

Lucy crumpled. She slipped and fell into the mud, landing hard on her back, right beside the motorcycle. She couldn't breathe. Her chest was a vacuum. Reality hit hard. Gates was ten times stronger than she was.

Gates fell on her, he dug his knees into her ribs and began to strangle her. The rain fell in her eyes. All noise went soft and muffled when her ears sunk under the mud.

She needed air. She clawed at his hands. One of her fingernails bent back and she cringed. She shook her hand out on instinct and his grip tightened. Her vision dimmed. Raindrops hurtled toward her in slow motion and landed cold on her cheeks. She looked at his frenzied face. She looked at the bleeding hole in his cheek.

Lucy reached up and dug her middle finger through that hole. She hooked her finger inside his mouth and yanked. The stab wound widened, the hole stretched, and Gates let go of her neck. He was holding his sagging cheek in horror.

She stabbed her fingernails at his eyes. One nail hit its mark. Right in the red. He grabbed at his eye and fell back, screaming. He lay groaning on top of the fallen motorcycle, pressing his fingers into his eye. He rolled around with his head on the back tire. The engine crackled underneath him.

She'd put a skid mark on his face. She grabbed the front handlebar and twisted the throttle. The spokes of the speeding back tire caught hold of Gates's long hair that was whipping off his shoulders. The whirring wheel kicked his head around, and snapped his neck.

Gates was dead. His neck was a Twizzler.

Lucy lay down in the mud.

41

HILARY'S PLIERS SCRATCHED ACROSS THE

enamel of the Freak girl's tooth.

"Stop squirming."

The Freak girl was small. Tons of freckles. Probably naturally a redhead, but her pixie haircut was chemical blue, and
her eyebrows were white. Her wrists were fastened to her
ankles by wire. Her ankles were fastened to the chair, which
stood in a clearing in the trash-filled basement. She'd woken
up just minutes before. She probably didn't even remember
Hilary whacking her in the back of the head with a two-by-
four.

Hilary had a grip on that tooth and she wanted it now. The
pointy jaws of her needle-nose pliers were jammed into the
pink of the Freak's gums. The girl's crying made her face
uglier. She wasn't much of a looker, but she had great teeth.

Hilary pulled. She squeezed just tight enough to keep even

pressure. The girl screamed into the old gray hand towel that Hilary had crammed into her mouth. Hilary tongued the gap in her own teeth as she strained. The pliers slipped off and snapped closed, her arm yanked back.

"Whore!"

Hilary kicked the girl's chair over and it fell on its side. The freckly girl shook her head violently. She made more sad honking noises. Hilary closed the metal jaws on the tooth again and imagined it was Lucy tied to the chair. She sat on the floor and got her feet in the Freak's face. She shoved one of her heels into the girl's open mouth, bottom of her shoe against the girl's upper row of teeth. Her other heel was in the girl's eye, pressing down on the lip of her brow. She pushed with her legs and pulled with her back, like she was using a rowing machine. The girl honked into the towel again.

Scream, Lucy.

Both hands crushed down on the rubber handles. The burning muscles of her forearm stood out like steel cables. Her thumb wanted to cramp. She gave it everything. The girl shrieked. Hilary heard a crack.

Something gave way inside the Freak's gums. It felt like tearing a drumstick off a chicken. Hilary stood up, still gripping tight on the pliers. The Freak coughed out the towel and screamed for her mother.

The tooth was beautiful. So long and pointy, like a normal

tooth with a unicorn horn on top. It might be a little too wide, but maybe she could grind it down.

She'd find a way to make it fit. She'd climb her way back up to the top, return to her former glory, and no one would ever know. That vile pig, Lucy, was the only one who knew her secret. Hilary was coming for her, and no one in McKinley could keep her away. Nothing could stop Hilary from yanking every tooth out of that bitch's head.

42

COLD RAIN PELTED WILL IN THE HEAD. THE raindrops were fat, and the downpour had doubled in strength in the short time since he'd been lifted out of the school. The crane had swung him away from the school, and was now lowering him down to the ground. He could hardly see a thing in the heavy rain. The harness pinched his skin. Thunder cracked. Wind whipped across his wet body and Will shivered.

His mind was on Lucy. What would happen to her? What was Gates doing to her right at that moment? Was he running her over to get back at him for leaving? Was he riding through the halls with her corpse laid over the motorcycle? Or dragging behind? Jesus. He should have waited, he should have stayed in McKinley another day, at least another few hours. Even though his mind would have started to break apart and he might not have gotten another chance to get out, and he might have died . . . he should have stayed.

Through the torrential downpour, he could barely make out the base of the crane in the distance. He was being lowered into a fenced-in area, on the lawn next to the school. Barbed wire ran along the top of the tall chain-link fences. The only thing inside the fenced-in area was an Airstream trailer. It looked like an aluminum Twinkie. His descent ended as his sneakers sank into the moist grass.

Will unfastened himself. He was glad to get the harness off. The wind surged again, blowing the rain sideways for a second. The harness rose back into the sky. He watched it go until he couldn't see it anymore.

He was freezing. There were lights on in the trailer. The square windows with rounded corners glowed a faint orange. He hugged himself and hurried over to the door. The rain sprayed off of its rounded roof.

He found the door unlocked. He opened it cautiously and poked his head in. There was no one inside, but a single lamp was on, filling the interior with warm, butterscotch-colored light. There was a bed, a small bathroom, a tiny kitchen with a stove and oven. Cereal boxes and bags of trail mix were arranged neatly on the kitchenette's counter. He saw a pile of books. The inside of the trailer was dry and he was about to walk inside when he heard someone shout his name.

"Will!"

He turned. There was a figure standing just beyond the fence. Will shielded his eyes from the rain. He couldn't make out anything more than the shape of a man, but he knew what this was. The second Will had realized that he was holding Sam's disembodied head in front of Sam's father, he knew he'd be in serious trouble when he hit the ground. He was going to have to talk his way out of this before Sam's father pulled out that rifle again.

"Sam was already dead! I didn't do it!" Will shouted to the man.

"That's good to hear," the man said.

Will swore he could feel his heart stop inside his chest. He knew that voice. Will ran toward the fence. The hazy figure brought a scuba mouthpiece up to his face as Will got closer. The mouthpiece stretched his lips out of shape, and his hair was brown now, and his eye patch was black instead of white, but it was him. Will had to hook his fingers through the holes of the fence to keep from falling over.

David was alive.

WANT MORE OF THE

QUARANTINE

SERIES?

LOOK FOR BOOK THREE FROM
EGMONT USA IN SUMMER 2014!